RECKLESS MILES

THE MILES FAMILY BOOK THREE

CLAIRE KINGSLEY

Always Have LLC

Published by Always Have, LLC

Edited by Elayne Morgan of Serenity Editing Services

Cover by Lori Jackson

ISBN: 9781710083613

www.clairekingsleybooks.com

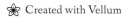 Created with Vellum

To Cooper. Your book is done. Will you be quiet now, please? Thanks.

ABOUT THIS BOOK

Reckless Miles: The Miles Family Book Three

"I love being naked. Naked is awesome."

For Cooper Miles, life used to be an endless party. He worked hard and played harder—as often as possible. But things change—people change—and lately the party life isn't doing it for him.

Enter Amelia Hale. Cooper doesn't see her coming. But it isn't every day you meet a girl in a wedding dress in a bar. A girl whose life just took a sharp left turn she wasn't expecting.

Kissing her is totally no big deal. She's had one hell of a day and a little kissing lesson by Cooper is bound to make her feel better. The invitation back to her hotel, however... that, he wasn't expecting.

Saying yes to her is reckless. Not because he's a stranger to a one-night stand. And not because she's in a wedding dress, and the words *this is my first time* cross her lips.

It's reckless because she makes him feel things he's

never felt before—big things. Nothing scares Cooper Miles. But this girl? She might be magic, and he has no idea what to do with that.

Author's note: Cooper Miles. He's sexy, hilarious, and deeper than you think. This former playboy has a heart as big as his personality, and when he finally falls in love, he falls HARD.

ONE
COOPER

ZOE-SITTING my pregnant sister-in-law was an important task, and I was determined to be the best Zoe-sitter ever.

Step one involved never telling her that I called hanging out with her when Roland had to leave *Zoe-sitting*. She'd hate that. Zoe was sassy under the best of conditions—one of the reasons she was my favorite—but now that she was hella pregnant, she was taking her sass to new heights.

I stood at the grill out on my deck, keeping watch on the steak. It smelled awesome, and Zoe had given it a thumbs-up after a sniff test. She'd had a rough almost-nine months, so step two was feeding her anything she wanted. She'd asked for steak for lunch. I figured she needed strength for the upcoming task of popping that tiny Miles person out of her vagina, so the protein was a good call.

"How you doing in there?" I called through the sliding door. My grill was on the deck—because of course it was, where else would I have put a grill?—and the late June sun beat down on my back. Thankfully it was cooler inside the apartment.

"Still fine," she said. "Just like last time you asked. Three minutes ago."

I heard the annoyance in her voice, but I gave her a pass. Everything annoyed Zoe lately, but I knew from my extensive research on pregnancy that this was normal. She was probably uncomfortable as fuck with that huge belly. And make no mistake, Zoe had popped out like she had a beach ball under her shirt.

Why had I done extensive research on pregnancy? Always be prepared. I'd never been a Boy Scout or whoever it was that said shit about being prepared, but it was a good motto anyway. Ben had taught me that.

I paused with the spatula in my hand, wondering if Ben had been a Boy Scout. That would explain a lot. He was the groundskeeper and handyman at our winery, and he knew how to do everything. Maybe he'd learned all his outdoor knowledge from Boy Scouts. And the guy was pretty much a saint, which sort of fit with the whole Boy Scout thing.

But I needed to be prepared, because even though Zoe wasn't *my* girl—she was married to my oldest brother Roland—she was one of my best friends. And from the moment they'd announced they were having a baby, I'd decided it would be good for me to know what's what when it came to pregnancy and shit.

"Coop, do you guys have any pineapple juice?" Zoe called from inside.

"Pineapple juice? Is that a thing people normally keep around? Because I don't think it is. That seems like a special request item. Which is cool, I can get some, but the chance of us already having pineapple juice, just in the house like we anticipated someone might want some, is pretty low."

"No, that's okay. It just sounds really good."

I flipped the steak to sear the other side and stuck my

head through the door. "I can go to the store after I finish out here."

"No, don't." She was lying on her side with a pillow between her knees.

I'd grabbed extra pillows from my room to help her get comfortable. Pregnant women needed a fuck ton of pillows. Maybe that's why girls love to have all those decorative pillows on their beds—it's like pre-pregnancy nesting. An instinct. I wondered if there was a correlation between the number of pillows on a girl's bed and the chances she'd want to rope a guy into marrying her and getting her pregnant. That would be really good information to have.

They were pillows from my room, rather than Chase and Brynn's room, because although my sister had a bunch of decorative pillows—I made a mental note to tell Chase about my *pillow quantity vs. chances of wanting to get pregnant* theory—I wasn't about to touch their fucking bed. No thanks.

I'd totally accepted the fact that Chase and Brynn were not only together, but married. It was fucking awesome, actually. Yeah, I'd kind of freaked out at first—if *kind of* meant I'd gone full-on batshit crazy asshole for months on end. Not my finest performance, I had to admit. In fact, I'd been a total dick about it, and I was still pissed at myself for not pulling my head out of my ass sooner than I had. Because Jesus, they were perfect together. I was just lucky that they were awesome enough to forgive me.

But that didn't mean I wanted anything to do with whatever was happening in their bedroom. She was my *sister*. It was bad enough I had to share a wall with them.

Of course, I also loved living with them, so it was a small price to pay.

Zoe grabbed her phone off the table.

"You aren't working, are you?" I asked. "You're not supposed to be checking on work stuff."

"What makes you think I'm working? I could be texting Roland. Or Brynn. Or your mom."

I raised my eyebrows at her.

"Fine, but I'm only checking in with Jamie. There's a big wedding today. I want to make sure everything is going well."

"Jamie has it covered. You focus on being pregnant."

She rolled her eyes.

I went back onto the deck to pull the steaks off the grill, then brought them into the kitchen. "Steaks are done, Zoe-bowie. Do you want something else with this? Because I'm just now thinking about the fact that all I made was steak, and I think girls usually like a side dish or some shit. Mom would be so disappointed in me. Don't tell her I didn't make you a side dish, okay?"

"Um, Coop?"

I added another pinch of salt to the steaks. "Yeah?"

"We have a little bit of a situation here. And I think you might need a new couch."

"Why? We just got a new couch. I was skeptical about that at first, but now I'm totally on board with the new couch. Although I don't think our old one was nearly as gross as Brynn said."

"That's not what I mean." Zoe was sitting up now, and she looked down at the cushions. "I think my water just broke."

There was a hint of panic in her voice and she stared at me, wide-eyed. Her hands were on her belly, like she was afraid the baby was going to rip out of her right here in my apartment, *Alien*-style. Or maybe she was just internalizing the fact that she was about to go into labor and have to push a human through her vagina.

And me? The buzz of thoughts constantly running through my mind quieted, and the world around me came into sharp focus. "Are you sure it was your water breaking?"

"I didn't just pee my pants."

"Are you having contractions yet?"

"I've been having small ones all day, but they're really irregular and not very strong."

"Sounds normal." I grabbed my phone and flipped to the app I'd downloaded for her this morning. "Here. Next time a contraction starts, hit the button. This will time them for us."

She took my phone and glanced at the screen. "You have a labor app?"

"Yeah," I said, looking at her like she was nuts. Because she *was* nuts if she thought I didn't have this under control. "Of course I have a labor app."

"Oh, there's a contraction." Her forehead tightened with strain and she hit the button on my phone. "I should call Roland."

"On a scale of one to ten, how intense was that contraction?" I asked when it seemed like it was over.

"Um, a five, I guess?"

"Cool." I grabbed a few towels out of the closet. "Want to clean up? I can run you a bath if you want. Warm water is supposed to relax your body and ease the pain."

"You're freaking me out right now."

I raised my eyebrows. "Why? Bath?"

"Let me call Roland first."

Roland was over in Tilikum, helping our sister Grace with some financial stuff. He'd only planned on being gone a couple of hours, so I was surprised he wasn't back yet.

With Zoe so close to having the baby, he'd been nervous about her being alone—hence me Zoe-sitting. If her water just broke, it would be go-time soon.

"Hey, honey," Zoe said when Roland answered. She held her belly again and I wondered if she was having another contraction. "You what? Oh god, are you okay? Are you sure?" She was quiet for a minute, listening. "Yeah, I'm fine, but my water broke. No, it's okay. The contractions aren't strong yet. It's really fine, I'll just wait here with Cooper until you can get back. Yes, I'll call my doctor, I know. Okay. Love you, too."

"What's up?"

Zoe let out a long breath as she put down the phone. "Someone hit Roland's car while it was parked. Whoever it was drove off, but it sounds like a bystander might have gotten the license plate number. He's waiting for the police."

"That sucks. Do you want your lunch?"

"Yes. But, no. But, yes. I don't know what I want, but Cooper, I'm having another contraction already and this one is really strong."

"Deep, slow breaths." I sat next to her and she squeezed my hands. "You're doing awesome, Z-Miles. Just breathe."

"Holy shit, that hurt," she said and took a few gasping breaths. "I think I need to pee, but I'm not sure."

"Let's go try."

I helped her stand and walked her to the bathroom. She went in and I waited outside the door. I heard her groan in pain, so I hit the button on the labor app. She was definitely having another contraction.

"How you doing in there?" I asked.

"Cooper, why is this happening so fast? These contractions are huge."

Glancing at my phone, I debated calling her doctor for her. Or calling my mom. But my gut was telling me she just needed to get to the hospital. This baby was on the way, and even though I was prepared, the last thing any of us needed was for her to pop the little human out in my bathroom. No one wanted to clean up that mess. I texted Roland to let him know to meet us there.

She came out, her eyes wide, one hand clutching her belly.

"Hospital," I said.

Zoe just nodded.

I got her out to the car, stopping twice while she had a contraction. I didn't bother timing them. She was in active labor, no question. I talked to her in a soothing voice, encouraging her to breathe. Let her squeeze my hand as hard as she wanted.

Fortunately, Echo Creek wasn't a big town, and the hospital was a short five-minute drive. I ran inside and got a wheelchair so she wouldn't have to try to walk in.

"You're doing so awesome, Zoe," I said as I pushed her into the lobby. "You're a freaking baby-delivering rock star."

"Thanks, Coop. Just get me inside."

In no time at all, a nurse brought us back to a room. I helped Zoe up from the chair, then turned my back while the nurse did her thing. She got Zoe into one of those blue gowns and got her situated on the bed.

When the nurse left, I pulled up a stool next to the bed. Zoe squeezed my hand while she had a long contraction.

"I've heard this before, but I'm telling you, whoever said women are the weaker sex never saw a woman in labor," I said. "Remember to relax between contractions."

She closed her eyes, taking a few deep breaths. "I knew

this would hurt, but holy fuckballs, this sucks. Where's Roland?"

I checked my phone. "He's on his way. I'll let everyone else know we're here."

"Okay. Oh god, here comes another one. Already? Are you fucking serious?"

I held her hand through the contraction, then got her a cold washcloth to put on her forehead before texting Mom, Brynn, Chase, and Leo. I texted Grace, too.

"You're doing so good, Zoe. Breathe and relax."

"Thanks."

"And just think, in no time at all, you're going to be holding your baby. How cool is that? I know you're doing all the hard work, but you get the reward, too. This little boy or girl is going to call you Mommy."

A tear trailed down her cheek. "Oh, Coop."

"Keep your eye on the prize, Zoe-bowie." I could see her body begin to tense up with another contraction. "You've got this. You're doing so great."

About half an hour later, Mom and Brynn showed up. Zoe managed to give them a little wave.

Mom came in and kissed Zoe's forehead. "You're doing great, honey. Do you want me to stay until Roland gets here?"

"No, that's okay," Zoe said. "Cooper's been great, and I'm sure Roland will be here any minute."

I puffed up at that. "Yeah, Mom, I've got it. I know the drill. Ice chips. Cold washcloth. Plus she can squeeze my hand really hard and it doesn't even hurt." *Much.*

"All right, if you're sure. We'll be in the waiting room. I'm so excited to meet my first grandbaby."

Zoe started having another contraction, so I talked her

through it while Mom and Brynn left. I was beginning to wonder if Roland would get here in time.

"Oh my god, where are my fucking drugs?" Zoe asked as her contraction eased. "My doctor said I could have the drugs."

I pressed the cold washcloth to her forehead. "You're doing so awesome."

The nurse came back in. "Hi, Zoe. I'm just going to check you really quick to see if you're ready for your epidural."

"I'm ready. I'm really fucking ready."

She smiled and moved the sheet, tipping Zoe's legs apart. I turned to give her privacy, even though I couldn't see anything over her belly anyway.

"Oh," the nurse said, and the surprise in her voice made me turn. "You're almost complete. I'll go find your doctor."

"What did she say?" Zoe asked, her voice going high-pitched as the nurse ran out of the room. "Did she say *almost complete*? That means ready to push. Oh my god, Cooper, I can't do this."

"You can definitely do this."

She closed her eyes again. "There's a baby in there and it's a lot fucking bigger than my vagina. How the fuck do women do this?"

Another contraction started, so I breathed through it with her. "You're going to do it because you're a mother-fucking goddess, you hear me? You're a warrior. And you're going to birth the shit out of this baby."

She squeezed my hand and cracked a little smile. "How are you the calm one right now?"

I just smiled and rubbed her arm while we waited for the next contraction. This was some crazy shit. I'd never thought I'd be here for this. But my pregnancy research sure had paid off. Be prepared, indeed. Ben's wisdom for the win.

"Breathe, Zoe," I said as she tensed up with another big contraction. "There you go. Breathe."

"Zoe, there you are." Roland burst into the room. He went around to the other side of the bed and took Zoe's hand. "I'm so sorry, baby. I got here as fast as I could."

"It's okay," she said, breathless.

"How are you doing? No epidural yet?"

I dropped her hand and stepped away from the bed. Roland was here now, so she didn't need me anymore. Which was as it should be, obviously. This was his wife. His baby. He should be here.

"She's almost complete," I said. "That means her cervix has dilated to nearly ten centimeters, and she's almost ready to push. The nurse went to find the doctor. I'm sure she'll be here soon."

"Thanks, Coop," Roland said, not really looking at me.

"Sure."

I wandered out to the waiting room. Mom was sitting with Brynn and Chase. She jumped up as soon as she saw me.

"Is the baby here already? How's Zoe?"

"No, not yet," I said. "Roland's here, so I'll just hang out with you guys."

I paced around the waiting room, waiting to hear what was happening. I hoped Zoe was okay. Did Roland know what to do? He'd taken those birthing classes with her, so I guessed he probably had it under control. I tried to sit down a few times, but I was bored. The TV couldn't hold my attention, either, so I just paced.

It was another two hours before Roland finally came

out. His hair was messy, but he had the biggest smile I'd ever seen on him.

"It's a boy."

Mom cried. Brynn cried. Chase smiled, hugging Brynn. I was happy as hell for them. He said Zoe was fine with us coming back to see the little guy really quick, so we did. Zoe kinda looked like shit, but that was to be expected. Although the way she looked at her son made her look pretty damn beautiful.

It was all so surreal. A few hours ago, it had just been Roland and Zoe. Now they were a family of three.

Mom passed the baby to me. He was wrapped up tight in a blanket, a little blue hat on his head. His face was all squishy and pink and he blinked his blue-gray eyes at me.

"Hey, slugger." I swayed a little as I held him. "Welcome to the ballgame."

"Did you decide on a name yet?" Mom asked.

"Hudson James Miles," Roland said.

I stared at his little face. Hudson James. This whole scene was so profound, I wasn't even mad that they hadn't named him Cooper.

Mom shooed us out after we'd all had a chance to hold Huddy, saying Zoe needed rest and the new parents needed time to bond with their baby. Brynn and Chase had already made plans for a date night, so they decided to go catch their movie. Mom invited me to come to her place, but I was in a weird mood, so I opted out.

My nephew was amazing. And maybe I just needed some time to grapple with the enormity of a new human coming into the world almost before my eyes. But I was unsettled and restless. So many things were changing. Chase was married. Zoe was a mom. It was all good stuff.

My best friends were growing up and moving onto new things.

Chase had Brynn now, and he didn't need me like he used to. Zoe had Roland again, and neither did she. And I was happy for them. I really was.

But I wasn't sure where it left me.

TWO

AMELIA

THE DAY WAS RUSHING by in such a whirlwind of activity, I hardly knew what was happening. Manicure, hair, makeup. Every step required a new professional, and took at least an hour. Before I knew it, I was being zipped into my dress and I had no idea how I was going to go to the bathroom.

My tummy fluttered with nerves. That was normal, right? I was about to get married. Brides were anxious. That didn't mean anything.

I'd been telling myself that all day. All week, really. The closer this day got, the more I felt like I couldn't sit still. My fingers and toes tingled, like they'd lost circulation. My stomach was raw, and I had no appetite. I'd barely eaten a thing in days.

At least I hadn't done the opposite and binged on tacos and ice cream all week. I'd been so worried my dress wouldn't fit. My mom had insisted I go down a size and lose a little weight before my big day. It had been a huge relief when Daphne, my maid of honor, had pulled the zipper all the way up. It was snug, especially around my boobs, but at least it didn't look like all my curvy parts were spilling out of the white fabric.

And I had plenty of curvy parts to spill.

"Amelia, you look beautiful." Daphne fussed with a curl of my dark blond hair, then fluffed my veil.

Daphne was the one who looked beautiful. My best friend had porcelain skin and dark hair. The tattoos that ran along her left shoulder and arm—deep blue and purple flowers—looked gorgeous against the pale lavender of her dress.

"Are you sure you're okay?" She paused and looked me up and down. "You're sure about… everything?"

"Of course I am. Why wouldn't I be? It's my wedding day. Obviously I'm great and happy and all the things a bride should be."

She didn't answer, although it was a good question. Why wouldn't I be okay? We were at a beautiful winery in the mountains. The weather was perfect. In fact, everything was perfect. The dress. The décor. The location. What more could I possibly ask for?

It was still kind of freaking me out that I was marrying Griffin Wentworth. He'd been my first crush. Our parents were friends, so we'd gotten to know each other at their dinner parties and country club events. We hadn't gone to the same school—I'd been in an all-girls boarding school— but we'd seen each other sometimes on weekends, and around the holidays. We'd always been friends, but I'd been too shy to tell him I wanted more.

We'd stayed friends all through college, and both of us had just graduated. He'd surprised the heck out of me four months ago when he'd said we should get married. He'd told me that he'd always cared about me, and he'd realized I'd been right there in front of him this whole time.

In that moment, it had felt like my dreams were all coming true. How many times had I snuggled up on the couch with Griff to watch a movie, wishing he'd reach over and hold my hand? Or lean in to kiss me? So many times. And there he was, suggesting we get married.

We were the friends who'd finally figured it out, like something in a book.

Except...

"Daph, do guys usually like kissing?"

"What?" She fluffed my veil again. "I think so. Harrison likes kissing. Why?"

"I don't know." I had no idea why I was asking about this now. It had been on my mind for the last few months, but I'd been afraid to bring it up—afraid it meant something was wrong with me. "Griff doesn't really like kissing."

"Did he say that to you?"

"Yeah, kind of. He made it sound like a lot of guys aren't into kissing."

"Amelia," she said, her voice taking on a motherly quality. "You've kissed him, right?"

"Oh yeah, of course I have." Which was true. Griff and I had kissed. It just... never felt like I thought kissing should feel. "Stop looking at me like you don't believe me. We've kissed for real. With... you know... tongues and everything."

"Well, maybe that's just not his thing. Or maybe he was holding back because he knew making out with you would lead to sex, and he's trying to hold out for tonight."

"Yeah, maybe you're right."

I took a deep breath. Talking about sex, when I was a few hours from finally having it, made my queasy stomach worse. I was still a virgin, but not because I had strong feelings about it. I just hadn't really had an opportunity yet.

Going to an all-girls school had been part of it. Not that

the other girls hadn't found boys to date. They had, Daphne included. She'd had a few boyfriends, and now she was engaged to Harrison, who was the coolest guy.

But I'd always been shy and kind of awkward, especially around boys. And being tall and a little chubby among a sea of petite skinny girls meant boys hadn't tried with me. Plus my parents had strongly discouraged dating. Since I hadn't exactly had anyone beating down my door to take me out, it hadn't been much of an issue.

It hadn't happened in college, either. Some of my friends had given me a hard time about it, which was annoying. Did they see me judging them for their sexual choices? No. I hadn't slut-shamed them, so why did they think they could virgin-shame me? I wasn't smug about not having sex. I didn't think I was better than them. In fact, it felt weird to be a twenty-two-year-old college graduate who was still a virgin.

That was all about to change. Because Griffin had figured out that marrying your good friend was a lot better than dating bimbos. Not that I was judging the girls he'd dated.

Okay, I was totally judging the girls he'd dated.

But he wasn't marrying them. He was marrying *me*. And it was what I wanted. The kissing thing had to be a fluke. Or maybe Daphne was right. Maybe he was holding back. I hadn't necessarily wanted to wait for our wedding night to sleep together. But since our engagement was so short, he must have figured we might as well wait. I'd gone this long, so why not stay traditional?

Surely it would just make tonight extra special.

"Come here." Daphne led me to a chair and helped adjust my dress so I could sit. "This has been a super-fast engagement, and you've had a huge wedding to plan, all while finishing college. Life has been insane. So if you're starting to feel a little bit freaked out right now, no one could blame you."

I nodded.

"But sweetie, if you're having doubts..."

"No," I said, my voice firm. "I'm not. Griffin is... He... You know I've always liked him. This is what I always hoped would happen, but didn't think could, because I'm not his type and we were just friends."

"I know, I know. You just seem like maybe... I don't know, you don't seem like *you* today. You haven't seemed like you all week."

"I'm just nervous." That was it. Normal nervousness. Brides got nervous, and it didn't have to mean something. "There are so many guests."

She squeezed my hand. "Yeah, but you won't even notice them. You'll just be looking at Griffin while he watches you walk up the aisle."

"Why do I feel like you're telling me what you think I want to hear? That's not like you. Why are you hiding something?"

"I'm not."

"You are. I can tell."

"I just think—"

The door opened, and my mother strode in, looking stately in her silver mother-of-the-bride dress. "Good, there you are. Where's Portia?"

Daphne and I both shrugged. Who knew with Portia. She was my only female cousin, and as such, it had been expected she'd be in the wedding. I guess the good news was, I didn't have any other Portias in my family who had to be in my wedding. One was enough.

"I haven't seen her," I said. "I figured she was getting ready with Aunt Veronica."

"No." Mom narrowed her eyes at me. "Are you wearing your Spanx?"

I glanced down at myself, noticing the way my stomach was not perfectly flat and my boobs looked enormous. "Yes, Mom, obviously."

"You can layer them, you know. Give you a little more help where you need it."

"Yeah, I know. I'm wearing two."

"She looks phenomenal, don't you think?" Daphne took my hands and helped me stand. "She's a perfect bride."

Mom gave me a pinched smile. "The dress is nice. We will not be starting this wedding late. If Portia doesn't appear in the next two minutes, we're starting without her."

"Okay, that's fine, I guess," I said. "I haven't seen her yet, so I don't know what to tell you."

It irritated me the way my mom seemed to be blaming me for Portia going missing. She'd probably met some guy last night and lost track of time. Portia wasn't exactly known for being responsible. And it was my mom who had insisted she be a bridesmaid. Well, really it was my mom's sister, Aunt Veronica, but that message had come through my mom down to me.

Just as Mom was leaving, Jamie, the winery's wedding coordinator, came in. Mom pulled her into the hall and spoke to her in a low voice. Jamie nodded along, then said something that sounded reassuring, but I couldn't make out her words. Mom left, her heels clicking on the floor as she walked down the hall.

"Hi, ladies," Jamie said with a smile. "It sounds like we're down a bridesmaid, but your mom would like to begin on time regardless?"

"Yeah, it's fine," I said.

Daphne rolled her eyes. "Portia's a brat and Amelia's aunt insisted she be in the wedding. I don't think anyone will be surprised if she flakes."

"Okay, then," Jamie said. "If you're ready, we'll get you two out to the staging area. Everyone else is waiting."

Daphne handed me my bouquet. "Ready?"

Deep breaths, Amelia. Deep breaths. "Yes, I'm ready."

My stomach did somersaults as I followed Jamie and Daphne. The wedding was outside, and Jamie led us through the back doors and down a path through the garden to a wide-open expanse of grass.

It looked like a sea of people. The two hundred guests looked like ten thousand, and my heart started to pound. The aisle up the center of the white chairs seemed a mile long.

If I thought things had moved fast earlier today, we were racing toward the finish now. Hands plucked at my dress and smoothed my veil. Voices spoke softly around me and I was vaguely aware of the string quartet playing at the front. The sun was dropping down toward the mountain peaks, but I still blinked at the brightness.

My hands were hot and clammy, and I wondered if my ring would still fit. Oh no—what would I do if Griffin couldn't get it on my finger? I had a horrible vision of standing in front of all these people while he tried to push the ring past my swollen knuckle.

Suddenly, my mom and dad were there; someone was talking about Portia again, and Daphne was talking to Jamie in hushed whispers. It was all happening too fast. I couldn't breathe. My dress was so tight, and the stupid double set of Spanx was suffocating me.

I looked up the length of the aisle, past the flowers and

tulle, to find Griffin. I was sure that seeing his face in this moment would calm my frayed nerves.

He wasn't there.

We'd gone through everything in rehearsal last night. Griffin and his groomsmen would be at the front. Portia would walk up the aisle. Then Daphne. Then me with both my mom and dad. There was no Portia, but that didn't really matter. People would quietly ignore the fact that there were two groomsmen and only one bridesmaid, then gossip about it at the reception.

But there were only two men standing in front of all the guests, and neither of them was the groom.

"Where's Griffin?" I asked.

Everyone stopped, slowly turning to look at me. Mom stood next to Dad—he did look very nice in his tux—and they both looked back and forth between me and Spencer, the best man.

Spencer's eyes darted around and he winced, then gave a subtle shrug of his shoulders.

"Wait, that's not Griffin?" Jamie asked.

"No, Spencer is Griffin's brother," I said. They looked so much alike, they were often mistaken for identical twins. "He's the best man. The other groomsman is Mark. But I don't see Griffin. Where is he?"

Jamie hugged her clipboard to her chest. "Oh dear."

I backed away from the rows of chairs, staring at the spot where Griffin was supposed to be standing. Mom was whispering something about car accidents, but our hotel was right next door. We'd walked over here to get ready.

Spencer quickly walked down the aisle toward us. Heads turned as he passed, more and more guests beginning to notice the knot of people at the back. And the fact that the wedding wasn't starting.

"What's going on?" Mom whispered. "Where is he?"

"I don't know," Spencer said. "I thought he was with Mark, and Mark thought he was with me. Then Jamie told us to go stand up there, so we figured he was with Amelia or something. But he's not with you guys either?"

"No, of course he's not with us," Mom hissed. "You're the best man, Spencer, you're supposed to make sure this doesn't happen."

"Okay, let's stay calm," Daphne said. "Spence, what did you guys do last night? Did you go out?"

"Just to the hotel bar," Spencer said. "We had one drink and went back to our rooms. I was in bed by eleven."

"And Griffin went to bed, too?" Daphne asked.

"As far as I know," Spencer said with a shrug. "I saw him this morning at breakfast, but he didn't stop to talk. He grabbed some food and went back to his room. He said he'd see me later. I figured he meant, you know, now."

The conversation continued, but I couldn't hear it over the sound of the blood rushing in my ears. Because no matter how many explanations they came up with, I knew the truth.

He wasn't coming. Griffin was standing me up on our wedding day.

THREE
AMELIA

I WAS NUMB. Daphne kept looking at me like she was afraid I'd break down sobbing, but I didn't feel much of anything.

She'd whisked me back to the bride's room while everyone else tried to figure out what had happened to Griffin. I stood at the window, looking out over one of the gardens. I couldn't see the guests from here, but I knew they were out there. Word had to be spreading. Griffin had left Amelia at the altar.

Well, I hadn't made it all the way to the altar. But the result was the same.

Spencer poked his head in. "Any word?"

"Nope," Daphne said. "You?"

"No. He checked out of his room earlier, but that's all the hotel could tell us."

"Well, that's useless," Daphne said. "Of course he checked out of his room. He was supposed to be with Amelia in the honeymoon suite tonight. He didn't need his room."

"He didn't have his bags sent up to the suite, did he?" I asked, although it wasn't really a question.

"No, I don't think he did," Spencer said.

"I didn't think so."

"I'll go see if my parents have heard anything," Spencer said, and closed the door.

"That asshole better be fighting for his life in a hospital," Daphne said. "That's the only excuse for missing your fucking wedding."

I stepped out of my shoes. They were already hurting my feet. I'd wanted different ones—something comfortable. After all, who was going to see my feet? Why not wear a pair of white Converse low tops? But my mother had been incensed at the suggestion. With her, there was a proper way to do things, and formal events meant heels.

Was it weird that I was contemplating my footwear while the question of whether or not I'd just become a jilted bride was still up in the air? Yeah, it probably was.

My stomach churned, and I started pacing. I had too much nervous energy; I couldn't sit still.

The door opened again, making me jump. I put a hand over my heart and took a deep breath as Daphne's fiancé, Harrison, came in.

"Hey, I was just wondering if you two are okay," Harrison said.

Even in a suit, Harrison looked every bit the rocker. He had a thick beard and neck tattoos that peeked above his shirt collar. He'd recently signed his first record deal, and he and Daphne were scheduled to fly to L.A. after the wedding.

"Hey babe." Daphne stepped into his hug. "I don't know what the hell is even happening right now."

"What's going on out there?" I regretted the question as

soon as it came out of my mouth. I wasn't sure if I wanted to know.

"People are just waiting for now," Harrison said. "Your dad told everyone there's a delay."

"A *delay*," Daphne said. She sounded like she was ready to spit nails. "Yeah, it's kind of hard to have a wedding when the groom disappears."

"I'm sorry, Amelia," he said.

"I'm sure there's a perfectly logical explanation," I said. "Something must have happened. Maybe he got a stain on his suit and he was trying to get it out, but rubbing it just made it worse. So he realized he needed to take it to a dry cleaner, and they were backed up and told him they couldn't get to it right away, but he explained that he needed it for his wedding, and he's still over there arguing with the owner."

"Um... yeah, maybe that's it," Harrison said.

"Or, you know, he left because he realized he doesn't want to marry me."

"Oh, sweetie," Daphne said.

"You need me to track him down and beat his ass?" Harrison asked. He'd lowered his voice, but I could still hear him.

"Maybe," Daph said. "I'll keep you posted."

Harrison nodded, then gave Daphne a quick kiss and left.

Daphne checked my phone, and I could tell by how quickly she put it down that I didn't have any messages. She grabbed hers and started flicking her thumb across the screen while I paced.

"What about all the food?" I asked. "And the cake? What happens when a wedding gets canceled at the last second? Does the cake just go to waste?"

"I don't know, but—" Daphne stopped mid-sentence and stared at her phone, her mouth open. "Oh my god."

"What?"

"Holy shit balls."

"Did he reply? Did you find him?"

"No, he didn't, but I found him all right." She shook her head. "This is unbelievable."

"What? You're killing me. What's going on? I wasn't right about the dry cleaner thing, was I? Because I was just babbling. You know how I am. I do that when I'm nervous."

"Yeah, sweetie, I know you do. He's not at the dry cleaners." She held up her phone so I could see her screen. "He's with Portia."

I grabbed the phone out of her hand. Right there on the screen, plain as could be, was Portia's tweet.

BRIDESMAID in my cousin's wedding. Kinda slept with the groom. Oops.

"WHAT DID I JUST READ? Is this real? Or is this a joke? Because if this is her idea of a prank, it's not very flipping funny."

"I don't think it's a joke."

"He slept with Portia?" I read it again. And again. Once more, just to be sure, but the words didn't change. "Griffin and Portia? When? Today was supposed to be... we were... she's my *cousin*."

Daphne gently took the phone from my hand. "Holy shit, there's more. She's been live-tweeting the whole thing."

I balled my hands into fists while Daph scrolled through Portia's tweets.

"Okay, it starts with the *oops* one. 'Oops' my ass, what a bitch. Then there's a picture of their luggage in his car. It says, *we're following our hearts*. That was this morning. Then there's a picture of them at the airport. This selfie is awful, by the way, they both look like shit. Then... oh my god, they didn't."

"What?"

"They went to Vegas."

"Vegas? Why would they... oh."

It felt like the air was being crushed from my lungs. The numbness burned away, red hot anger crisping the edges, like a piece of paper turning to ash. Only I wasn't burning to dust. I was metal. Hot steel turning to molten liquid, the anger searing through me at terrifying speed.

"Sweetie, I think they're getting married." Daphne held up her phone again to a photo of a crappy-looking wedding chapel.

"He left me to take my cousin to Vegas so he could flipping marry her?" I asked through clenched teeth.

"It looks like it. Oh... oh yeah. She tweeted again. It's another shitty selfie and she's holding up her hand. She has a ring on her finger."

I looked down at myself, clad in a voluminous white wedding gown. A gown I didn't even like. I was supposed to be getting married to Griffin, right this second. But he'd left me. He'd slept with my cousin and run off to Vegas to marry her.

"This is so unrealistic," I said. "Can you imagine if this was a movie? The girl thinks she's about to marry the guy she's had a crush on since she was thirteen, and everything is going great, like her dress fits and the weather is beautiful. But then she finds out that not only did her fiancé sleep with her cousin, he took her to Vegas and married her instead. I'd never believe it. I'd throw popcorn at the screen and boo and tell everyone not to watch because who would believe that could ever happen?"

"Amelia..."

"No, I'm being serious. This is just silly. This wasn't supposed to happen. And now there are two hundred guests out there who expected cake, and what are they going to get? Nothing, that's what."

"I don't give a flying fuck about the guests. I want Griffin to die a slow and painful death, preferably after losing his genitals to leprosy."

"I don't know if that's how leprosy works. And can't they just cure that now? It's not like there are people walking around in rags, shouting that they're unclean so people won't get near them."

"No... that's not the point." She shook her head. "God, Amelia, I'm so sorry."

"You're right."

"About what?" she asked.

"Leprosy. Of the genitals. That's what he should get. I'm so mad I don't know what to do with myself."

"Good," she said. "Mad is good. Let's stay mad. You know what we need to do? Before this gets out, we need to hit him where it hurts."

"He's in Vegas. I can't kick him in the jimmy from here."

"Not his balls," she said. "His bank account. You have access to it, right?"

"No."

"Damn."

"But the one for our honeymoon is a joint account."

A slow smile crept across her face. "We need an ATM. Now."

"You want me to withdraw money from the honeymoon account?"

"No, I want you to decimate that account, and any other account you can access. He's probably paying for that fucking Vegas trip with *your* honeymoon money. Gut him, Amelia."

I went for my purse, but paused. "Wait, there's a limit on how much money you can withdraw from an ATM. And I don't think I can leave this room anyway. There are two hundred people, including my mother and Griffin's parents, out there and I can't face them, Daph. Maybe not ever. You're going to have to explain to the winery that I have to live here now and I can't ever leave."

"Shit." She crossed her arms and tapped her elbow with one finger. "Can you access the bank from your phone?"

I knew I was babbling again, but Daphne was good at cutting through the nonsense flying out of my mouth when I was anxious, and focusing on the important parts. "Yeah."

She grabbed my phone and tossed it to me. "Do it."

My hands were surprisingly steady as I logged in to the account. I decided the best place to put the money was my trust fund. I wouldn't be able to spend it. The account was managed by a trustee, although I'd been set to gain access to it after I got married. I wasn't sure what would happen to it now, but I didn't really care. I knew one thing for sure—if I put the money in my trust, Griffin would never see it again.

"There."

I felt a surprising sense of empowerment as I tapped the button to request the transfer. Like this wasn't something happening *to* me, outside of my control. I was hitting Griffin where it would hurt. For all his good points—although I was having a hard time remembering what those were just now —he did have a huge preoccupation with money. His parents had gobs of money, but they were young and healthy. He would inherit millions, but not for decades. He had a trust fund, like mine. Both our parents had set them up similarly, with conditions for disbursal, designed to make sure we were responsible adults before we had access to the funds.

Although I didn't know the details of Griffin's trust fund, a sickening thought hit me. "Daph, what if Griffin only wanted to marry me to get his trust fund?"

Her eyes widened. "Is that a thing? He has to get married to get it?"

"I don't know," I said. "It's one of the conditions of mine."

"What in the ever-loving fuck? Did he know that?"

I shook my head. "No, but he might have guessed. Although we didn't talk specifically about my parents' money."

Because that's what it was—theirs. I'd never thought of it as mine. They'd set up a fund for me when I was a baby, but used it to pay for tuition, both for private school and college. Which was fine with me. That's the type of thing it was supposed to be for. If there was money left over—I actually didn't know how much was in it—I really wanted to use it to open a horse rescue. I'd already been doing research on locations and start-up costs, figuring I'd get going on it after my honeymoon.

Obviously that wasn't going to happen.

"Sweetie, I'm incapable of holding back at this point," she said. "I'm telling you right now, this is the best thing that's ever happened to you."

"That's a very weird thing for you to say. You'd think the best thing that's ever happened to me would not be this humiliating."

"I know." She took my hands. "But Griffin showed you his true colors today. I know you guys have been friends for a long time, but what kind of friendship was it, really? He only wanted to hang out with you when he was in between girlfriends. And his sudden *you were in front of me all along* thing sounds really sweet and romantic, but clearly he didn't mean it."

"Oh god, Daphne. I was going to marry him. Like, marriage, which is forever. Or at least it's supposed to be. But if he could just... I mean, he ran off with my cousin. With flipping *Portia*. She's the worst. He wants to be with her more than me? I mean, she's skinny and beautiful, so of course he wants to be with her more than me. Who wouldn't?"

"Um, any guy who has a brain?" Daphne said. "Don't even start on the fact that you aren't a size zero. You're gorgeous. Not to mention smart and sweet. Griffin never deserved you. He did you a big favor today. I still hope he gets genital leprosy, but thank god you didn't marry him."

Anger was still smoldering in my stomach, so in that moment, it was easy to believe her. He had done me a favor. I'd just dodged a bullet—one with a life sentence. If Griffin was the kind of guy who could do this, who could cheat on me with my cousin and leave me on my wedding day, imagine what kind of husband he would have been. He hadn't been much of a boyfriend—although it wasn't like we'd dated for a long time, so he hadn't had much of a chance—but I'd figured we would get through our wedding and settle in with each other. But this? This was the kind of man he was? Screw him.

"You know what? You're right. I'm glad this happened." My anger hardened into resolve. This wasn't my fault, and I wasn't taking the blame, no matter what.

"Here's what we're going to do," Daphne said, her expression brightening. "We're going to spend the rest of the night celebrating your freedom. That's how we'll get you through this, okay? We'll have a few drinks and ruin your dress. Then we'll eat your wedding cake. Or maybe take it out somewhere and smash it. What do you think?"

I smiled—a real, genuine, honest-to-goodness smile. And considering what was happening, that was an amazing thing. "Yeah, I—"

The door opened and instantly my smile evaporated into thin air. My stomach clenched tight and a wave of dread poured through me. It was my mother.

"Well, this is a disaster," she said. "Griffin apparently ran off to Vegas with Portia."

I gaped at her. She had no idea that I already knew and had been processing this for the last ten minutes. That was how she told me? "I know."

"You know? How?"

"Portia's been live-tweeting," Daphne said.

Mom's lips pressed into a thin line and she exhaled through her nose. "Why does this generation insist on documenting their idiocy so publicly?"

I just stared at her.

"I need to go out there and work on damage control," Mom said. "Amelia, you should come out and be seen speaking to the Wentworths. We need to make sure it's clear this isn't the beginning of a feud between our families."

There was no way I was going out there. I could already feel the anxious swirl of chaos in my brain. I'd take one look at all those people—staring at me, judging me, wondering what I'd done to drive Griffin away—and start babbling.

Didn't my mom realize that? I was terrible in front of people, especially when I was stressed.

"What? No."

"Excuse me?" Mom folded her arms across her chest. "This is important. We need to smooth this over as quickly as possible."

"Do you think maybe it would be better if Amelia disappears for a little while?" Daphne asked, adopting her *deal with Mrs. Hale* voice. "No one would expect a bride to socialize in this situation."

Daphne and my mother had the strangest dynamic. Mom made no secret that she didn't approve of my best friend. Daphne wasn't from the right sort of family. I'd met her at the private boarding school my parents had sent me to, but she hadn't been there because her family had money, like the rest of the students. Both of her parents were teachers there. My biggest—only, really—act of rebellion was being friends with Daphne.

Despite the fact that my mother disapproved of Daphne, she listened to her. I'd never understood why. But Daphne had a way with my mom. It didn't always work, but sometimes, when Daph could tell I was about to buckle under pressure, she'd step in and magically redirect my mother. I'd always wished I had the same ability.

"True," Mom said.

"How about I go out there with you, Mrs. Hale," Daphne said. "You and I can make the rounds and smooth things over."

"Very well," Mom said.

"I'll be right there," Daphne said. "Just give me a minute with Amelia."

"We'll sort this out," Mom said, looking at me. "Just keep yourself together."

Was that her attempt at comfort? I wasn't sure why I'd thought I might get more out of my mother—she'd never been the nurturing type—but seriously?

Daphne turned her back on my mom as she left, and rolled her eyes.

"Thanks," I said.

"Anytime. Listen, I'll handle the crowd. You go back to the hotel. If you slip out now, no one will notice. We'll get the wine flowing and they won't care that you aren't there. Or that there wasn't a wedding. I'll be over there as soon as I'm sure your mom won't bug you again tonight."

I stepped in to hug her. "Thank you. Again. So much. All the thank yous."

She pulled away. "Do you want to get out of this dress first?"

"No, it's fine, I can take it off myself."

"Are you sure you're going to be okay for a little while?"

"Yeah," I said. "As long as I don't have to go out there. I'll see you in a bit."

"Definitely." She squeezed me again. "You're going to get through this. I promise."

We heard the click of my mother's heels outside, so Daphne rushed out to intercept her.

When I was sure they were gone, I put my shoes back on and poked my head out the door. The coast was clear, so I crept down the hallway toward the front entrance. There were a few people in the lobby, but they weren't here for my wedding, so I just told myself all they saw was a woman in a wedding dress—not a jilted bride running off in shame.

I wanted to cry. I really did. But there was no lump of sadness choking me. I was humiliated, and embarrassed, and pretty darn angry. But none of it made the tears come.

The hotel was right next door, but I hesitated. I didn't

want to go back to my room and sit there, dejected and alone. I knew Daphne would come as soon as she could, but what was I supposed to do with all this nervous energy?

I was angry. I was sick of being good and doing what people told me to do. I wanted to do something unexpected. Something crazy. Crazy being a relative term, but since I never did anything *actually* crazy, that made it easier. I wouldn't go back to my hotel. Not yet.

Hitching up my dress so I wouldn't trip, I turned and marched toward the line of restaurants and shops on the other side of the entrance to Salishan Cellars. Because not far up the street, I'd seen a sign, and it was exactly the sort of place I had my mind set on right now: a bar. I was going to a bar. In my wedding dress. And I didn't care what my mother was going to say about it.

FOUR
COOPER

MOUNTAINSIDE TAVERN WAS QUIET TONIGHT.
That was both a relief and a disappointment. I didn't want
to sit here alone, surrounded by couples and happy groups
of friends having a good time. But it meant no one I knew
was here, either, so I was basically doomed to fly solo
tonight.

I slipped onto a stool at the bar. There was a group of
girls near the pool tables, and they might have been cute,
but I barely paid attention. Which was weird and fucking
stupid. But picking up girls wasn't nearly as fun without
Chase. In fact, it was barely fun at all, and I'd basically
stopped doing it since he'd started dating my sister. There
was an emptiness to the whole scene that had never bothered me before. But now, even the thrill of the hunt didn't
hold any appeal. And really, that's what I'd always loved.
The chase. The challenge. It was fucking fun, or it had
been. Now, not so much. And if it wasn't fun, what was the
point?

The bartender came over and I ordered a beer. Noticed

there was someone sitting next to me. Her eyes were on her drink, which looked mostly untouched.

"Rough day?" I asked. The bartender handed me my beer and I took a long swig.

"You could say that." She didn't look up.

"Me too. I really don't know what's going on with me lately. I had a perfect life, you know? Everything was great. And now it's all messed up and the reasons why make me think I must be a much bigger asshole than I previously would have thought."

"What do you mean?"

There was something in her voice. A sweetness. Like warm maple syrup slowly spreading over freshly made pancakes. Just the sound of it was slowing me down. Instead of blurting out a reply, I thought it over for a second.

"My best friend married my little sister a few weeks ago. And I think I'm jealous."

"That seems understandable," she said. "Do you think feeling jealous is a bad thing? It doesn't sound like it to me. Unless your jealousy is making you be mean to them, because that would be bad."

"No, I'm not mean. Not anymore. I was being a total dick for a while, but I stopped when I realized what a dick I was being. And that was before they got married, anyway. But what kind of asshole isn't happy for his best friend when his best friend is this unbelievably happy? Chase is the best guy ever and he's crazy about my sister and they're great together, and here I am, sulking over a beer because I don't get to hang out with him tonight. I also became an uncle today, but that's good news."

"That's wonderful," she said. "Congratulations."

The brightness in her voice made me look at her again. Her eyes were on me, rather than on her drink, and they sparkled. She had dark blond hair, far as I could see in the dim light, done up all fancy and shit. Lot of makeup, too, which I could tell at a glance she didn't need.

"Thanks. It is awesome. The kid... well, he looks like a newborn, so that means he's that cute-ugly that everyone says is adorable. I guess because you're supposed to think babies are adorable, even when they have warped heads and wrinkled faces."

"Oh, I know," she said. "I'm pretty sure babies don't get cute for at least a couple of months, but everyone freaks out when you say they look like a Shar-Pei with no teeth."

"Right?" I asked, a flare of excitement hitting my chest. She got it. "I know. So yeah, my nephew is great and all that, and it's awesome for Roland and Zoe. Roland is my brother and Zoe is his wife. They're all happy and shit, which is awesome, so I'm happy for them. But now it's like, fuck. Chase and Zoe were who I always hung out with the most. Now Zoe is a mom and Chase is this devoted husband. Which he better be, because he married my sister, and if he was here hanging out with me, I'd kick his ass. But I want him to hang out with me. Life is confusing."

"So confusing." She shook her head slowly. "This is water, by the way. I don't want you to think I'm cooler than I am, like I'm sitting here drinking alone. I didn't know what to order."

The sadness in her voice hit me then, like a punch in the kidneys. I turned on my stool so I was facing her. "What's the matter, Cookie?"

She blinked at me a few times, her lips parted. Pretty eyes. More hazel than green. Not a color you saw often.

"Well, I mean..." She trailed off and looked down at herself.

And that's when I realized she was wearing a wedding

dress. There was a veil sitting on the bar next to her water, and her dress was big and white. I didn't like it. The dress didn't look like her, and it seemed to me that a woman's wedding dress ought to be *her*. Brynn had looked like the best little Brynn ever in her dress. And Zoe had rocked her red dress when she'd remarried Roland. This dress looked like a fairytale nightmare.

But it also meant—

"What the shit? Cookie, I'm sorry. I'm sitting here running my mouth about my pitiful problems and you're... well, you're here in a wedding dress, and I don't know why, but I'm going to have to guess it's not because the wedding was so much fun you decided to keep the party going."

"No. I didn't get married."

I almost blurted, *well, that's a fucking relief*, but something stopped me—which had happened to me exactly never. But it was what I thought, and what I felt in a deep place in my chest. I was really relieved this girl hadn't gotten married, although I had no idea why.

Maybe it was my sudden sense of confusion that had kept me from saying the first thing that popped into my mind, but whatever the reason, I was glad. Because the second thing I thought was a much better reply.

"Damn. I'm sorry. I'm Cooper, by the way. Do you want to talk about it?"

She looked at me for a long moment, and I hoped she'd start talking. I really liked the sound of her voice, and I hated the sad look in her eyes. I wanted to see if there was something I could do to make it better.

"I'm Amelia. And you probably won't believe me. Although I do have proof. Portia live-tweeted the whole thing. Because why wouldn't she? She's having a great day. Unlike me, who's having the worst, most humiliating day of my entire life. Two hundred guests, Cooper. Two hundred people were there. And now they're probably eating the food I didn't pick and drinking wine and talking about how pathetic I am. They all saw me in the back, looking up at the empty place where he should have been, and I must have looked like a crazy person, just standing there, staring." She paused and took a deep breath. "Sorry, sometimes I babble. Especially when I'm nervous or upset."

"Me too."

"Really?"

"Yeah, except I pretty much do it all the time. What can I say, my brain moves fast. If people can't keep up, that isn't my fault."

"Brain moves fast. I never thought of it that way," she said. "Anyway, I should back up. As you can see from my dress, I was supposed to get married today. But he left. With my bridesmaid. Who is also my cousin."

"Whoa."

"I know. Who would even believe me? I've been friends with Griffin for years, and then he wanted to get married. I mean, cheese and rice, it was *his* flipping idea. He asked me. Why would he ask me if he was just going to sleep with my cousin and run off with her to Vegas to marry her instead?"

"Wait, wait, wait." I couldn't believe what she was telling me. And not because the story sounded too outrageous to be true. It just seemed outrageous that someone could have done this to *her*. "He slept with your cousin and then took her to Vegas? Today?"

"Yes, today. He was supposed to be here, marrying me, but then there's Portia live- tweeting their... their... thing."

"Is it weird that I want to kill this assgoblin?"

"No, it's not weird. I think Daphne wants to kill him too. Daphne's my best friend, although she's nothing like me, and I wonder why we've stayed friends sometimes. I mean, she has tattoos and a rocker fiancé. We're so different. But she said he did me a favor. If he's capable of this, what would being married to him have been like?"

"That's a great question, Cookie." I took another swig of beer and put my bottle down on the bar. "My guess is, it would have been a goddamn nightmare. How long did you two date?"

"Well, not long. We didn't date, in the traditional sense. We were friends for a really long time, and then he proposed."

"Sweetheart, I don't even know what to say, except I think your bestie sounds like an awesome friend and I think she's right. He did you a huge favor today. You can't marry the assgoblin. I need you to make me a promise, right now. I need this from you."

"Okay..."

"Promise me you won't ever marry him," I said, and I meant it. "Even if he comes crawling back with some excuse that sounds really believable and he declares his love for you and is really fucking convincing. Don't take him back, and please, please, Cookie, don't marry him."

She looked into my eyes. Jesus, she was beautiful under all that makeup. Big eyes, full lips. Her cheeks were a little round, which was cute as fuck.

"All right, I promise. Even if he comes crawling back and is very convincing, I won't take him back."

Some of the pressure in my chest eased when she said that. I hated the idea of her going back to that prick with a lot more intensity than made any sense. Why did it bother me so much? Was it just because she looked so sad?

It certainly wasn't because I was attracted to her. Couldn't be. I mean, I *was* attracted to her, she was fucking adorable. But she was in a wedding dress. That was basically my kryptonite. I wasn't the marrying type. Roland and Brynn could take on the get-married-and-give-Mom-grandchildren duties for all of us. Because I certainly wasn't ever getting married, and judging by my brother Leo's status as an agoraphobic hermit, neither was he.

In fact, Amelia broke too many rules to count. Yeah, she was gorgeous and sexy and all sorts of yummy things. But considering she'd been about to marry a guy she hadn't really been dating—and who had probably friend-zoned her for years—she obviously wanted marriage. That was strike one. She also seemed like awesome girlfriend material. The type of girl who'd be sweet and loyal, and would expect—and deserve—the same in return. That was strike two. I wasn't the boyfriend type, so it would be a dick move for me to go for a girl who wanted that.

"Can I ask you a question?" she said out of the blue.

"Sure."

"Do you like kissing?"

The sound of her voice kept cutting through the cascade of thoughts in my brain, so I was laser-focused on her. "Shit yeah, I like kissing."

"I don't just mean kissing, you know, before other stuff. I mean kissing for the sake of kissing."

That was a great question. I paused to think about it for a second, because she deserved a good, solid answer. "Yes. I do like kissing just for the sake of kissing. I really like it when it's leading somewhere else, because let's be honest, I'm a guy, and guys always get excited if we get to take our pants off. But yeah, kissing feels good. I like it."

She nodded slowly, like she was thinking about my answer. "Griffin said he didn't like kissing. But now I keep thinking maybe he just didn't like kissing *me*."

There was this thing in my chest that kept ticking toward rage. The more she said about this fuck-nut she was supposed to marry, the more I wanted to find him, drag him out to one of our unused fields, and make sure he was never seen or heard from again.

"That couldn't have been the problem."

"Why not?" she asked. "He obviously didn't want to marry me."

"Tell me this," I said, angling toward her. "Did you like kissing him?"

She licked her lips, which was really distracting. Between those lips of hers and all this talk of kissing, I was having a hard time keeping my dick from taking over.

"I'm not sure. Maybe I was doing it wrong. I, um... I don't have a lot of experience. Maybe I'm a bad kisser."

"I guess that's possible. Not everyone is born with innate kissing abilities," I said. She bit her bottom lip, and fuck I was getting turned on. "But maybe you were just kissing the wrong guy."

"I guess."

"I know what we need to do." I shifted closer so our legs touched and looked her straight in the eyes. I was serious as fuck about this. "We need to figure out if you're actually a bad kisser, or if it was him. I'm going to put my money on assgoblin, but there's one way to find out definitively."

"How do we do that?"

I grinned. This was going to be fun. "I need to kiss you."

"You... oh... I don't know."

"Here's why." I held out my hand so I could tick the reasons off with my fingers. "I'm an awesome kisser, so if there's a problem, we'll know it isn't me. I have a feeling you're actually a great kisser and you just don't realize it. You look sad, and I don't like it when you're sad, even though we just met, and kissing makes me happy, so I bet it will make you happy, too. Finally, all this talk about kissing is making me watch your mouth while you talk, so now I really want to know what you taste like."

"Um..."

I was getting the biggest *yes* vibe right now, even though she was blinking at me like she'd forgotten how to talk. And damn, I wanted to kiss this girl. Maybe it wasn't one of my smartest ideas, but fuck it. I liked being reckless. It was like crack to me.

"Come on, Cookie," I said. She was watching my mouth now, so I dragged my teeth over my bottom lip. "It's for science."

"Oh, well, if it's for science, I guess that's okay."

Hell yes.

I moved in slowly, touching her cheek with my fingertips. Like a glass of good wine, I was going to taste her properly. Our noses brushed, but instead of going straight for her lips, I slid my cheek along hers so I could get a hit of her scent. My eyes rolled back. God, she smelled good—like birthday cake.

Her breath was feather-light on my skin and the barely audible sound of her gasp made the hair on my arms stand on end. This girl was giving me motherfucking goosebumps. I took in another lungful of her, breathing in deeply while I let my hands go where they wanted. One slid around the back of her neck. The other rested gently on her thigh—or at least, on the mountain of white fabric covering her thigh.

Man, I'd have loved to get under all that white nonsense and see what she had underneath.

But that wasn't what was going down tonight. I was just having a little fun with her. She'd had an absolute disaster of a day, and making her smile a little was the least I could do.

And this bullshit about that assclown not wanting to kiss her? I was going to cure her of any notion that it was her fault.

Unless, of course, she really was a shitty kisser, in which case, I'd fix that too.

I traced a path back to her mouth, letting my scratchy jaw brush against her soft skin. Then I settled my lips over hers and exerted gentle pressure.

Hesitating there, I let us both sink into it. I quested out with my tongue, drawing it along her bottom lip. That earned me another little gasp that I felt all the way to my groin. The blood in my body was quickly heading south, but I kept my attention on the kiss.

Except as she parted her lips and our tongues started to explore, I lost track of what I was doing. Or at least, why I was doing it. Because everything else faded into the background. All I could feel were Amelia's lips. Her tongue. The warm wetness of it as our mouths tangled.

My heart beat faster and I clenched a fistful of her dress. There was something happening inside of me. Sparks and crackles and pings of electricity. I was going to pull away. I'd only meant to kiss her a little bit. But then...

I.

Couldn't.

Stop.

Kissing Amelia was the best thing I'd done in a long time. And that was saying something, because mostly my life was awesome. But this. Holy fuck. Her lips were full and soft, her tongue wet and velvety. She tasted like mint and rainbows and motherfucking candy. I probably tasted like beer, but judging by the way she eagerly lapped her tongue into my mouth, she didn't seem to mind.

She'd asked me if I liked kissing, and I'd given her an

honest *yes*. But in this moment, I didn't just like kissing. I loved it. I loved it so much, I wanted to keep kissing her as long as possible. Deep to shallow. Long, slow drags of our tongues against each other, followed by gentle kisses on the lips. Then mouths opening, deep again, tongues delving in, anxious for more.

We were making out right at the bar, and it wasn't like I gave two shits, but I did hear the bartender clear his throat a few times. I didn't want to get her kicked out—and if I got kicked out of here again, it would probably be a while before they let me back in.

Still wasn't enough to make me stop. At least, not for another few seconds. Then, very reluctantly, I pulled back. I kissed her lips a few more times before I pulled away fully.

I was drunk on her. Fucking plastered. I blinked my eyes open, my lids heavy, my head spinning.

"Cooper," she said, her voice soft. "I've decided something. I'm going to ask you a question, and I need an honest answer. I need this from you right now, do you understand?"

I swallowed and blinked again, trying to kick-start my brain, but I felt sluggish. Oddly calm. "I understand. Tell me what you need, Cookie."

"Will you come back to my hotel with me?"

FIVE

AMELIA

COOPER HAD a dopey half-grin on his face and his eyes looked heavy. I didn't blame him. I felt the same way. The only thing stopping me from diving in for more kissing was my resolve to see this through. I'd decided something while he kissed me, and I was determined.

I was going to have sex with Cooper.

This was, without a shred of doubt, the most reckless thing I'd ever done in my entire life. He was a stranger. He could be crazy, or a murderer. I might be bringing the cause of my death back to the honeymoon suite.

But I didn't believe that. Not for a second. Cooper was a stranger, but that was a lot of his appeal. Granted, he was dripping with appeal. Sex appeal, to be specific. He was ridiculously attractive. Tall—certainly taller than me, which I loved—and his body was thick with muscle. Unkempt dark hair made him look a little boyish, but that jaw was all man. Add to that a set of bright blue eyes that sparkled with his smile, and rough hands that looked strong, and I was ready to swoon off my stool.

He was the type of guy who'd normally have me so

tongue-tied, I'd never get a word out. But I *could* talk to him. I wasn't sure why. Maybe I just didn't have anything else to lose. I'd been stood up on my wedding day. Who cared if I sounded like a dork in front of a hot guy?

And oh my god, he was hot. The hottest guy I'd ever been this close to in person. And he'd just kissed the heck out of me.

I wanted more. A lot more. I wanted to be reckless, and Cooper was perfect.

"Did you just ask me back to your room with you?"

I nodded. "Yes."

He bit his bottom lip again and his eyes flicked up and down. "That's... not what I expected you to say."

My heart sank a little. I'd spoken so quickly, I hadn't thought through what I'd do if he said no.

"Well... I mean, if you don't want to, it's fine. I realize that sounds silly, since I'm sitting here in a wedding dress after having been publicly rejected in basically the worst way imaginable. So it would seem like I'm putting a huge amount of pressure on you not to be the second man who rejects me today. But I'm being honest when I say it's fine. I wouldn't want you to come back to my room with me if you don't want to. That would be worse than you telling me no right now. Because I'm not asking you to come back to my room to hang out or watch TV or something. I'm asking you because... you know. I want to sleep with you. And by that I mean have sex."

He coughed, then hit his chest with his fist a few times. "Sorry, Cookie. You just took me by surprise, and not many people manage to do that. I'm usually the one shocking people, so it's a weird feeling to be on the other end of it. It's odd. You think someone is going to say one thing, like, *kiss me again Cooper, that was the best kiss I've ever had.* And instead she says, *come back to my hotel room because I want to have sex.* I mean, it's fucking awesome, I'm pretty excited that you said it, I just didn't expect it."

"You're excited?"

"Shit, yeah. Why wouldn't I be? How was the kiss, by the way? Because from my end, it was amazing. You're a badass kisser, and assgobin is a dumbfuck if he thought you weren't."

"It was... so good." Which was such an understatement it was practically a lie. It was the best kiss of my entire life, by orders of magnitude.

"See? I told you I was a good kisser. I'm really good at sex, too. I have to warn you, if we do this, I'm going to ruin you for all other men. Is that a risk you're willing to take?"

"Yeah, I think so."

"This is not how I thought my night was going to end, but I'm not complaining. You're sure about this?"

I took a deep breath, making sure it pushed my boobs up higher. This dress was a lot of things, but it did make my boobs look pretty great. Cooper definitely noticed.

"Yes, I'm sure. Positive. Completely. One hundred percent."

"That's very convincing." He touched my face and gently ran his thumb down my cheek. "Okay, beautiful. Let's go back to your room."

Did he just call me *beautiful?* God, he was making me all warm and melty inside.

Cooper tossed some money on the bar and I sent a quick text to Daphne.

Me: I'm OK but going to bed and turning off my phone. Talk in the morning.

Daphne: U sure?

Me: Yes. Sure. Just need to go to bed. We can do the fun revenge stuff tomorrow.

Daphne: I feel bad leaving u.

Me: Don't. I'm good for now. Pinky promise.

Daphne: OK. I'll check on you in the morning. Luv u.

Me: Luv u too.

"Ready?" Cooper asked as he helped me down from the barstool.

I took another deep breath. "Yes. I'm ready."

Cooper laced our fingers together, holding my hand on the walk to my hotel. It was a very sweet gesture. It felt... intimate. Which was an odd thing for me to think, considering I'd just asked him to come get *very* intimate with me. Why did hand-holding feel special? I wasn't sure. But it did, and it felt good, so I enjoyed the warmth of his hand as we walked to my hotel.

"We should see if there's a back or side entrance or something," I said when we got close to the hotel. "I don't want to run into anyone from the wedding. I don't want to have to deal with their pity smiles when I know they'll gossip about me two seconds later."

"I know five ways to break into the Lodge, so we're good."

I laughed. "I have a key, so we don't have to break in."

"That does make it easier," he said. "Follow me. I've got you."

He squeezed my hand and led me around the edge of the parking lot. Suddenly, he yanked on my arm, pulling me down behind a car. I crouched next to him, which was seriously awkward in my dress, but he put a finger to his lips.

With a quick wink, he popped up, then back down again. "We're clear. Let's move."

We stayed low as we moved across the lot from one row of cars to the next. He stopped me again, crouching between two cars, while he popped up to look.

"Make for the door. Go."

My hand was still clasped in his as we rushed to the back entrance. I fumbled in my little clutch for my room key. Cooper swiped it for me and the lock clicked. A second later, we were hurrying down the hallway to the elevator.

I was giggling by the time the elevator doors closed behind us—which was a weird sensation, all things considered. But the whole *groom left me for my cousin* thing was far from my mind in the presence of Cooper. Sneaking him back to my room on what was supposed to have been my wedding night seemed perfect, somehow.

It wasn't a revenge thing. I wasn't going to tweet about this in the morning to rub Griffin's face in the fact that I hadn't slept alone on the night he should have been sleeping with me. I was doing this for one person, and one person only: me. In fact, this might have been the first time I'd ever done anything that was truly just for myself.

My dress rustled around my legs as we walked down the hall toward the double doors of the honeymoon suite. Someone had tied pearly white balloons to the doorknob and a sign read *Congratulations Mr. and Mrs. Wentworth*. I ripped the sign down and tossed it on the floor while Cooper swiped my key card and opened the door.

As soon as the door clicked closed behind us, Cooper grabbed me. I was glad he didn't wait, or ask if I wanted to sit down and talk or anything like that. I didn't know how this one-night-stand thing was supposed to work, really, so I was happy to let him take the lead.

And I wanted him to keep kissing me, because oh my god, that felt good.

I stepped out of my heels as he backed me into the bedroom. His hands slid around my waist, across the satiny fabric of the dress that I hoped he'd get to work taking off, and his nose brushed against mine. Our lips touched, briefly, sending a shiver down my spine.

Then he bit his lower lip, grinned, and kissed me.

His mouth on mine was something out of a dream. The way he'd kissed me at the bar had made my knees weak—and for the first time in my life, I understood what that phrase really meant—but this was something else entirely. This wasn't a kiss like anything I'd ever experienced before.

It was mouth sex.

His hands tangled in my hair—it was completely ruined now—and the things his tongue was doing... It was wet and delicious, with all these sensations skittering across my skin, dancing like lights. I couldn't have opened my eyes if I'd tried.

He pulled away and I let my eyelids flutter open. I was panting, my chest heaving against my dress. *Heaving?* Such a cliché, but it was the only word that would do.

I wanted this stupid dress off—now—but I knew there was something I needed to tell him first. I was most assuredly going to be horrible at this. I was never good at anything I did on the first try. With some practice, sure, I could get better. But I didn't want him to think there was any other reason for what was about to occur.

His lips left a hot trail down my neck and the way his tongue lapped against my skin—who knew I'd love being licked so much?—almost broke my brain entirely. Almost.

"Um, Cooper." My voice sounded completely foreign to my ears. Breathy and full of lust. "I need to tell you something first."

"Sure," he said in between lavishing the base of my neck with wet, sloppy kisses.

"Uh..." His mouth on my neck and his hands sliding up my back to find my zipper were making it very hard to concentrate. As was the very persistent throbbing between my legs. "I've just... I need you to know... I've never done this before."

"Hmm?" His voice humming against my collarbone sent a shiver through my body.

"This is, um..." Oh my god, he needed to stop that with his mouth or I was going to collapse before I could get the words out. "This is my first time."

He froze with his lips against the base of my neck and his hands splayed across my back. "What was that, now?"

"This is my first time," I whispered. I hated feeling like it was something to be ashamed of.

Cooper stepped back and looked at me. A groove formed between his eyebrows and his eyes were so intense I could have sworn they almost glowed.

"Amelia, I need you to be really straight with me right now," he said. "Talk to me like I'm three and I don't fully grasp all the ins and outs of the English language, because I'm telling you, there is not a lot of blood in my brain to make all the braining happen. So, I need to hear this in one simple sentence of about three or four words. Okay? Do you get me? I need this from you right now."

I nodded, understanding him perfectly. "I'm a virgin."

"Whoa," he said, backing up a few steps. "That felt like being hit by a big board, right here in the chest. Okay. Let's calm down." He started moving around the room, gesturing as he spoke. "This is a big deal. I mean, this is really huge. Cookie, I'm going to need a minute to process what you just told me, because I'm not sure what to do with it yet. That word is kind of rolling around my head, like it's one of those bouncy balls. Do you remember those? They're little and colorful, and you bounce them and they go way higher than you think. I have one of those bouncing around my head, except it's not a ball, it's a word, and it's hitting all these different parts of my brain, and I just need a second."

I swallowed hard, trying to prepare myself for the crash. The disappointment. It was coming. He was going to leave. He was going to say no, and I'd spend tonight alone in this stupid suite. Still a virgin.

But I was determined to hold myself together, at least while he was still here. God, this was the stupidest thing I'd ever done in my entire life.

On the other hand, it really wasn't. Agreeing to marry Griffin probably took that honor.

So I squared my shoulders, adjusted my dress, and waited for Cooper to make up his mind.

He stopped and stared at me again. I felt as naked as if he'd just walked in on me coming out of the shower. My cheeks blazed hot. I had to keep myself from looking down at my chest, because I was positive I was turning red all the way down to my boobs.

"Holy fuck," Cooper breathed. "Oh my god, you're fucking sexy. I mean, really. I'm so turned on right now it isn't even funny. Like, this hurts. My dick is so hard it feels like it's going to burst right out of these pants."

"Um, thank you? I think."

"I don't want you to think you being a virgin is a bad thing, okay? It's not a good thing either. It's neutral, like it shouldn't be a thing, because who cares if you've slept with tons of guys or none, it doesn't matter to me. That's not why I'm freaking out over here. It's just that, it's a lot of responsibility. You're asking me to be your first and that feels really important."

"Okay. I can understand that."

"I know you can." He took a few steps closer. "And that's the other thing. You're scaring me a little bit."

"Why would I scare you?"

"Because I've never been with a virgin. Not even when I was one. But you know what? That's not even it. I'm just using that as an excuse. I'm scared of you because I think you might be magic, and I don't know what to do with that."

"I'm not magic, Cooper. I'm just a girl. I'm ordinary."

"What? Who told you that?"

"Told me what?"

"That you're ordinary. Was it that guy I saved you from marrying?"

"Um, I don't know, and you didn't save me from marrying him," I said. "He left me, remember?"

He waved his hand like it wasn't important. "Details. I basically saved you. It's fine, you don't need to gush about how great I am, I already know. But I am getting the very disturbing impression that you don't realize how great *you* are. It has nothing to do with having a virgin pussy. I mean, yeah, that's probably pretty great, but not because it's virginal—just because it's you." He brushed a lock of hair back off my face. "I'm looking at you, Amelia. And I really like what I see."

A single tear escaped from the corner of my eye and slid down my cheek. That was the nicest thing anyone had ever said to me. And it was said by a random hot guy I'd picked up at a bar who barely knew me. Talk about unexpected.

"Thank you," I said, my voice quiet in the small space between us.

"I just call it like I see it, beautiful," he said. "And by the way, I'm in."

"Yeah?"

"Fuck yeah. This is an enormous responsibility you've given me. But you know what? I'm honored. I'm honored that you would choose me to share this with you. And baby, you chose right. The things I'm going to do to you tonight…" He traced his fingers down the side of my cheek. "I won't let you down, Cookie."

And then his hands were back in my hair as he kissed me again, and I melted against him.

SIX
COOPER

AMELIA SOFTENED AGAINST ME, putty in my hands. She might not have been experienced, but she was one hell of a kisser.

Being a girl's first? That was some heavy shit. But I was up to the task. Throw in some revenge sex on what was supposed to be her wedding night, and I had a feeling tonight was going to blow my mind. I was going to blow hers, that was for sure.

I slid my hands around her back to lower the zipper on her dress, kissing down her neck and shoulder as I went. How did she taste so good? I wanted to lick her all over. I pulled the zipper down and it took both of us to get the dress off her. She giggled softly, her cheeks flushing pink as she stepped out of all the white fabric.

She kicked the dress away. "I won't be needing that again."

Her hands strayed to her waist. She was wrapped up like a fucking mummy. Not just a bra and panties. She had layers of nonsense all over her.

"What is all this?" I asked.

"Spanx," she said with a shrug. "You know, to hold me in and keep everything contained. I guess this stuff is supposed to make you feel more confident, because it smooths you out, but right now I'm wishing I wasn't wearing it because oh god, I'm going to take it off and I just don't know how I feel about this."

"Shh." I put a finger to her lips and kissed her nose. "You're fucking beautiful. If by the end of tonight you don't feel like the goddess you are, I've failed you."

She bit her lip and nodded. "Maybe I should just..." She gestured toward the bathroom.

"Whatever makes you comfortable, Cookie."

She went into the bathroom and when she emerged, she was dressed in nothing but a strapless bra and white lace panties.

My eyes nearly popped out of my head as I took her in.

Amelia was all curves and softness. Full tits, tapered waist that flared to her round hips. She was thick and soft and there was so much for me to grab onto.

"Holy fuck, Amelia." I brushed the hair back from her face and leaned in close to whisper in her ear. "You're really going to let me touch you?"

She gave me a subtle nod.

So touch her I did. I let my hands roam, getting to know the lines of her gorgeous body. Smelled her hair and kissed her neck. Her bra clasp came undone and she gasped, but let it drop.

"Lie down, beautiful."

Her breath came faster, and she seemed both eager and nervous. It made me want to devour her. I pulled off my shirt while she got on the bed, then kicked off my shoes and unfastened my jeans. She watched me, licking her lips as I undressed. I pulled a condom out of my wallet before I tossed my pants to the floor, but didn't rush to get naked and put it on. I set it on the bed so it would be ready. But I was going to get her ready, first.

"Oh my god," she said. "You're... wow. I can't believe I'm doing this. Actually, I can't believe you're doing this. Look at you, you're... wow. I said that already. You're so gorgeous."

I grinned at her and adjusted the waistband of my boxer briefs over my erection. Her eyes darted to my cock and she made a cute little noise in her throat.

After climbing on the bed with her, I helped her slip her panties down her legs. My hands trailed up and down her soft skin, just getting the feel of her. I palmed one of her tits —she was more than a handful—and she gasped again.

"Do you like it when I touch you?" I murmured as I lapped my tongue against her neck and squeezed her tit, feeling her nipple harden.

"Yes," she breathed.

Working my way down, I licked her hard peak, letting my hand trace a path toward her belly. Just her quiet whimpers had me so turned on I could barely stand it. But I moved slowly, lavishing her nipples with attention from my tongue. Licking, kissing, sucking. She trembled and tipped her knees open of her own accord when my hand moved closer to the apex of her thighs.

This girl wanted to get fucked. I wasn't sure why I got to be the lucky bastard to do it, but I wasn't complaining.

She shuddered as I let my hand slip down to her beautifully waxed pussy. Her skin was petal soft. I moved back to her mouth and kissed her lips while I gently stroked outside her slit, letting her get used to the feel of me touching her.

"You like this?"

"Yes," she breathed.

"Do you want more?"

"Yes, please." She twitched a little. "Should I be... doing something else?"

"Shh." I kissed her and gently swiped my thumb across her clit. Her hips jerked. "We'll get to that. Just relax and let me make you feel good."

She gasped as I slipped a finger inside her. I didn't move too fast. I wanted her to feel safe with me so she could let go —so I could take her places she'd never been. I took my time, stroking her, feeling her warm wetness. When I thought she was ready, I slid a second finger into her pussy.

"How does that feel?"

"So good," she said, her voice soft. Her eyes were closed and I could feel her body relaxing as I carefully stroked her.

I gradually fingered her harder, rubbing her g-spot and caressing her clit in a steady rhythm. Her body responded, moving with me, her hips thrusting against my hand. Soft whimpers escaped her lips and I sucked on her nipple as I brought her closer. Felt her pussy heat up as her orgasm built.

"That's it, Cookie." I picked up the pace. God, she was so wet. I needed to be inside her like I needed to breathe, but I wanted to make her come. Kissing and nuzzling her neck, I murmured in her ear. "Come for me, beautiful. Your pussy feels so good. I can't wait to be inside you."

She moaned, her eyes still closed.

"I'm going to fuck you so good," I said, and she bucked her hips against my hand again. Her pussy started to clench around my fingers. Making a girl come was such a rush. I fucking loved it.

"Oh my god," she breathed.

I felt her come apart, and the sight of her voluptuous body writhing against the sheets was glorious. Leaning in to gently nuzzle her neck, I waited while she took quick breaths, coming down from the high.

"How did that feel, beautiful?"

"I don't even... how did you... that was amazing."

"Good. And baby, we're just getting started."

I kissed her again—even just kissing this girl was a hell of a lot of fun—and grabbed the condom. Once I had it rolled on, I nudged her legs apart and settled on top of her.

Her skin touching mine felt incredible. I didn't know what it was about her. She didn't just feel good. She felt *insanely* good, and I wasn't even inside her yet.

"Are you ready?" I asked.

"Yes."

"I'll go slow, but if something hurts or feels bad, just tell me," I said softly. "And if it feels good, tell me that too."

She smiled, her cheeks still flushed, her eyes a little glassy. "Okay."

I aligned the tip of my cock with her opening and pushed in. Just the tip. She gasped, her hands gripping my back.

"Are you okay?"

"Yes," she said.

It was hard to hold back, but I didn't want to hurt her. Slowly, I pushed my cock inside her pussy, feeling her walls wrap around me. She was wet from coming already, and so hot. So ready for me. I slid in deeper and our eyes locked. Those pretty hazel eyes held mine, holding me hostage, and an intensity I'd never felt before flooded through me.

I felt close to her. Like we were sharing something huge and important. And I was really fucking glad it was me.

"How does that feel?" I asked. "Does it hurt?"

"A little. But mostly it's... oh god, so good. So good I can't think."

I pulled out halfway and pushed in again. Slow. Careful. Every cell in my body wanted to pound the shit out of her, but instead, I amped up slowly. Moved just a little faster, thrust just a little harder.

Groaning, I shut my eyes. "You feel so fucking good."

She whimpered a reply.

I kissed her eager mouth while I picked up the pace. Her body responded, her legs falling open wider, her hips thrusting up to take me in deeper. As she relaxed into it, her hands moved over my skin, caressing my back and shoulders. I loved the way she touched me, her hands smooth and warm.

Holy shit, she felt good. I lost myself in her, my mind going hazy, sensation taking over. Her soft skin. Her scent. Her fantastic pussy and the fluid movements of her gorgeous body. We flowed together like we'd been made for this. Like we'd done this a thousand times and knew all each other's secrets.

She pressed against my lower back and lifted her knees, drawing me deeper inside her. I groaned. I was ready to die, she felt so fucking good. Tension built in my groin and my muscles flexed. I moved faster, daring to thrust harder, and was rewarded with needy whimpers.

Our tongues lapped out, kisses messy. My cock throbbed inside her, my balls drawing up tight. Leaning my face into her neck, I grabbed her ass with both hands, digging my fingers into her soft flesh. Driving my cock in hard.

"Yes," she breathed into my ear. "Yes, yes, oh god, yes."

Instinct took over as my orgasm built, almost to the breaking point. Her body moving in sync with mine and her refrain of *yes*es in my ear drove me on. Her pussy was so hot, clenching around my dick. She moaned, I thrust, she clenched, I growled, she pulled her legs back.

And I lost my fucking mind.

I exploded into her, the rush of orgasm eclipsing everything. My muscles clenched and released, and my dick throbbed as the hot waves burst through me. Her pussy tightened around me, her breathless moans in my ear the only thing I could hear. We rolled and moved and thrust and held onto each other as if the power of our shared climax would sweep us away.

Slowly, I came back to reality. We were both breathing hard, our arms holding each other tight. My mind was a haze of happy brain chemicals, my body light and tingling. And there was something else. A feeling uncurling inside my chest that I wasn't used to. I wasn't sure what it was, but it felt really good, and made me want to hold her.

I lifted up to look at her and touched her face. Her cheeks were flushed the cutest shade of pink and she slow-blinked at me a few times.

"How was that?"

"I... yes... oh... it was... I can't... Cooper."

"Me too."

Reluctantly, I rolled off her so I could deal with the condom. I brought back a warm washcloth. There wasn't much to clean up, but it was her first time, and I wanted to make sure she was comfortable.

"Thank you," she said.

I got back in bed and gathered her in my arms. I wanted to keep her close. Hold her and snuggle her and breathe in her scent.

She relaxed against me, her body languid, and tucked her head below my chin. I wrapped my arms around her and let my eyes drift closed.

"Cooper?"

"Yeah, Cookie."

"Was that... well... I'm just wondering... I guess I'm trying to ask something but it's kind of hard. But I feel so good right now and that was one of most amazing things that's ever happened to me, but I can't imagine it was that good for you."

"It was that good for me."

She shifted so she could look at me. "Really?"

"Baby, you're incredible. I just hope I'm lucky enough to get to do it again. But I don't want to hurt you."

"It wasn't too bad. I think I'll be sore later, but right now I just feel... amazing. Is it always like this?"

I took a deep breath and squeezed her against me. "No. It's not. But I said you might be magic. I think I was right."

She nestled her head against my shoulder and traced soft circles across my chest. A hum of contentment buzzed inside me as I enjoyed the feel of her in my arms. I was relaxed, sated, happy. Happier than I'd been in a long time. I wasn't sure why. Great sex was awesome, but this was more than a fantastic orgasm. I hadn't just fucked this girl. I'd connected with her. And I liked it.

She *was* magic. I'd known it as soon as I'd kissed her. Somewhere in the back of my head, I wondered why that didn't scare the hell out of me. Why drifting in bliss with her right now wasn't triggering my instinct to bolt. But it wasn't, and as I felt her soft breath against my skin, I decided to just go with it. I closed my eyes and drifted off to sleep, feeling more whole than I ever had before.

SEVEN
AMELIA

SLEEP RETREATED SLOWLY. The bed was comfortable and my body so relaxed I felt like I was floating. Reaching my arms above my head, I stretched, then drew the comforter over my shoulder and curled up again.

Something touched my lips and my eyes flew open. Cooper. It was Cooper touching my lips. Kissing them, to be precise. I startled, but quickly melted at the feel of his mouth on mine. I slid my hands along the hard planes of muscle in his back and shoulders while he leaned over me, his erection pressing against my hip.

"Morning," he mumbled between kisses.

"Morning." I giggled into his mouth.

I couldn't believe he was here. Cooper was by far the hottest guy I'd ever met, and here he was, lying in bed naked with me. Kissing me good morning. I'd expected him to leave last night, but we'd fallen asleep together.

It had been fantastic. Magical. Incredible. He'd told me he'd ruin me for all other men, and I had a feeling he was very, very right.

"How'd you sleep?" he asked.

"So good. You?"

He brushed his nose against mine. "Really good. Like, suspiciously good. I didn't wake up once."

"Do you normally wake up at night?"

"Yeah, most of the time." He reached over me and tilted the alarm clock toward us. Nine thirty-seven. "Holy shit, it's late."

"I'm sorry," I said. "You probably have to go."

"No, I just don't usually sleep in." He grinned. "You wore me out."

"You don't feel worn out." I wiggled against his hard cock.

He groaned and nibbled on my bottom lip. "Worn out is relative. I'm always down to fuck. Especially with you, apparently."

I laughed, last night's euphoria still making me smile. I knew, somewhere in the back of my mind, that I was going to crash from this high—and crash hard. Sooner or later, I was going to have to face the reality of my life.

But it was hard to think about that when Cooper was lying next to me, his skin touching mine. He felt warm and safe.

It meant something—something big—that Cooper's presence was enough to drive away thoughts of Griffin. I'd have to face that, too.

"You feel so good, Cookie, but I need to pee and it's going to take me like five minutes just to get my dick to cooperate. And that's if I'm alone in the bathroom. He won't budge if you're anywhere near me."

"Oh, okay. But why will it take you five minutes? Wait, that was a weird question. I'm sorry. I just... I don't have brothers or anything, and before you, I wasn't exactly acquainted with anyone's male anatomy. I don't know that much about how they work."

He grinned again. "You didn't seem like an amateur last night. Of course you have me, and I'm a great teacher, so there's that. But guys can't pee with an erection. At least, not easily. So I gotta go in there and think of all the least sexy things I can to get him to calm the fuck down. How about you go first, then I'll go, then we'll take a shower."

"That sounds nice."

"Jesus, I shouldn't have said shower. Now all I can picture is you naked and soapy. Fuck, my bladder hurts." He rolled onto his back, wincing.

"Are you okay?"

"Just go." He waved in the direction of the bathroom with one hand, grabbing his crotch with the other. "I can't deal with your hotness right now. I'm closing my eyes. I can't even look at you or I'll never be able to pee and my bladder will explode and I'll die."

I laughed. He really had closed his eyes.

"Okay, okay, I'm going."

I slipped out of bed and into the bathroom. My makeup was smudged, so I washed the last of it off my face. My hair was crazy, but there wasn't anything I could do about that until I showered. Too much hair spray. I felt a little self-conscious, but Cooper hadn't said anything about me looking messy. So I put on one of the bathrobes and decided not to worry too much about it.

Cooper went into the bathroom after I finished. I sat on the edge of the bed, wondering what was supposed to happen next. He'd mentioned a shower. Did that mean more sex? God, I hoped so. I was achy between the legs, but I'd have given just about anything for more.

But what about after that? What was a girl supposed to

do after sleeping with a stranger? Invite him to breakfast? Was he going to leave and I'd never see him again?

I had no idea how any of this worked.

The shower turned on, so I pushed those thoughts aside. I'd face reality later. Right now, I had a ridiculously hot guy who wanted to shower with me.

I was just about to go into the bathroom when there was a knock on my door.

My heart leapt into my throat. Oh god. What if it was my mother? It was late; she would have expected me to make an appearance by now. Of all the things I wasn't ready for today, dealing with my mother was at the top of the list.

Please let it be housekeeping. Please let it be housekeeping.

I walked out into the living room—the suite was huge—took a deep breath, and opened the door.

"Hey, sweetie." Daphne pushed her way in, dressed in a black tank top and jean shorts, her face all sympathy. "How are you doing this morning? Have you had breakfast yet? Do you want to eat? I feel like I should have stayed here with you last night. Are you okay?"

I pulled my robe tighter and let the door close. My relief that it wasn't my mother was quickly replaced by alarm. The sound of the shower roared in my ears.

Crap. I needed to get Daphne out of here.

"Um, yes, I'm okay. And no."

"No you haven't had breakfast, or no you don't want to eat?"

"No, I haven't had breakfast. But I'm fine. I'll, um... I'll get something later."

She went to the window and threw the curtains open. "The room is on Griffin's credit card, right?"

"Yeah."

"Then we need to order room service. All the room service."

She went into the bedroom and drew those curtains open. Something small and shiny on the floor caught my eye. Oh god, it was a condom wrapper.

Don't look down, Daph. Don't look down.

"That's okay, I don't feel like eating yet." I moved back into the doorway, hoping I could shoo her out.

She paused and raised an eyebrow. "Is your shower on?"

"Oh." I looked toward the bathroom, the door slightly ajar. "Yeah, I was going to get in the shower when you knocked. I was um... letting the water warm up. So, I'll just do that and text you later?"

"Why are you trying to get rid of me?"

"I'm not. I just want to take a shower. I have all this hairspray in my hair from yesterday."

She pulled at my matted hair. "Yeah, you have quite the nest going on up there. Did you sleep okay?"

"Yeah, slept fine."

"Really? Amelia, you're acting weird. Although, I don't blame you. Yesterday was horrible. But sweetie, you're going to be fine. We're going to get through this together, okay?"

"I know, it was horrible, but I'm okay. I swear. I just want to go take my shower."

The water turned off.

Daphne blinked at me. "Did the shower just turn off?"

"Um, yeah, I think it's a water conservation feature," I lied. "If the shower is on too long, it shuts off automatically."

"I took like a thirty-minute shower last night and it never turned off."

"Well, no one is in there, so it turned off because it isn't being used."

She raised her eyebrows. "How does the shower know if someone is using it or not?"

"I don't know how it works. I didn't invent the technology. Maybe it has a sensor in the floor. I'm just saying, no one is in there to turn off the water, so obviously it turned off by itself. The most likely explanation is that it's a water-conserving shower. I actually think this is a great development and I'd recommend this hotel based on their ecological friendliness alone."

Daphne opened her mouth like she was going to reply, but her eyes slid past me and widened. My back stiffened, and I didn't need to turn around to know what—or rather, who—she was looking at.

"Cookie, did you want to get in? I was waiting for you but... Oh. Hey."

The deep male voice behind me shouldn't have made me startle—I knew Cooper was in the shower—but I jumped nonetheless. I glanced over my shoulder to find him standing in the doorway of the bathroom. Naked. He had a towel in his hand, which he casually draped over his crotch, but other than that—naked.

Oh god, he was incredible. Dripping wet, messy hair, his skin a little flushed from the hot water. He had the coolest unicorn tattoo across his ribs. I'd noticed it last night. Not the kind of thing you normally saw on a guy, but it was amazing on him.

He grinned at Daphne and I thought my knees might buckle.

"Holy shit," Daph said, looking Cooper up and down.

Cooper wrapped the towel around his waist and held it low around his hips. With that sexy grin still on his face, he came closer and stuck his hand out toward Daphne.

"I'm Cooper. Let me guess, best friend? Here to make sure she's okay after being left at the altar? Awesome."

Daphne shook his hand slowly, her mouth hanging open.

"This is Daphne," I said, since she wasn't introducing herself.

"Amelia, can I see you over here for a second?" she asked, not taking her eyes off Cooper.

"I like your tattoos," Cooper said, gesturing to her shoulder. "Peacock orchids. Nice choice."

"Thanks," Daphne said, looking bewildered. She grabbed my arm and hauled me toward the window while Cooper retreated to the bedroom. "Oh my god, what is going on in here? Who is that guy?"

"Cooper."

"Yeah, he told me his name. Who is he? And why is he naked in your room?"

I hadn't planned on hiding this from Daphne. I would have told her. Eventually. At this point, there was no reason to tell her anything but the truth. "I picked him up at a bar last night."

"You what?" she whisper-yelled.

"I went to a bar last night and I met him there. And then, well..."

"I need more details before I decide how I feel about this."

"What details?" I glanced back into the bedroom, but I couldn't see Cooper from where I was standing. He was probably getting dressed so he could leave. That was a depressing thought.

"How did you end up here? And did you..."

"I asked him to come back to my room with me, okay? I realize my former—yes, *former*—virginity was well-known.

And you know what? I was sick of it. I was sick of that being my thing. And stupid Griffin left with stupid Portia, so I went to a bar, and I met Cooper, and I asked him to come back here with me. And then we had sex. And it was amazing."

"Amazing is an understatement, Cookie," Cooper said from the other room. "It was fucking mind-blowing."

"Wow." Daphne's eyes lit up and her mouth curled into a smile. "This is... wow. Okay. I need a second. Amelia picked up a hot guy at a bar and had sex. Oh my god, I'm so proud of you."

"Yeah?"

"Shit, yeah. I would have suggested it last night if I'd thought there was any chance you'd actually do it. Wait, you weren't drunk, were you?"

"No."

"Okay. And Cooper?" She jerked her thumb toward the bedroom. "He seems... well, he's hot as hell, so I guess that's all he needed to be. He got the job done?"

"Twice, babycakes," Cooper called.

"How can he hear us?" Daphne asked.

I shrugged.

"Did he have a tattoo of a unicorn across his ribs?" she asked, lowering her voice to a whisper.

"Yeah, isn't it incredible?"

She blinked at me. "Um, sure. So, is he leaving, or what?"

"I don't really know what's going on. Oh god, Daphne, I have no idea what I'm doing. What am I supposed to do now?"

Cooper sauntered in, shirtless, buttoning his jeans. "Daphne, darling, I'm betting you're in here trying to make plans with Amelia for the day. Find ways to take her mind off things. I get it. She's been through a lot, and you're the best friend, it's your job. But I need to interrupt, because I'm starting to worry you're going to take her away from me, and I don't think I'm ready for that yet."

My heart soared a little. But not too much. A tiny soar. More of an extended jump, rather than actual flight. "You're not?"

"Nope."

"Okay, that's... nice." Daphne looked back and forth between me and Cooper. "But I think I should take it from here. Thanks for everything, Cooper. It was nice to meet you."

Cooper's eyes were locked with mine, vivid and intense. "Have you checked assgoblin's social media to see if he's updated?"

"I... well, no, actually." It was true. I hadn't even thought about looking.

"I didn't think so. Tell you what, this is entirely up to you. I'm not here to make you do anything you're not into. If you want to hang out with Daphne, that's fine." He moved in closer, crowding me with his bare upper body, and tilted my chin up. "But if you want me to, I'd really like to stay. I wasn't finished with you."

I stared into Cooper's eyes, like he'd hypnotized me. A part of me wondered why I trusted him. I didn't know him. Well, I knew him in the sense that I'd slept with him, which was pretty intimate knowledge.

But beyond his sexual prowess—and even without anyone to compare him to, I knew without a doubt he was excellent—I didn't know much about him. I didn't even know his last name. Was it safe to stay with him? What did he want to do today? Staying in the room and having sex again was enormously tempting. But then there was the problem of my mother, and Griffin's parents, and we were supposed to be leaving on our honeymoon tomorrow morning, so what was I going to do now?

"Hey," Cooper said, his voice soft. He touched my chin again. "Where'd you go just then?"

"My life exploded yesterday, and I have no idea what I'm doing."

"Oh sweetie," Daphne said. "Cooper, you seem like a nice guy, but I think you should go. Amelia's life really did explode yesterday, in ways you couldn't understand. Sweetie, I'll have Harrison change my flight and I'll come stay with you at your parents' until we figure out what to do next."

"I can't ask you to do that."

"I don't mind," she said. "We'll make it work."

Cooper looked back and forth between us a few times. "Harrison? Flight? Cookie, I need you to catch me up."

"Harrison is Daphne's fiancé, and he's here for the wedding, but they have to drive back to Seattle today to catch their flight to L.A. in the morning. Harrison got a record deal and he's going to be a rock star."

"Bad ass," Cooper said.

"Well, I don't know about rock star," Daphne said. "He is incredibly talented. But... okay, not the point. Amelia, we need a plan. I'll go talk to Harrison—"

"I like my plan better," Cooper said.

"What's your plan?"

He grinned. "Giving Amelia so many orgasms she forgets assgoblin's name."

I squeaked.

"We'll get out and do some fun stuff, too," he said, his voice casual, like he hadn't just said anything about orgasms.

"I'm off today, and I have some awesome ideas. Cookie, how long do you have this room? Is it paid for?"

"Another night," I said. "And yeah, it's on Griffin's credit card."

"This day just keeps getting better," Cooper said. "Daphne, go grab your rock star. I hope you're hungry. We're ordering all the room service."

The corner of Daphne's mouth turned up in a smile. "Room service is a good idea, I'll give you that."

"I know, I'm full of good ideas," he said. "Meet us back here. But give us a good hour."

"An hour?" she asked.

"At least," Cooper said. He turned that intense gaze back on me. "She still needs a shower."

COOPER *WAS* full of good ideas. And we really did need that hour. I'd never realized a girl could have so many orgasms in such a short period of time.

We ordered two of everything on the room service menu and had a giant picnic in the suite's living room. Cooper won over Daphne and Harrison easily. Harrison was giving him the side-eye for a while but gave him a back-slapping hug when he and Daphne left.

I convinced Daph not to change her plans, and still go to L.A. Nervous as I was about what would happen tomorrow—when I could no longer hide in my hotel suite and had to face reality—I didn't want to disrupt her life.

Avoiding my parents was a priority, so I group-texted them, saying I was staying in the hotel one more night, and I'd see them at home tomorrow. Apparently the universe decided to be kind to me, and neither of them came banging on the door to convince me to go home with them today. Dad replied that he'd send a driver for me. Mom reminded me not to forget to pack my wedding dress in the garment bag so it wouldn't get ruined.

Really, Mom? She was worried about the dress?

After Daphne and Harrison left, Cooper and I lay on the bed, clutching our stomachs. We'd ordered enough food for ten people, and the four of us had eaten a lot of it.

"I'd say I regret that last piece of French toast, but that would be a lie," Cooper said. "It was worth it."

"Me too. The worth it part, I mean. I've barely eaten all week. It feels good to be full. We should do this again for dinner."

"I'd feel bad for freeloading meals off you, but freeloading meals off assgoblin is perfectly acceptable," he said. "Are you ready to go have some fun?"

It was hard to imagine anything more fun than what we'd done this morning. But I couldn't wait to see what he had in mind. "Sure."

He got up and refastened his jeans. "Awesome. Bring the dress."

"What dress?"

"The wedding dress."

"What do we need that for?"

He winked. "You'll see."

We left the hotel by the same side door we'd come in through last night. Cooper said his truck was still parked at the bar, so we walked to it. I was dressed comfortably in shorts and a t-shirt, and Cooper carried the garment bag with my wedding dress unceremoniously stuffed inside.

I still wasn't sure where we were going as we drove through town. He took us down a long road, then made another turn. We pulled up to a small building with a tall fence behind it. The sign said *Paintball.*

"What are we doing here?"

He turned to me with a smile. "Do you trust me?"

"Yes."

"Then come on."

I had a feeling I knew where this was going. Were we going to trash my dress?

We went inside, and Cooper asked me to wait while he talked to the guy who worked there. They seemed to know each other. I glanced around at photos of people in paintball gear on what looked like a big obstacle course. There were tractor tires, wooden walls, shacks, and metal barrels.

"Okay, Cookie, Nolan here is going to get you geared up," Cooper said. He still held my garment bag over his shoulder. "There's a group here already, but it's a bunch of younger kids, so it's perfect. You won't get hurt. I'll meet you out there."

"Wait, Cooper, what are we doing? Are we going to shoot paintballs at the dress?"

"Something like that."

Cooper went through a door behind the counter while Nolan brought out an armful of stuff. He helped me into a dark gray jumpsuit over my clothes, then gave me gloves and a helmet to put on.

"Have you ever done this before?" Nolan asked as he helped me adjust the helmet to fit. It had a visor over my eyes and covered my whole face.

"No, and I'm starting to get scared."

"Don't be scared," he said. "You'll be fine. There are some kids out there, but they're young. The hard-core guys are usually in later."

"Okay," I said, but I wasn't so sure about this. Where was Cooper? If we were shooting paintballs at my dress, why did I need the helmet? Although it was probably just standard procedure.

I followed Nolan through the back door. Outside was a huge field set up with the obstacles I'd seen in the photos—

tires, walls, stacks of concrete blocks. A bunch of kids ran around, ducking behind barriers, shooting at each other. Nolan gave me a paintball gun and showed me how it worked. It seemed straightforward, although I was nervous. The kids out in the field seemed like they were having fun, but there were some yells that might have been pain.

"Ready for this, Cookie?"

I turned at the sound of Cooper's voice and nearly dropped the paintball gun. He was wearing my wedding dress.

Granted, *wearing* was a loose term. The dress didn't fit. The skirt hung down from his waist and stopped just above his ankles. His tan boots stuck out the bottom. The bodice was pulled up almost to his chest, and secured with silver duct tape over his long-sleeved shirt. He had a helmet that matched mine and a paintball gun in his hands.

He looked ridiculous. And absolutely fantastic.

I practically squealed with excitement. My parents were going to murder me for ruining the dress, but I didn't care.

With a paintball gun in my hands, the world tinted slightly yellow from the visor, I squared my shoulders and took a deep breath. "I'm so ready."

"See you out there," Cooper said and jogged away, the dress swishing around his legs.

Nolan led me to a tall wall made of wooden planks. "Cooper's over that way. Once I'm clear, you're free to start."

I still felt like I had no idea what I was doing. Putting my back to the wall, I gripped the paintball gun in my gloved hands and watched Nolan jog back to the building. My heart raced in my chest and a trickle of sweat ran down my back.

Nolan was gone, so it was now or never...

I peeked out from behind the wall and saw a flash of white fabric. He was going to be easy to spot in that thing. He'd ducked behind a wall, so I waited, peering around the edge of my cover.

Cooper dashed for one of the big tires. I fumbled the gun as I brought it up, but managed to get a few shots off before he disappeared behind the tire.

He knew where I was, so I didn't want to stay put. The object might be to ruin my dress, but he had a paintball gun, too. If I didn't move, I was a sitting duck.

There was a stack of barrels nearby, so I peeked out again, then dashed for the barrels. The screams and squeals of the kids were getting louder. I looked again, but no sign of Cooper, and he hadn't shot at me.

A blast of pink splattered on the barrel next to me. I shrieked and scrambled out of the way as a few more bursts of paint hit nearby. Cooper had circled around behind me. I jumped to the other side of the barrels for cover, took aim, and fired.

A splotch of blue spread over the dress, right at Cooper's waist. He tried to spin around behind another barrier, but the dress tangled in his legs. I took the opportunity for all it was worth and fired as fast as my finger could pull the trigger. My aim wasn't great, but I hit him once more, this time with green.

He disappeared behind a stack of cinder blocks, so I made a run for it. A kid darted in front of me and I almost crashed right into him.

"Get the guy in the white dress!" I shouted, pointing in Cooper's direction.

The kid nodded and kept going. And that gave me an

idea. I needed to find allies. With more people on my side, we could do some damage.

The anger I'd felt yesterday churned in my tummy again. I hadn't even wanted that dress. Daphne had said it looked good on me, but I think she'd been trying to make me feel better. It was too fancy. Too big. Too much. I was self-conscious enough about my size, and I'd had to try to stuff myself into that stupid thing. And for what? For Griffin to leave me at the last second?

Screw that.

I followed the sounds of the kids deeper into the course. There were a couple of taller people—adults, I presumed—hiding behind a barrier. I waved, then held my gun up as I approached so they wouldn't shoot me.

"Hey," I said, a little breathless. "This is going to sound so weird, but I was supposed to get married yesterday, and I didn't, and now I'm here with my, um... my friend and he's wearing my dress and I need help destroying it."

"Guy in a wedding dress?" one of the men asked, sounding confused.

"Exactly," I said.

The two men looked at each other and shrugged. The first guy started calling names and in seconds, the kids gathered.

"Okay, crew, here's the deal," he said. "The enemy is out there, dressed in disguise. He's in a white wedding dress, but don't let that fool you. Shoot him, and aim for the white."

The kids—seven of them had gathered—all nodded or gave a thumbs-up before spreading out in search of their prey.

"Have fun," the first guy said.

"Thanks!"

I scurried toward another barrier, then peeked around the edge. There were two kids just ahead of me, crouched behind a tire. The course was eerily quiet. It felt like the calm before the storm.

And just like that, the storm broke.

Cooper jumped out and aimed his paintball gun at me. But I wasn't alone. The two kids behind the tire stood and started firing, sending a flurry of paintballs at him. Some found their mark, splashing him with globs of color. More kids came running, shouting at the top of their lungs, and firing as fast as they could.

"Shit!" Cooper yelled and took off running.

I fired, sending a line of paintballs at him. I was pretty sure the pink and purple splotches that bloomed across his back were mine.

He disappeared around a tall stack of cinder blocks. The kids and I spread out, stalking him. A heady sense of euphoria swept through me. This was the most fun I'd ever had in my life.

A paintball whizzed past me, then another hit me in the leg. It hurt a little, but not too much. Sort of like being shot by a rubber band. I squeaked and ducked behind a tree.

I glanced down at the splatter of green paint on my jumpsuit, oddly proud of that mark. I'd been hit by a paint-ball and survived. I felt like I could do anything.

The kids gathered around me, hiding behind barrels, walls, and stacks of logs nearby. They signaled to each other —they were surprisingly organized—and the two men brought up the rear.

"Give it up, dress guy," one of the kids shouted. "We have you surrounded."

"Never!" came Cooper's voice from up ahead. "You'll never take me alive!"

He jumped out from behind a wall, yelling as he sprayed paintballs like an action hero shooting a machine gun at an army of bad guys.

Laughing so hard I could barely aim, I joined the insanity as the kids and I pummeled Cooper with paintballs. The kids screamed and yelled, the two men shouted at them not to get too close, and Cooper—and my dress—were hit with a rain of multicolored missiles.

Cooper dropped his gun and clutched his chest, then crumpled dramatically to the ground, like we'd killed him. The two men called the kids off, and they all ran in the opposite direction, shouting as they went.

I dashed over to Cooper, who lay on the ground, unmoving. Kneeling beside him, I pulled off my helmet. "Are you okay?"

He pushed his helmet off too. "I think so. Did we win?"

I looked at the paint-splattered dress. "If by winning you mean thoroughly ruining the dress, then yes."

"That's exactly what I mean." He winced as I took his hand and helped him sit up. "That's going to hurt in the morning. Shit."

"I'm sorry."

"Don't be. It was fucking fun. Did you have fun?"

"Yeah, I had so much fun."

He grinned. "Then it was worth it. Uh oh, did you get hit?"

"Just once." I looked down at myself and noticed a second splotch of paint. "Oh! No! I got hit twice!"

"You're a badass, Cookie." He winced again as we both stood up. "Those kids were merciless."

"Yeah, that was kind of my fault. I told them to go for the guy in the dress."

He smiled at me again and his eyes swept up and down.

"Good thinking. I'm proud of you. But now all I can think about is how much I want to rip that jumpsuit off you."

"This thing looks like a bag." I held out the loose fabric. "There's nothing sexy about it."

He stepped in and slipped his arm around my waist, drawing me close. "Not true. You're sexy as hell in that thing. Your hair's messy and you have dirt on your cheek and I want to fuck the shit out of you right here."

My entire body lit up at his suggestion. My cheeks flushed hot, and warmth pooled in my core. The pressure between my legs made me want to rub up against him.

"But... we can't... I mean, there are kids here."

That smile of his was going to take me down. "I know. I'm crazy, but not quite *fuck you on a paintball field with kids around* crazy. So how about we go back to your hotel and I get you dirtier before we get clean."

I was so breathless, I could barely speak. "Uh-huh."

"Awesome." He kissed me, his lips warm and soft. "I love how tall you are. I barely have to lean down to reach. It makes you so kissable."

"Really?"

"Of course. I wouldn't lie about something like that."

I bit the inside of my lip to keep from tearing up. We were supposed to be having fun, not being serious. But I'd never been comfortable with my height. It was worse than my weight. "Sorry, it's just... boys used to tease me for being tall."

"What kind of little pricks did you grow up around?" He kissed me again, deeper this time. "Yep, so damn kissable. They didn't know what they were missing."

"You're very kissable too."

"You bet I am." He bent down to pick up his paintball gun, then looked at me. "You were supposed to go on a honeymoon, right? I'm not trying to remind you of assgoblin. In fact, I'm working pretty hard to keep your mind off that douchebag. But that was the plan? Leave tomorrow?"

"Yeah, that was the plan."

"How long was the trip?"

I picked up my paintball gun, wondering why he was asking about my honeymoon. "Two weeks. We were going to Hawaii, but now I have no idea what I'm going to do."

"I have an idea." His mischievous grin was back.

"What?"

He slid his hand around my waist again. We must have looked ridiculous. Me in a gray jumpsuit, my hair a mess. Cooper in a paint-splattered wedding dress, duct taped around his chest.

"Stay," he said, and my heart did a little jump at the word. "You were supposed to be gone for two weeks anyway, so you might as well. You can stay in one of the cottages at Salishan and we can hang out more."

Hang out with Cooper? That was so very tempting. But this was starting to make me nervous. When we'd met last night, and I'd asked him to come to my hotel with me, I'd never dreamed it would lead to more than one wild night together. But here we were, having fun in the light of day, and he was asking me to stay longer. Spend more time with him.

But he had a point. I didn't have anywhere else to be. I'd just be going back to my parents' house until I could figure out what to do with my life.

"I don't think Salishan rents those cottages," I said. "We checked into lodging when we were planning the wedding, and those aren't for rent."

"Oh, no, my family owns Salishan," he said. "I'm Cooper Miles. Did I not mention that?"

"No, I don't think we ever got to last names. Mine's Hale. Amelia Hale."

"Well, Amelia Hale..." He leaned in and placed a wet kiss on my lips. "I have it on good authority that the Miles family would be more than happy to let you stay in one of the cottages. And this particular Miles boy would love it if you did."

He made me feel so squishy and melty inside, it was hard to think. With his arm around me, his nose touching mine, and his lips oh so deliciously close, I felt like I'd do anything he asked. Stay longer with a guy I'd just met after being dumped on my wedding day? Sure, what could possibly go wrong?

"Okay, I'll stay. Instead of a honeymoon, I'll have a Cooper-moon."

"Yes!" he said, his eyes widening. "That's exactly it. Fuck yes, I knew this was a good idea. Holy shit, Cookie, we're going to have so much fun. Your Cooper-moon is going to be the best."

We were going to have fun. And it was about time I had a little fun in my life. I deserved it.

NINE
COOPER

I HAD to be up early Monday morning to get to work. Reluctantly, I left a sleeping Amelia in her hotel. It would have been much more fun to stay and play with her. For a girl who'd been a virgin a few days ago, holy shit she was frisky. I'd never met a girl who could keep up with me, but Amelia was insatiable.

I'd kept my promise to get her dirtier after paintball. Then I'd fucked her up against the wall in the shower. After we'd gorged on more room service, we'd turned on a movie. But halfway through, she'd started nuzzling against me. Tracing her fingers across my abs. Rubbing her toes against my leg. I'd sprung on her like a predator attacking its prey.

There was something about her. I didn't have an iron-clad one-night rule, but I always kept things casual. I liked to have fun, and I loved sex, but I'd never been interested enough in any one girl to take it further. So most of the time, I did keep it to one night. But with Amelia, I couldn't get enough. I was as insatiable as she was. Five minutes after leaving her, I was already thinking about how long I'd have to wait until I could see her again.

I didn't contemplate what that might mean. I was just happy she was staying longer. It would have been depressing as fuck to have to say goodbye to her today. Particularly because my first order of business this morning was decidedly less pleasant than the sweet girl I had back at the Lodge.

The sun was just rising above the mountain peaks as I drove through my vineyards in the utility vehicle. My crop was looking perfect, the plants thriving. We'd planted a new grape variety—Sangiovese—this year, and I was excited as hell to see how it would turn out. If it did well, we could plant more over in the east vineyard next season.

Dust billowed as I pulled the utility vehicle to a stop behind a car. A sick feeling rolled through my stomach before I even saw him. He got out of the car and it got worse. I clenched my hands around the steering wheel and took a deep breath.

Stay calm, Coop. Just get this over with.

My father shut his car door and put his hands in the pockets of his gray slacks. I got out of the utility vehicle, but kept my distance. God, I wanted to punch that asshole.

"Well?" I asked.

"Hi, Cooper."

"Don't *hi* me, dick," I said. "We both know neither of us wants to be here."

"You'd go a lot further in life if you quit acting like a punk kid," he said.

"I don't need your life advice, thanks."

He sighed. "I need to make sure our arrangements are firmly in place. I can't have anything go wrong."

"Nothing will go wrong."

"You're sure Leo isn't monitoring those fields?"

"No, he thinks they're empty," I said. "He doesn't have a reason to monitor them."

Dad scowled like he didn't believe me. "If you fuck this up, it's over. Even if I don't get Salishan in the divorce, I'll bury your mom in legal fees and she'll have to sell anyway. It's in your best interest to make sure this works."

It took every bit of self-control I possessed not to punch him in his stupid face. It probably wasn't healthy for a guy to hate his father so much, but the seething rage I had for mine only grew every time I was forced to see him.

"Yeah, I get it."

"The crop will be ready for harvest sometime in September. And once it's ready—"

"Jesus, I know. Make sure your crew gets in to harvest the shit without getting caught. I told you already, I'll make it happen. Just make sure you hold up your end of the bargain."

"Oh, I will. I don't want a legal battle any more than your mom does."

"You're not getting this land." I looked him straight in the eyes. I hated seeing some of myself reflected back at me. Why did my father have to be such a prick? "Even if your fucking crop dies and this all goes to shit. I'm not letting it happen."

"If my crop dies and it all goes to shit, you bet your ass I'm getting this land," he said. "But as long as you do your part, that doesn't have to happen."

I didn't answer. Just took another deep breath to keep myself from killing him.

"Don't text me unless there's a problem. I'll contact you."

"Fine."

He got back in his car and I watched him drive off.

Piece of shit. I hated everything about this, but the asshole had me by the balls. What the fuck was I supposed to do? I'd do anything to protect my family's land. Even sell my goddamn soul.

Which was basically what I was doing.

Secrets and lies. I hated this shit so much, it made me sick. When Dad had first approached me with his plan, I'd told him to fuck off. There was no way I was cooperating with anything he wanted to do.

But then he'd countered Mom's divorce settlement offer and demanded Salishan. All of it. Every acre my grandparents and great-grandparents—on Mom's side—had bought. All this land they'd worked and cultivated. The hills and fields. This was *my* fucking land. My dirt. And that prick was not taking it.

Now I was backed into a corner. Roland had admitted he was worried. Even if the courts didn't award Dad everything he was after, they might make us parcel off the land and sell it piece by piece if Mom couldn't afford to buy him out—which I was pretty sure she couldn't. That was unacceptable. If I did this—sick as it made me—it would be worth it, if it meant keeping our land and getting rid of Dad for good.

I just had to make it to September.

His plan—which wasn't a very good one, but he hadn't wanted my opinion—was to grow a huge cannabis crop in one of the big unused fields on the north side of our property. Nothing had been grown there for years. It was tough to get the harvesting equipment back there, and the soil required a lot of maintenance to keep it fertile. I planned to cultivate it again in a few years, but the rest of our crops kept me busy.

Dad knew about the unused land, and he thought he

could make a shit ton of money on his stupid pot plants. They were legal here now, but you had to have all sorts of permits and licenses to grow it—all of which cost money, and I was sure Dad hadn't bothered getting them. He claimed he had a buyer already lined up and once he cashed in, he'd give mom her divorce and go away.

But to do all this, he needed someone on the inside. Which, unfortunately, meant me.

I hated this. I hated everything about it. But I was going to suck it up and handle it so the rest of my family didn't have to. Then Mom could get divorced, and Dad could drop off the edge of the fucking planet as far as I was concerned.

It was a good thing I had a full day of work ahead of me. I needed to move and sweat and wear myself out, or I was going to pop a blood vessel.

The thought of Amelia, however, calmed the raging storm in my head. I had her to look forward to, and that was pretty fucking great.

I TOOK a break midday to help Amelia get her things over to the Blackberry Cottage. I'd sent my mom a text to say I had a friend who needed a place to crash for a couple of weeks, and of course she didn't mind. No one was using it, since Brynn had moved in with me and Chase. And it looked beautiful. The flowers I'd planted for Brynn were blooming and the whole place smelled amazing. I did good work.

By dinner time, I was worn out from a long day in the fields. It was pushing ninety and I'd been outside all day. Chase texted to say he and Brynn were having dinner at my mom's. That sounded awesome, but I didn't want to leave Amelia alone, either.

So after stopping home for a quick shower—seriously, I smelled terrible—and downing a gallon of water, I went straight for Amelia. Mom was always happy to feed an extra person or two. I liked win-win situations. In fact, I was pretty sure anything could be turned into a win-win if you tried hard enough. Tonight, Amelia wouldn't be alone, and I wouldn't miss dinner at Mom's. Perfect.

Amelia answered the door, her pretty smile lighting up her face. "Hey. You're sure it's okay if I stay here?"

I went inside and shut the door behind me. "Yeah, why?"

"I saw some guy walk by and he stopped and looked. He didn't get close, but I think he was trying to look in the window."

"Was he a tall older guy, or a dude with long hair and a beard?"

"Um, tall older guy, I guess? He had a beard, but not long hair."

"Don't worry about it," I said. "That was Ben. He works here. I didn't see him today, so I didn't have a chance to tell him you're here."

"Oh, okay."

"Hungry?"

"Yes, starving. I was hoping you'd come over, but I wasn't sure. And I was going to text you, but then I thought maybe I shouldn't because I didn't want to bother you while you were working, and you already took the time to come help me move my stuff over here. And then I thought maybe I was supposed to fend for myself—which I can totally do, I'm not a spoiled princess."

"I never got the impression you were a spoiled princess," I said. "But that's still good to know. Anyway, we're going to my mom's for dinner."

She stared at me, like I'd just said we were going to eat gum off the sidewalk. "We're what?"

"Eating at my mom's. Chase and my sister are eating dinner there, which means Mom will make enough food for twenty people. I didn't want to leave you alone tonight, and this way I can introduce you to my mom, since you're staying here and everything."

"Oh. I guess that makes sense."

I could tell she was hesitant, but I couldn't figure out why. "If you'd rather not, it's no big deal. But my mom is an amazing cook, so you'd be missing out. I'm just going to be up front about that."

"No, it sounds fine, it's just... that's a lot of new people to meet when I just met you."

"It's just dinner, Cookie. It's not a big deal. They don't bite." I stepped closer and grabbed her hips. "I might, though."

Her cheeks flushed a light shade of pink. "You make it hard to think."

I laughed. "Wanna fuck first?"

"What?"

"I'm just asking. We don't have to, it's cool either way. But if you want to fuck real quick, you know I'm down. Except it won't be *that* quick, because it's me."

"I don't... I'm not... I think... maybe just dinner?"

"Sounds good. I'm going to drop dead if I don't eat soon, so I'm with you. Let's go."

"Should I change?" she asked. "I'm not dressed in dinner clothes."

"It's my mom's house, not a palace." I gestured at my jeans and t-shirt. "I'm wearing this. You're dressed fine."

She tugged at her shirt and started fussing with her hair, so I gently grabbed her wrists and backed her up against the wall.

"You're cute when you're flustered."

"You're cute all the time," she said. "I can't believe I just said that."

"It's true, I'm cute as fuck. But so are you." I dove for her lips—kissed her hard and deep. Because why not? Kissing her felt good. And it seemed to relax us both. The tension melted from her body and the hum of noise in my brain quieted.

"You're so good at that," she whispered when I pulled away.

"We make a good team." I grinned and took her hand. "Let's go."

We walked the short distance to my mom's house. The front door was wide open, and the sound of voices drifted out. I squeezed Amelia's hand and led her in.

Mom was at the big dining table with Chase, Brynn, and Leo. They were huddled around a board game, laughing. Or at least, everyone but Leo was laughing. I needed to figure out how to get Leo to loosen up. It was bad enough that he stayed here all the time. The dude needed to smile once in a while.

"Hey, family."

Everyone looked up and Amelia shifted closer.

No one said anything—just stared at us. I wondered if my hard-on was showing. It wasn't like I was wearing gray sweats. My jeans kept things contained. And I couldn't help it. Amelia smelled really fucking good and I was still a little kiss-drunk.

"This is Amelia," I said. "Mom, is it cool if she joins us for dinner? She's the friend I told you about who's staying in the Blackberry Cottage, and I didn't want her to be alone tonight. Figured we could make room."

I squeezed Amelia's hand again and she made a little squeaky noise in her throat. She was so adorable.

Mom blinked a few times, her mouth partially open.

"Mom? You okay? Hey, if there's not enough food, we'll go out. I just figured you always make too much food anyway, so one more person wouldn't be a problem."

"No, no, it's fine. I just didn't expect... You said friend, and I didn't think..." Mom shook her head a little. "I'm sorry, Amelia. It's so nice to meet you."

"It's nice to meet you too," Amelia said. "Thanks for letting me stay in the cottage. And for inviting me to dinner. Although you didn't really, Cooper did, and I think you're surprised to see me here. Which, of course, I don't blame you, I'm surprised to be here, myself. So we sort of have that in common."

Mom smiled. "I guess we do. I hope you like spaghetti. It's not fancy, but Chase requested it."

"Oh my god, Mom's spaghetti is the bomb. Good choice, Chasey."

"That sounds delicious," Amelia said. "Thank you."

"Intros," I said, and pointed to everyone in turn. "My mom, Shannon. My sister, Brynn. Chase used to be mine before Brynn stole him from me. And that's my brother, Leo."

"Hi. I'm Amelia. He already said that, but maybe you forgot. It's okay if you did, I'll probably forget your names, so I apologize in advance if I have to ask."

"Don't worry about it," Mom said. "Just make yourself at home."

Mom went into the kitchen and Leo got up to put the board game away. He scowled at me but walked away before I could ask what his problem was.

There was a bench on this side of the table—chairs on the other—so I took a seat on the end and pulled Amelia onto my lap. This way I could keep my hands on her, which was much better than not touching her. Mom started bringing in dinner and Chase got up to help. When everything was on the table, we all dished up. I kept Amelia on my lap and just pulled her plate over next to mine.

"Um, should I move?" she whispered.

"Why?"

She made a subtle gesture toward the others at the table. "Because, we're at your mom's?"

"You're fine," Mom said quietly and winked at her. "Cooper's actually staying seated. It's a nice change."

"So, how do you two know each other?" Brynn asked.

"I met her at Mountainside Tavern," I said around a mouthful of spaghetti.

"Okay, this is making more sense," Brynn said.

"It was funny because I was wearing my wedding dress and he didn't even notice at first," Amelia said, talking fast. "It was like, how do you not notice the mile of white tulle hanging down off the barstool around my legs, right? But he didn't."

"I'm sorry, wedding dress?" Brynn asked. She glanced at Chase, who shrugged.

"Oh, right, I should back up. I was supposed to get married on Saturday. Here, actually, and the winery is so beautiful. But my fiancé left me and ran off to Vegas with my cousin. That's why I was at a bar in my wedding dress. I don't make a habit of doing that sort of thing. I don't make a habit of bars in general, but especially not in a wedding dress. In fact, I got a water because I had no idea what else to order. I think I need someone to teach me about alcohol. That's the kind of thing most kids learn in college, but I didn't really hang out with that crowd."

"I can teach you all about that, Cookie," I said, then turned to my family, who were staring at us for some reason. "And now Amelia's my friend and she's staying in the Blackberry Cottage for her Cooper-moon."

"Exactly," Amelia said.

Brynn leaned close to Chase. "Oh my god, I think she speaks Cooper."

"I'm sorry to hear about your wedding," Mom said.

"Thanks. I don't think it's really hit me yet. But I'm glad it happened, even though I know that sounds weird. I wouldn't have thought he was capable of something like this, so it's better that I found out now."

"You're absolutely right," Mom said, her voice soft. "It's much better that you found out now."

It squeezed my heart to hear her say that. For obvious reasons—my existence being a big one—I was glad my parents had been together. But Mom had suffered a lot, and it wasn't over. I wanted to tell her I was doing everything I could to make it all go away. That I was taking care of this for her. But of course I couldn't.

"Thanks. It's all a little weird now, but I should probably stop talking because I babble when I'm nervous and I think I'm on the verge of oversharing, if I haven't already."

"Not at all," Mom said. "What else can you tell us about you?"

"Well... I love horses. I grew up riding. My parents own four, and there was a riding program at the boarding school I went to. I even taught horseback riding lessons for a while. Oh, and I just graduated college."

Brynn cleared her throat. "Just graduated? That must make you about my age."

"Oh yeah? I turned twenty-two in April."

"Yep, I'll be twenty-two soon," Brynn said.

Chase caught my eyes and gave me a look.

"What?" I asked.

"Nothing," he said, his voice full of fake nonchalance.

"Congratulations on your degree," Mom said.

"Thanks."

"Zoe and Roland took baby Hudson home yesterday,"

Mom said. "They're all doing well. He's just the most beautiful baby boy."

"I thought I was the most beautiful baby boy," I said, winking at Mom.

Leo snorted. "Shut up, Cooper."

I laughed and shifted Amelia a little so I could reach my dinner better. It would probably have been easier to eat with her sitting next to me, instead of on me, but I liked her here.

Mom and Brynn talked forever about how cute Hudson was. Dinner was great, though. When we all finished, I reluctantly moved Amelia off my lap so I could help clear the table.

Chase followed me into the kitchen with a stack of plates.

"What's going on, Coop?" he asked, putting the plates down next to the sink.

"I don't know. I had dinner and now I'm helping clean up because I'm an awesome son."

"I mean the girl."

"What about her?"

He glanced toward the dining room and lowered his voice. "Twenty-two?"

"Yeah? I actually didn't know that about her until just now. But, so?"

It looked like he was trying not to smile. "She's Brynn's age."

"And?"

"Come on, dick, you gave me endless amounts of shit about Brynn's age. And now you bring this girl home and you expect me to keep quiet about it?"

I scowled at him. "I don't see how that's the same. You got engaged to Brynncess really fast."

"Cooper, you've never once brought a girl home to meet your mom."

I started to reply, but I realized he was right. I never had brought a girl home for dinner before. "Huh. That's interesting."

"Was she really supposed to get married on Saturday?"

"Yeah."

Chase shook his head. "Okay, dude. I don't know what your game is, but I hope you know what you're doing."

"There's no game."

"Don't bullshit me. With you, there's always a game."

"I'm serious." I put my hands up. "No game. She had a shitty thing happen and we met and she's awesome. She was supposed to go on a honeymoon, so I talked her into staying here for a Cooper-moon instead. That's it."

He raised an eyebrow. "Okay."

Brynn came in and put her hands on her hips. "Cooper, what are you doing?"

"I literally just had this conversation with Chase."

"I'm serious," she said. "You bring a girl home for the first time ever, but she was supposed to marry someone else two days ago? And now she's with you?"

"Oh, no, she's not *with* me," I said. "Not like that. That would be crazy, even for me. She's just a friend."

Brynn raised her eyebrows. "Just a friend? You, *just friends* with a girl?"

"Hey, I resent what you're implying. I've had lots of girls who were just friends."

"Name one who isn't Zoe."

I opened my mouth to answer, but Zoe was the one I'd planned on pointing out. "Okay, maybe Zoe is it, but she proves my point anyway."

"So you're friends with Amelia like you're friends with Zoe?"

I almost gagged. "No, I've never slept with Zoe. Gross. Why are you interrogating me?"

"Because she seems really nice and I don't understand what's happening," Brynn said. "We've always been afraid the first girl you brought home would be a stripper named Cinnamon or something. Amelia seems so... so normal. Although she appears to understand your weirdness, so she can't be *that* normal."

"I don't know why you guys are making this into a thing. Amelia is my friend and I'm helping her get over assgoblin." I was about to say she'd be leaving in two weeks when her Cooper-moon was over, but I couldn't quite get that part out. If I said it, I'd have to think about it, and thinking about it was depressing. No sense in dwelling on it.

"Assgoblin?"

"The bitch-monkey she was supposed to marry. He has a name, but fuck him."

"Doesn't she have anyone else?" Brynn asked. "Wait, don't interrupt me with how you're perfect for this, I'm sure you are. I just mean, doesn't she have family, or a best friend or something? Why is she out here alone?"

"No, she does. Her BFF is Daphne, but she's engaged to Harrison who's going to be a rock star. They were already leaving for L.A. And I don't know what's up with her parents, but I think she's avoiding them. So you see, sister-who-doubts-me-but-shouldn't, staying here and hanging out with me as much as possible is clearly her best option."

"Oh-kay," Brynn said.

"Makes sense," Chase said. "You know, if you want to be a child predator and bang a girl who's so much younger than you."

"I'm twenty-six, dick. She's not that much younger."

"You're twenty-seven, dumbass," he said. "Saying you're twenty-six forever won't actually keep you from turning thirty."

"It might."

Chase punched my arm. "Good luck with that. And be nice to her. She seems really cool."

"Oh, I will be," I said. "Very nice."

Brynn rolled her eyes. "Ew."

"Don't even get me started on *ew*, Brynncess," I said. "I share a wall with you two."

She smiled. "I know."

"I'm done with both of you."

I went back into dining room and hauled Amelia back into my lap. She fit so nicely, and I liked it when any part of my body was touching her ass. That was the great thing about having a girl in your lap. It was like naughty touching on the downlow.

Mom brought out dessert—lemon cakes with sugary frosting, and holy shit they were good. Then Amelia helped me clean up the dishes, even though Mom told us we didn't need to. She splashed some soap bubbles on me, which turned into a bubble fight in the kitchen. We had to clean that up, too. But it had been fun, so it was worth it.

Afterward, we said goodbye to everyone. With my arm around Amelia's shoulders, I led her back to the cottage. I was tired after the long day and big meal, but not *that* tired. I'd been thinking about this sweet girl all day and I couldn't wait to get her naked again. And judging by the way she grabbed me when we got inside, she felt the same.

ELEVEN

AMELIA

THE SWEET SCENT of flowers drifted in the morning breeze. Salishan was basically paradise. Lush green lawns and gardens bursting with color. This time of year, the mountain peaks surrounding the winery were a patchwork of green and brown, and I wondered what they'd look like covered in white snow.

I wandered along a trail that wound through the grounds. It was early, and the air was warm, but not yet too hot. I'd been here for the better part of a week, and the longer I stayed, the more I enjoyed this place.

Cooper was at work, but he said he'd try to finish up early so we could do something fun. I couldn't wait to find out what he had up his sleeve.

I'd never met anyone like him before. He was so free. He did what he wanted and didn't seem to worry about what other people thought. Spending time with him was the perfect antidote to my wedding disaster last weekend. We had so much fun when we were together, it was hard to think about anything else.

Moments like this were harder. I had a little more than a week left. Then what was I going to do? I couldn't stay here. Going to my parents' house was an option, but not a great one. Their house hadn't felt like home even when I was a kid. I'd spent more time at boarding schools than I ever had there.

My best option was Daphne. She'd already offered to let me come stay with her and Harrison in L.A. The idea of seeing a new city was exciting, although Los Angeles wasn't exactly my first choice. But it wouldn't be bad, and at least I'd have friends there.

Now that I was no longer marrying Griffin, my future stretched out before me like a wide-open expanse of nothing. Nothing specific, at least. It was scary, but a little bit exhilarating. I'd always gone from one thing to the next, in quick succession. My parents had sent me to camps and summer school in between school years. I'd spent the summer after high school interning at a horse ranch before starting college. And I'd been about to get married just weeks after graduating.

One thing to the next. Never giving myself a chance to just *be*. To breathe and figure out who I was.

Now I had that chance. I just needed to figure out what to do with it.

My phone rang, so I took it out of my pocket. It was my dad.

"Hi, Dad."

"Amelia, are you still at Salishan?"

"Yes. I told you, I'm staying for two weeks."

"Griffin is back in town," he said, and my stomach lurched at the sound of his name. "He's staying with his parents."

"Okay."

"And Portia," he said, then cleared his throat, "is with your aunt and uncle."

"I don't know why that pertains to me at this point."

"I think Griffin is quickly realizing the gravity of his mistake. I wouldn't be surprised if he gets in touch with you soon."

"Dad, I don't want to talk to Griffin. He cheated on me and left me at the altar. I don't have anything to say to him."

"We've known his family for years. They're an important connection for us to maintain. Griffin... got carried away. Young men can be like that. Impulsive and rash."

"Well, he has to live with his choices," I said. "He humiliated and betrayed me."

I could hear my mom's muffled voice.

"Your mother would like to speak with you."

Mom got on the phone. "Amelia, I realize you're going through something at the moment. Your father and I are trying to give you space, since that's what you seem to require. But you have to meet us halfway."

"What is that supposed to mean?"

"Boys will be boys," she said. "Part of marriage is learning to live with that."

"Are you really telling me I should consider taking him back? You can't be serious. Even if he did call me—which he hasn't—I'm not speaking to him."

"Don't be unreasonable."

"I don't think I'm being unreasonable," I said. "If you want me to call the Wentworths and assure them I'm not mad at them, I will. They're nice people and it's not their fault their son did this to me. But Griffin made his choice. If he doesn't want Portia, I'm sorry to hear it, but he can't come crawling back to me."

Mom sighed. "I simply want to remind you what our

relationship with the Wentworths means to us. And I hope you'll be cooperative in repairing it."

"I'll be perfectly cordial the next time I see them. But you're going to have to accept that whatever was between me and Griffin is over."

"You should come home," she said. "There's no reason for you to stay out there."

I sighed at her change of subject. "I'm fine where I am. Oh, look, Daphne's calling me back. I missed her call yesterday, so I should take this. Talk to you later."

I hung up and I didn't even feel bad about the lie.

Why did my parents act like they were royalty and needed to marry me off to form an alliance with Griffin's family? It was ridiculous. Their preoccupation with their social standing had always baffled me.

The garden area where I was supposed to have gotten married was a little further down the path. It was empty now. No rows of chairs or decorations, just neatly clipped grass and pretty plants. No sign of the sharp left turn my life had taken here on this lawn.

My phone dinged, so I pulled it out of my pocket again. I had a text from Cooper. He'd sent me a selfie—hat on backwards, sunglasses on his face. He was smiling but sticking his tongue out to the side. I made a silly face and snapped a picture to send back to him.

Smiling again, I put my phone away. He made me feel so good. Even just a funny text melted my worries to nothing. And after all, I was on vacation. Wasn't that what vacations were for? Forgetting your troubles for a little while?

I walked back to the cottage. It was so cute, with blackberries on the curtains and bedding. I'd tried to get Cooper's mom to let me pay for my lodging, but she wouldn't hear of it. Without access to my trust, and no job, I didn't have a lot of money, but I had some. Enough to live on for a little while I figured things out.

I hadn't been back long when someone knocked on the door and my heart fluttered. Was it Cooper already? I took a deep breath and opened the door, but it was his sister, Brynn.

"Hey," she said. "Sorry to come over unannounced, but Cooper just texted me about five hundred times. He's worried you're bored, and that you didn't pack the right clothes to wear. I think that means he wants me to take you shopping. Sometimes it's hard to tell with him."

I'd liked Brynn from the second we'd met at her mom's house the other day. She was shorter than me, with long dark hair and pretty eyes, and she'd been so friendly to me at dinner.

"I did say I wished I'd packed different clothes. I was expecting two weeks on a beach. That's sweet of him."

"Yeah, it is sweet of him," she said, and it sounded like she was surprised by that. Or confused. "Chase is working today, but I'm off, so I figured why not. Want to go shopping?"

"Sure, that sounds great." I grabbed my purse and followed Brynn out.

Echo Creek's downtown area was just outside the entrance to Salishan, so we walked into town. Brynn led me past a restaurant and a few shops to a clothing boutique with hats and dresses in the window display. It looked cute.

The clerk said hello when we walked in. We wandered through the shop for a few minutes, plucking at the shirts and dresses on the racks. I nibbled the inside of my lip, growing increasingly anxious. Should I start a conversation?

What should I talk about? I was afraid if I started talking, I'd just babble.

Apparently, I couldn't help myself. "Cooper told me you just got married, which is really exciting. Congratulations. I bet your wedding was beautiful. Mine was going to be beautiful, too. I just mean your family's winery is so beautiful, so of course it would have been. I don't mean I'm jealous that you had a wedding and I didn't. It's better that mine fell apart."

Brynn gave me a sympathetic smile. "Are you doing okay with everything? I can't imagine what the last week has been like for you."

"You'd think I'd be a puddle of sadness, wouldn't you? It's probably telling that I'm not. I don't know what I feel, to be honest. Maybe I'm still in shock."

"Were you with him for a long time?"

"No. We were friends for a long time, but we didn't really date. Which, in hindsight, wasn't a good thing. I just..." I hated to admit this, now that the whole thing had blown up in my face. "I had a secret crush on him for years. So when he proposed, I thought it was all my dreams coming true. But nothing was like I thought it would be, even before he left me at the altar."

"Wow," she said, pausing with a shirt dangling from her hands. "I can relate to the secret crush. I had a crush on Chase for as long as I can remember. But he didn't notice me when we were younger."

We moved further into the store. I searched through a rack of peach dresses, but they were all a size small. "What changed?"

"He saw me with another guy," she said with a laugh. "That sounds terrible, but it's true. Things were kind of a whirlwind for us. But once we were together, we just knew."

"That's what was missing," I said, dropping the hem of a turquoise shirt. "I didn't *know*. I thought I did, but I was just telling myself I knew because I thought I *should* know. He was supposed to be everything I'd ever wanted, but maybe I was more in love with the idea of him than the real him. Because it's the weirdest thing. I'm not sad about losing him. I'm hurt, and embarrassed, and pretty flipping angry. And I don't know what I'm going to do with my life now. But I'm not sad."

"Then I think you're right, it is better that yours fell apart."

"I'm sorry. I'm oversharing and making this awkward. I'm really nervous because you're so nice and pretty, and I talk too much when I'm nervous."

"It's okay. You don't need to be nervous." She held up a strappy lilac tank top. "This would look pretty on you."

I eyed the thin wisp of fabric. "I don't think that tiny thing would fit me. It would look great on you, though."

"Hmm, maybe. Should we try some things on?"

"Sure."

We loaded up our arms with outfits, and the clerk opened two dressing rooms for us. I started with a pink dress. I turned back and forth, studying my reflection. Clothes shopping was always an exercise in frustration. I wasn't terribly overweight—at least I didn't think so—but I was thick and curvy. It always seemed like clothes were made to hang off stick-straight bodies, not women with lumps and bumps. And I had plenty of those.

"Are you ready?" Brynn asked through the door.

I went out and tried to resist the urge to cross my arms

over my stomach. Brynn was wearing a pink and orange tie-dyed maxi dress that looked unbelievably cute on her.

"That's the cutest thing ever. You look adorable."

"Yeah?" She stepped in front of the full-length mirror and looked from several angles. "It is fun. Maybe I'll splurge a little. But oh my god, look at *you*."

I smoothed the dress down and turned in front of the mirror. It had a retro cut, with a sweetheart neckline and a skirt that flared from the waist.

"Do you like it?"

"That's so hot on you," she said. "You look like a pinup girl."

"Thanks." I turned again. It did work with my shape. And I loved the color. "It's so hard to find things that fit right. It's like designers forget some women have hips and boobs."

Brynn laughed. "And let's be honest you have great boobs. I'd love it if I had more curves. I guess we always want what we don't have."

"We do, don't we? Why do we do that to ourselves?" I sighed and did a twirl in front of the mirror. "You know, I've never worn anything like this before. It's a lot sexier than my normal clothes."

"Then we need to get you more like this," Brynn said. "Let's bring out your inner Marilyn. You know what you need? Sexy pumps. Show off those long legs of yours."

We spent the next hour trying on more clothes. Brynn grabbed everything she could find with the same retro feel as the pink dress. Before I knew it, I had a bunch of cute clothes that actually fit—and made me feel pretty darn good.

After we finished shopping, we walked back to Salishan. I invited Brynn to stay for some iced tea. The weather was gorgeous, so we brought two chairs out in front of the cottage and sat outside. A few bees buzzed around the plants and the scent of flowers wafted on the breeze.

"This place is so beautiful," I said and took a deep breath. "It even smells wonderful."

"That's Cooper's doing," Brynn said. "He planted all these flowers for me when I was staying here."

"That's so sweet."

"It was ridiculously sweet. He's like that, though. This was his way of apologizing for something. He could have brought me flowers, or—I don't know, something normal brothers do. But not Cooper. He planted a garden."

I glanced around at the flowers. They were so pretty. "Wow."

"Can I ask you a personal question?"

"Sure."

"I know you said you had a crush on your ex. But were you in love with him?"

I fiddled with my straw. "No, I wasn't in love with him. I think that's why I'm not sad. I knew it wasn't right, but I kept trying to convince myself that it was—that we'd grow to love each other and everything would be fine. I feel pretty stupid about it all, to be honest."

"I don't think you should feel stupid." She smiled. "Those childhood crushes can be powerful things."

"Yeah, and sometimes you *should* marry your childhood crush," I said, my heart warming at her big smile. She was obviously smitten with Chase, and from what I'd seen, he loved her just as much. "But not if he's the type of guy who will sleep with your cousin the night before the wedding."

"I don't even know your ex, and I hate him. I can't believe he did that. Did he really take her to Vegas to elope?"

"I guess so."

"What did he say to you about it?"

"Nothing. I haven't talked to him."

Her mouth dropped open. "What?"

"It's crazy, right? He left me at the altar, and I still haven't heard from him. I guess he assumed I'd figure it out when he didn't show, but it would have been nice to get a heads up that he wasn't going through with the wedding."

"What an asshole."

I took a sip of my iced tea. "Yep. I'm glad he hasn't called me, though. I don't want to talk to him."

"No, I guess I wouldn't either. My ex cheated on me with my roommate, and I'd be totally fine with never seeing either of them again."

"Are you kidding me? With your roommate? What is wrong with people?"

"I have no idea." She took a drink and eyed me over her glass, one eyebrow lifting. "So... Cooper seems to like you a lot."

I felt my cheeks flush. "Does he? That's a silly question, of course he likes me. We're... friends, I guess? Most people like their friends."

Brynn laughed softly. "Yeah, they do. What's with the nickname? Did he make that up?"

"What nickname?"

"He calls you *Cookie*," she said. "He even did it in his texts earlier."

"Oh, right. I think he just made it up. It's funny, I barely notice. It sounds so normal for him to call me that, I don't even think about it."

"Wow, you really do speak Cooper."

I shrugged. "I guess so."

"It's cute." She absently stirred her tea with her straw.

"By the way, this was really fun. I know I was kind of doing Cooper a favor, but I like hanging out with you. I don't know how long you'll be in town, but I'd love to do it again."

"You would?"

"Totally."

I tried to play it cool but failed miserably. I was so fidgety with excitement, I was practically bouncing in my seat. "I liked hanging out with you, too. So much. My friend Daphne is super nice, and I've known her forever, but she has her own life, and she's getting married. Of course, you're married, but you're here, not in L.A. because your man isn't a musician. Sorry, I'm babbling again, I'm just trying to say thank you because this was really fun and I'd like it if we could be friends."

"Done deal," she said. "We'll hang out again. Maybe go get our nails done this time."

"That sounds perfect." I clicked my mouth closed before I could launch into another ridiculous babble-fest.

Cooper pulled up in his truck and parked in front of the cottage. He and Chase jumped out, and almost before I had time to stand, Cooper ran over and picked me up. With his arms around my waist, he spun me around a few times.

He held me tight and buried his face in my neck, breathing in deeply as he set my feet back on the ground. I laughed and flung my arms around his neck while the world tilted. I was dizzy.

"I missed you today," he whispered in my ear.

"I missed you, too."

He pulled back and planted a hard kiss on my mouth, then started kissing me all over my face and neck. "You're yummy."

I laughed again and squirmed in his arms. Brynn and Chase were staring at us.

"Thanks for taking care of my Cookie for me, Brynncess," Cooper said. "Did you girls have fun?"

"Yeah, we did," Brynn said.

"I knew you would." He kissed me again. "Dinner?"

"Hey Coop, you should take her somewhere nice," Brynn said, winking at me. "She has a new dress she really needs to wear."

Cooper's eyes lit up. "Yeah? I wanna see. What color is it? No wait, let me guess. Blue. No, it's not blue. Hang on. It's pink, isn't it?"

"It is pink," I said.

"Hell yes. I'm good. Okay, you go change and get pretty. Although you already are pretty, but that's a thing girls do, right? I'm dirty as fuck, so I should get cleaned up at home." He turned to Brynn and Chase. "You guys wanna double date? Can this count for a double date, because I think it can."

My heart skipped a beat. Double date? Did that mean Cooper and I were going on a *date*? Was it a single date if Brynn and Chase didn't come? Were we *dating* now?

I felt dizzy again, but not from Cooper spinning me around. I liked Cooper—a lot—and I was having fun with him. But dating? I didn't know if I was ready for that. This was just a crazy fling. Wasn't it?

"You all right?" Cooper brushed my hair back from my face. "You look a little pale all of a sudden."

"Just dizzy," I said. "And probably hungry. I'll go get changed."

"Okay. I'll run home and shower, then swing back by to pick you up in an hour. Chase, you guys in?"

"Let's do it," Chase said.

"Awesome."

Brynn was still watching me, and I wondered if my feelings were written all over my face. I took a deep breath to pull myself together. This was fine. Dinner would be fun, no matter what we called it. I'd wear my new dress and go out with Cooper and his sister and brother-in-law. That wasn't a big deal. I was still just a girl having fun on my Cooper-moon.

TWELVE
COOPER

I LEANED BACK SO I could get a look at Amelia's legs as we walked out of the restaurant. She looked hot as hell in that pink dress. I'd almost fallen over when I'd picked her up for dinner. It highlighted her curves in all the best ways. I wanted to eat her up.

But Chase and Brynn had been there—Chase drove—so I'd settled for kissing her in the doorway until Brynn had complained that we were gross and going to be late for dinner.

"Cooper, everyone can see you checking out her ass," Brynn said as we walked to the car.

Amelia glanced at me over her shoulder.

"What?" I put my hands up, feigning innocence. "I wasn't. Okay, I was, but that's not all I was doing. I was checking out her legs, too. Brynncess, I owe you big for that shopping trip. This dress is bananas."

Amelia laughed, and Brynn shook her head at me.

Double dating with Chase and Brynn was super fun. Technically, I'd never done that before. Not like this. Picking up a pair of girlfriends at a bar, like Chase and I used to do a lot, didn't count. There was something different about bringing a pretty girl in a hot dress to a restaurant. Sitting at a table with your best friend and his wife—who was also dressed up—while you had dinner and drinks.

The restaurant, however, hadn't been ideal. Or at least, the waitress hadn't. I was trying my best to play it cool, but she'd been rude to Amelia all through dinner. I didn't know what her problem was. I'd slept with her once, like four years ago. There was no reason for her to be nasty to my date.

"Here," Brynn said, handing something to Chase. She'd lowered her voice, but I could still hear her.

"What's this?" he asked. "Did you take the tip off the table?"

"I only took half, and we both know she didn't deserve it."

Chase said something else I didn't catch. Brynn looked my direction and I gave her a little chin tip, acknowledging her awesomeness. That had been a good call. But then she widened her eyes at me. She knew exactly why the waitress had been rude. I winced and shrugged. She just rolled her eyes.

I wanted a distraction before Brynn made this weird. We didn't need to talk about the waitress, we just needed to keep double-date night fun.

"Chase, dude, what was the name of that bar with the live music?"

"Which one?"

"The one in Seattle."

He pointed at me. "The Office."

"Yes, that's the one.

"A bar called the Office?" Amelia asked. "That's cute.

So when someone doesn't want to admit where they were, they can just say they were at the Office, and it's not even a lie."

"Exactly," I said, then looked at Chase. "So?"

He held out his fist so I could bump it. "Let's do it."

"Mini road trip!"

"Yay," Brynn said. Before I could get in the back seat with Amelia, she hip-checked me out of the way and got in.

"Hey, you took my spot."

"You can ride up front with Chase," she said.

I groaned and got in the front seat. Chase started the car and headed toward the highway. Seattle was almost two hours away, but it wasn't even eight o'clock. And the Office always had live music late on weekends. Chase and I had been out there a bunch of times.

The girls talked and giggled in the back seat as we drove. I glanced at them, wishing Brynn hadn't ousted me from my rightful place. It was cute that they were having fun together. But it would have been more fun if I could have spent the drive making out with Amelia. I caught Chase looking at Brynn longingly in the rear-view mirror. Apparently I wasn't the only one less than satisfied with the seating arrangements.

We got into the city and found parking. As soon as we got out of the car, I grabbed Amelia and kissed the hell out of her. I'd been waiting to do that for the last two hours. I had a feeling Chase was doing the same thing to my sister, but I purposely ignored them.

The Office was tucked away on a side street downtown. I put my hand on the small of Amelia's back as we followed Chase and Brynn inside.

And yes, I totally checked out her ass again. Then grabbed it for good measure.

Music filled the dimly lit bar. Aside from some haphazard string lights and bar signs, the only attempts at decorating the bare concrete walls were posters and newspaper clippings chronicling Seattle's music scene. The place was a total dive—small and dingy—but they always had great local bands.

The long wooden bar was packed with people, as were most of the tables. We managed to find one near the stage that only had two chairs, but that was plenty. Chase and I went to the bar to get drinks, then he hauled Brynn into his lap and I put Amelia in mine.

I was stoked to see it was Incognito on the small stage. They were an awesome rock cover band, playing everything from classic rock to grunge. And they were on fire tonight.

Amelia sat in my lap, her arm draped around my shoulder. I slid my hand up her thigh, making her laugh and squirm. We listened to the music and a couple of drinks later, Amelia and Brynn were both singing along to the chorus of *Jukebox Hero*.

"Okay, which one is hotter?" Brynn asked, gesturing to the guys on stage when they were in between songs. "Singer, guitarist, drummer, or the bass player?"

Amelia shifted, eying the band with a finger to her lips. "The singer is hot. But I can't see the bass player very well. It's like he's keeping to the shadows at the back."

"I was thinking the drummer, but I want a better look at the bass player, too," Brynn said.

"Why do you think he hangs back like that?" Amelia asked. "Do you think he's shy?"

"That's so cute," Brynn said. "The shy bass player. I hope he moves so we can see his face."

Incognito started a new song, and it was like they'd

heard Brynn's request. The guitar player moved back and the guy playing bass came to the front of the stage.

Amelia and Brynn both stared at him, their mouths open. Even I had to admit, he was a good-looking dude. He didn't look like a rocker—not like the rest of the band. He was wearing a plain black t-shirt and jeans. No visible tattoos or piercings. Just a guy rocking out on his bass, and clearly loving it.

"I changed my mind. Bass player," Amelia said.

Brynn nodded, her mouth still open. "Oh my god, same."

"Good call," I said. "I'd hit that, if I was into dudes."

"For sure," Chase said.

Amelia laughed. "You think he's hot?"

I tightened my grip around her waist. "I'm secure in my manhood. I can admit when a guy is objectively hot."

Brynn gave Chase a wicked smile. "It doesn't make you jealous?"

His mouth turned up in a grin. "Baby, I know who you're going home with tonight."

We stayed until Incognito finished their set. Brynn had to work tomorrow afternoon, so Chase stopped at a twenty-four-hour coffee stand for a triple shot Americano before we hit the freeway for the long drive back to Echo Creek. And this time, I insisted on sitting in the back with my Cookie.

It was well after three in the morning when we got to Salishan. I wasn't remotely ready to leave Amelia—I planned on spending every second of the weekend with her —so I was glad when she asked me to stay. This girl was a hell of a lot of fun, and we were just getting started.

I WOKE up late the next morning with my legs tangled in the sheets and a naked Amelia sprawled across my chest. Holy shit, she felt good. I'd slept through the night—which was so weird; I still wasn't used to that—and the feel of Amelia's warm skin on mine was the best thing ever. I twined a finger through her hair and played with it while she slowly came awake.

"Morning, beautiful." I kissed her forehead. "How'd you sleep?"

"So good." She nuzzled her body against me. "You?"

"Really good." Which was true, but I was starting to get restless. We'd been out late, so we'd slept in. I wanted to get up and get moving, but Amelia snuggled against me like she had no intention of getting out of bed. Although she felt great, I was getting antsy. I drummed my fingers on the bed and bent one knee so I could tap my foot.

But then Amelia reached up and rubbed my earlobe between her finger and thumb. It was like she'd hit a chill-out button I'd never known I had. Instantly, my entire body relaxed, all the excess energy melting away. The thoughts starting to race through my mind quieted. I stopped tapping and draped an arm around her while she rubbed my ear and traced circles across my neck with her thumb.

I was used to girls turning to putty in my hands, but I was putty in hers. I couldn't remember ever being so relaxed and awake at the same time. Usually I was either going a mile a minute, or sleeping. Or drunk, but that was a different feeling.

I liked this. A lot.

"So what's the plan today?" she asked, still rubbing my ear.

"Plan?"

"Yeah. Yesterday you said you had something planned. Are you going to tell me what it is?"

I took a deep breath, filling my lungs with her. She was right, I did have something planned. "I do, but no, I'm not going to tell you. It's a surprise."

"Surprises are fun."

"They *are* fun." I caressed her bare back and glanced at the clock. "And this fun surprise means we need to get out of bed. Although I think I could do this all day."

"Me too. Or at least until I got too hungry."

That made me smile. I'd been about to say the same thing. "Exactly. We can get breakfast on the way."

We grabbed breakfast burritos at a little restaurant in town, then headed out for my surprise. I hadn't told her what we were doing, but I'd suggested she wear jeans. She looked fantastic in a bright pink halter top, her hair up in a ponytail. She said Brynn had helped her pick out the clothes. I was going to have to thank my sister again. The shirt made Amelia's boobs look fucking phenomenal.

She had such a banging body, and I'd been having all kinds of fun playing with it. She still acted self-conscious sometimes when I got her naked, but she'd relaxed a lot since the first time. I hated it when she said she didn't like the way she looked. She was sexy as fuck, with gorgeous curves in all the right places.

"Can I ask you a personal question?" she asked as she crumpled her empty burrito wrapper into a ball.

"Sure, Cookie."

"It's about penises. Well, yours specifically, since that's the one you have experience with. Does it feel weird just hanging there? When you're naked, in particular. It seems like it would be weird to have something hanging off the front of your body like that."

I kept my hands on the steering wheel and glanced at her. She was nibbling her lower lip. She was so damn cute.

"It doesn't feel weird, but I'm used to it. I guess if someone woke up with a dick when they didn't have one before, it would feel pretty crazy to have it just hanging there, though."

"Oh my god, can you imagine? Well, you can imagine because you have one, but that's not what I mean. I guess the equivalent for you would be waking up and *not* having one."

I swerved a little and had to correct so I didn't run us off the road. "Jesus. Don't even joke about something like that."

She giggled. "Sorry. It's not like that would ever happen."

"It better not happen. I'm really fond of my junk."

"I'm pretty fond of it, too."

"It does fit inside you really well."

This conversation was quickly making my dick stand up and take notice. I had to shift and adjust the crotch of my pants. He could totally tell we were talking about him. And thinking about the way I fit inside Amelia's fantastic pussy was really getting his attention.

"Does it?"

"Shit, yeah. Your pussy feels amazing when I'm fucking you. But Amelia, if we keep having this conversation, I'm going to have to pull over and fuck the hell out of you. Or turn around and take you back to my place. Or something. Because talking about my dick and your pussy and fucking you makes me really want to act on it."

"Sorry. I'm just curious about these things."

"And I highly encourage your curiosity in all things related to my dick. Feel free to explore anytime."

She giggled again. "Are you always so funny?"

"Baby, I'm a fucking delight."

I pulled my truck to a stop outside Rob and Gayle McLaughlin's farm. As soon as Amelia had told me she loved horses, I'd wanted to bring her here to go riding. It was hard work, thinking of things to keep her mind off assgoblin. But I figured I was doing a pretty good job. She seemed happy, at least, and making her happy was addictive. Every time I brought out her smile, it made me want to do it again.

Making her come was like that too, but we'd get to that later.

"Well? What do you think? Want to go for a ride?"

The way her eyes lit up pulled at something deep in my chest. She looked so excited.

"Are you serious?"

"Of course I'm serious," I said. "I'm man enough to admit I'm not the best on a horse, but I can hold my own. You said you like to ride, so here we are."

"Oh my god, Cooper. This is amazing."

She got out of my truck, literally bouncing with excitement. I followed, and Rob came out to greet us.

I'd known Rob and Gayle for most of my life. They were longtime fixtures in Echo Creek. I'd called a few days ago to see if they'd mind me bringing Amelia over to go riding, and they said they'd be happy to have us. Score another one for the Coopster.

Rob took us on a quick tour. I knew grapes and vineyards and all about making things grow. But horses were outside my zone. Amelia, on the other hand, looked like she'd been born and bred here. She and Rob talked as we walked around, and I understood about half of what they said.

But I didn't mind. I asked a few questions and Amelia

excitedly explained things to me. Her eyes were bright and her smile so big. It was fun just to see her like this.

Rob brought us out to a fenced pen where a brown horse stood nearby.

"This here is Lola." He clicked his tongue a few times. Lola walked over and nuzzled his hand, sniffing it like she was hoping for a treat. "Be careful with her. She's a sweet girl, but she's a diva."

"Hi, Lola," Amelia said. She stepped forward and held out her hand for Lola to sniff. "Hi there, pretty girl."

I watched, enraptured while Amelia talked to the horse in a soft, sweet voice. She ran her hands along Lola's neck. In no time, Lola was nuzzling Amelia like they were old friends.

"She sure likes you," Rob said. "And that's saying something, because Lola is picky about who touches her."

"Aw, sweet girl," Amelia cooed. "She's lovely. Do you mind if I take her around?"

"Please do," he said.

I jumped up on the fence and sat while Amelia mounted. She moved so effortlessly, hoisting herself up into the saddle like it was nothing. She took the reins and patted Lola's neck, still talking to her in that same soft voice.

I watched in awe as Amelia rode Lola around the wide pen. At first she walked her, but after a few minutes, she started to trot. Her hair blew back in the wind and the look of pleasure on her face was stunning. I didn't even care that I was just sitting on the sidelines. Seeing her like this was amazing.

"You ready, Cooper?" Rob led another horse out toward me. "This here is Skip. He'll go easy on you."

This was going to be interesting. Rob helped me get up

into the saddle and I took the reins. Amelia came closer on Lola.

"If you go out that way," Rob said, pointing, "there's a nice trail to follow. It makes a loop, so you'll wind up right back here."

"Perfect, thank you so much." Amelia looked at me, raising her eyebrows. "Are you okay?"

"Yeah, I'm good. Lead the way, Cookie." I leaned down and whispered to Skip as she rode out of the pen. "You're my wingman out here, Skip. Make me look good for the girl, okay, buddy?"

He definitely nodded.

I was good enough on a horse for a trail ride, and Skip took his wingman job seriously. He stayed mellow, even when Lola seemed to get a little excited. But Amelia handled her like an expert, talking in that sweet, soothing voice.

She was so much fun, but she seemed to carry a lot of self-consciousness around with her. Here, that all melted away. She was certain and confident. She looked wild and free on the back of that horse. And damn, I loved seeing it. I wanted that for her all the time.

We rode side by side along the trail, surrounded by pine trees and blackberry bushes. The horses' hooves made soft clumping sounds in the dirt. It didn't take long before I got used to the way Skip moved beneath me, although I couldn't tell if he was responding to my nudges, or following Amelia and Lola.

"My dad was cheating on my mom and he had a secret family we never knew about," I said suddenly, breaking the short silence.

"You're kidding," she said. "That's awful."

"Sorry to just blurt that out. I'm not sure why I said it. I guess I just want you to know that about me."

"When you say *secret family*, do you mean he was married to someone else? Or had kids?"

"He didn't marry her, but they did have two kids together. And she's not the only one. I don't know how many others there were. I don't really want to know. He was with someone new when my brothers found out. He went to her when my mom kicked him out of the house."

"Your mom kicked him out? I'm impressed."

"I was really proud of her. It sucked balls, but she was really strong."

"Wow. I'm sorry you all had to go through that."

"Thanks," I said, swaying a little with the movement of the horse. "It sucks that my dad's a dick. My mom's great, though, so that makes up for it. What about your parents? What are they like?"

"Distant," she said. "The older I get, the more I realize I don't know them very well. I've always spent more time away from them than with them. I always had nannies and went to boarding schools."

"That sucks."

"Yeah, although time away from my mother isn't a bad thing. She's very critical. It sounds weird, but I think that's her way of caring. She wants me to be the best I can be, so she points out my flaws, as if that will help. But I don't think either of my parents ever really understood me."

"How could they? It sounds like they don't know you."

"That's true." She was quiet for a long moment. "Kind of makes you want to do better, doesn't it? Some people grow up and repeat the same thing with their kids. My grandmother was just as sharp and critical as my mom is now. My mom raised me like she was raised. But I don't want to do that. If I ever have a family, I don't want to repeat the same mistakes."

"Yeah," I said, letting what she'd said sink in. I'd never thought much about having a family. Always figured I'd be a bachelor forever. But if I ever did have kids, I wouldn't be like my dad. Not even close. "You won't be like your mom. And hey, maybe one thing our parents did is show us what *not* to do."

"That's true," she said, her voice bright. "Maybe that's a little silver lining."

I smiled at her, a deep sense of relief washing over me. I'd told her something pretty shitty about me and she hadn't freaked out or judged me for it.

Kind of made my heart swell with... something. A feeling. A big feeling.

After we came back from our ride, Gayle invited us to have lemonade with them on their porch. Amelia and Gayle talked about the horses, and Amelia's experiences riding and teaching. It was fun to see her in her element. And they had cookies, which made it even better.

I held Amelia's hand on the drive back to Salishan. She kept thanking me, but I wanted to thank her. I didn't know how she did it, but she made me feel relaxed and happy all at once. I'd had a fun day with her, and I was excited for more.

THIRTEEN

COOPER

I STOPPED by the cottage to see Amelia before work on Thursday. It was early, but she was up. Plus, I brought donuts, and who didn't love fresh donuts in the morning?

She let me in, dressed in pajama pants and a t-shirt, her hair in a messy bun. As soon as I could dump the donut box on the counter, I grabbed her. She was so cute first thing in the morning. I loved the way she looked, all sleepy with no makeup.

"Morning, beautiful," I murmured into her ear. I hugged her tight, then ran my hands down her back and over her curvy hips. Grabbed her ass.

She giggled against my neck. "Morning."

"I can't stay, but I wanted to snuggle you before work."

"I'm glad you came," she said. "You're so good at snuggling."

"I *am* good at snuggling." I stopped grabbing her ass and went back to hugging her. "I'm glad you appreciate my talents."

"Yes, I appreciate all your talents. A lot."

She was making me hard, but that was pretty much

always. This girl could smile at me and I'd have an instant hard-on. Sadly, I didn't have time to stay and play. I gave her a few quick kisses, then let her go.

"Have anything planned for the day?" I opened the donut box and grabbed a chocolate one.

"Actually, I do. Brynn doesn't have to work until this afternoon, so we're getting mani-pedis."

"Awesome," I said through a mouthful of donut.

"It'll be fun. Your sister is really sweet. I like her a lot. I'm glad I get to hang out with her today, since I'm not sure when I'll see her again. She's spending tomorrow working at Chase's shop and then she's helping with winery events all weekend."

"Yeah, but that's just a few days. Why wouldn't you see her after—" And then it hit me. Amelia's Cooper-moon was almost over. "Oh. Right. Shit, you're..."

I couldn't bring myself to say *leaving soon*.

"I talked to Daphne. Their apartment is really small, but they're happy to have me come down for a while. I figure I'll go to my parents' first, then make arrangements to go to L.A."

"Right. Good." I set my half-eaten donut on the counter. My chest felt like it was going to cave in.

"I don't think my parents are going to be thrilled with my plan. I haven't talked to them yet and I'm totally dreading it."

"Yeah."

She put a hand on my arm. "Are you okay?"

I felt like I was going to crawl out of my own skin. I was not okay, but my brain was kicking into overdrive, moving too fast for me to stop and try to explain. Plus, I couldn't have explained it even if I did try. I didn't know what was wrong with me.

"Yeah, fine. Just a lot on my mind. I need to get to work."

I hugged her again and gave her a kiss. Two seconds later, I was out the door.

I barely remembered driving out to the south vineyard. There was too much going on in my head. I couldn't focus. It took me a solid hour of wandering up and down the rows before I finally calmed down enough to get anything done.

Last season we'd battled an outbreak of powdery mold in this area, but this year, my babies looked fantastic. The weather had been good so far and I made a mental note that we might be looking at an early harvest.

Growing anything, especially on a large scale, required a great deal of surrender. There was a lot I couldn't control. The number of days of full sun. The rain. Unforeseen nutrient deficiencies in the soil. The ripening time. There were a thousand variables to account for. My grandfather had taught me that the best thing to do was listen to your vineyards. I'd learned from a young age to let the land and the vines speak to me. They always told me what I needed to know. From there, I could adjust our plans as needed. So far, this season was looking good.

It was past midday when I went back to the utility vehicle. I took off my hat and wiped the sweat off my forehead with the back of my arm. It was getting hot. I'd left my phone on the seat, so I checked to see if I had any messages.

The text from Amelia made me smile. She'd sent a picture of her with my sister holding up their hands to show their nails. So fucking cute.

I had another text and I hesitated before opening it. The number wasn't in my contacts, but I knew who it was. Dad.

Back entrance. Monday.

Me: k

I sent the text, then erased his message and my reply. I knew what it meant. He had guys coming in to work his crop. I had to make sure they got in and could get their work done without anyone knowing. It sucked, but if it brought us one step closer to getting rid of Dad forever, it would be worth it.

Hearing from my dad did not improve my mood. Neither did being hungry. I hadn't brought any lunch out with me, so I drove back to the main grounds. I stopped by Mom's house first. She wasn't home, but she always had leftovers in her fridge. Best mom ever. I scrounged and found some chicken Alfredo. Felt a little better after I ate. I still thought I might burst out of my skin, but at least I wasn't starving anymore.

This Amelia thing was a serious problem. The thought of her leaving in a few days made me panicky. Like my lungs wouldn't fill with enough air.

I wandered outside and noticed Chase's truck over by the work house. I found him inside with Ben doing maintenance on one of our machines.

"Hey bros." I clapped Chase on the back.

Without looking up, he lifted his fist and I bumped it with mine.

"Cooper," Ben said with a nod.

"You guys look busy. Are you busy?"

"Just about finished." Chase stepped back and grabbed a rag to wipe his hands. "This looks great. I don't think you'll have any issues."

"Good. Thanks, Chase," Ben said.

"Anytime. What's up, Coop? You look like shit."

I took my hat off and scrubbed my hand through my sweaty hair. "I have issues, bro."

"Yeah, we know," Chase said.

"No, I mean I have a problem. Come on, man, I'm trying to open up here and you're going to pitch me shit? Be a friend, dude."

Chase laughed. "Okay, Coop. What's going on?"

"Amelia's Cooper-moon is almost over."

"What's a Cooper-moon?" Ben asked.

"Coop's new plaything was here to get married, but that crashed and burned, so instead of a honeymoon, she stayed on a Cooper-moon."

"I see."

"She's not my plaything, she's my friend, and she's leaving in a few days. She's going to fucking Los Angeles. *California.* I am *not* happy about this."

"Huh," Chase said.

"What?"

"I'm just surprised you're not already getting bored."

"With Amelia? She's the opposite of boring. She's fun as fuck. Have you met her? Seriously, dude. She's awesome and I don't want her to go. And you know what's weird? It's not even about me. I mean, it's partly about me. I like hanging out with her. And I want to keep doing it. But what's really getting me is that I think if she goes to L.A. she's going to be miserable. I hate that idea so much I want to punch something."

Ben was eying me with that mysterious look he got sometimes. Like he could see through me. "Why would L.A. make her miserable?"

I started to blurt out something about L.A. being hot and the air quality being shit, but I stopped myself. That wasn't the point, and I knew it. What Ben was asking was important, so I closed my mouth, took a breath, and started again, giving my brain a chance to slow down.

"She's not going to L.A. because it's what she wants.

She's going because that's where her best friend is, and she doesn't think she has a better option."

Ben and Chase glanced at each other with raised eyebrows.

"What? I just want her to have a good option. She's an awesome girl and she deserves that."

"And ideally, you'd like it if that option meant staying here?" Ben asked.

"Yes," I said, my eyes widening. "That's exactly it."

Ben rubbed his bearded jaw. "I talked to Rob McLaughlin the other day. He told me you took her riding last weekend."

"Yeah, but you're going to have to drop some more info, because I don't know what this has to do with Amelia's Cooper-moon ending. I'd love to tell you how amazing Amelia is with horses, because she's fucking brilliant and she loves it and god, she lights up like the sun. But I have a problem, here. Can we focus?"

"Slow down, Cooper," Ben said. "Rob and Gayle were really taken with her. Said she was a natural. And I happen to know that they're looking to hire someone new. I don't know if that presents an option for Amelia, but—"

"Holy shit," I said. "Are you serious right now? Tell me you're serious."

"I'm serious," he said. "I can't promise it'll work out. But it might be worth asking. You could mention it to Amelia and see if she's interested. If she is, have her give Rob and Gayle a call."

"Oh my god, Ben, you're the man. Jesus, this is perfect. I knew there was a solution."

"I'm in on this being perfect," Chase said. "You've been hanging out with Amelia so much, Brynn and I have had the apartment to ourselves. You know I love you, dude, but last night Brynn was in the kitchen in just her t-shirt and underwear and—"

I opened my mouth to stop him, but Ben beat me to it.

"Chase," he said. "Discretion, buddy."

"Thank you," I said.

Chase put on his best shit-eating grin. "Sorry."

"The kitchen?" I asked. "Don't even tell me the rest of that story, because I don't want to know, but we talked about this. Bedroom, man."

He just smiled bigger.

"For fuck's sake, Chase." I pointedly turned to Ben. "How'd you know the McLaughlins are hiring?"

Ben cleared his throat. "I know the woman who's leaving."

There was something in Ben's voice that caught my attention. "You know her? What does that mean? Like you know her because she's lived here forever and so have you? Or you *know* her, know her?"

"She's lived in the area a while, but it's a bit more than that."

"Dude, you can't say shit like that and leave it," I said. "Back me up here, Chase."

"Yeah, Cooper's right. What the hell, Ben?"

"We were seeing each other," Ben said.

I stared at Ben. I couldn't remember him ever mentioning being with a woman. Not a specific woman, at least. When I was younger, he'd talked to me about girls. But it had always been in the abstract. Ben liked to drop wisdom bombs on me, especially if we were out working in the vineyards. He always had, since I was little. But he'd never talked about his own relationships.

"Holy shit. I always figured you were a monk or something. You've been getting some action? Ben, you dog. Why didn't you ever say something?"

Ben's mouth turned up in a small smile. "A gentleman doesn't need to boast about his conquests."

"Whoa," Chase and I both said.

"I'm kind of freaking out right now." I paced, not moving too far from Ben and Chase, but stretching my legs. Ben was blowing my mind. "You mean to tell me you've been out there getting laid all these years?"

"I'm a single man, Cooper. I've had relationships with women. I just don't parade them around."

"Old school," Chase said. "That's awesome."

"So what happened?" I asked. "Is she your girl? Does that mean your girl is leaving? What's up with that?"

"No, I ended things a little over a year ago," Ben said. "But we stayed on good terms. She met someone else and she's moving to Montana to be with him. I'm glad for her."

"What about you?" Chase asked. "Just enjoying the single life, or do you have another secret girlfriend you're hiding from everyone?"

Ben rolled his eyes. "No, I'm not seeing anyone at the moment. Haven't since her."

The timing of all this wasn't lost on me. But I stopped myself from blurting out the first thing that came into my head. I was about to say that it sounded like Ben had broken up with his girl around the time my mom had kicked my dad out, and wasn't that an interesting coincidence. But before I spoke up, I realized that would probably be a shitty thing to say.

I didn't really know how Ben felt about my mom. I had my suspicions. I saw the way he looked at her now. But maybe there was a reason Ben hadn't made a move. And maybe me poking at him about it would be a dick move.

So I changed the subject. "Thanks for the heads-up about the job. It's perfect for my Cookie. I can't wait to tell her."

"Sure." Ben patted me on the back. "Just remember, Cooper, sometimes timing is everything. Your clocks need to be in sync. Don't get ahead of yourself."

"Yeah, okay." I wasn't sure what he meant, but that was how Ben was sometimes. He'd tell me things that didn't make sense until later. I just rolled with it. "Cool, bros. I gotta bounce. Catch you later."

I left, feeling a million times better. If Amelia got a job at the McLaughlin's ranch, she'd have a great reason to stay. It was a hell of a lot better than moving to L.A. She was going to be psyched, I just knew it.

And if my Cookie had a reason to stay, it meant I didn't have to say goodbye this weekend. And that was awesome.

FOURTEEN
AMELIA

THIRTEEN DAYS after Griffin left me at the altar, he finally tried to make contact.

I stared at my phone, his name blazed across the screen. It used to give me butterflies to see his texts—I'd hope it meant he was in town and wanted to hang out. That happened off and on, although when I thought about it now, it was always shortly after he'd broken up with his latest girlfriend. He'd go silent for months when he was dating someone else, even though he and I were supposed to be good friends.

Seeing his text now didn't give me butterflies. It gave me the opposite of butterflies, if there was such a thing. Instead of a flare of excitement and anticipation, I felt a flash of anger. It had been almost two weeks since I'd stood in a wedding dress waiting for him, and he hadn't even had the decency to break up with me properly.

Griffin: I think we should talk. Can I call you?

Me: No.

Griffin: Please. I don't want to do this over text.

Me: Do what? It's already done. I'm sure you and Portia will be very happy.

Griffin: Just answer your phone.

Seconds later, my phone rang, Griffin's number on the screen. I rejected the call. There was no way I was answering. I didn't want to hear his excuses. I didn't even want to hear his voice.

I didn't get angry easily as a general rule, but right now, Griffin had me so angry I wanted to swear. "Flipping Griffin."

Obviously I wasn't very good at swearing.

He texted again, but I didn't read it. What did he expect from me? He'd cheated on me and left me on our wedding day. And now two weeks later, I was supposed to be nice? Screw that.

The sound of Cooper's truck outside dampened my anger. In fact, there were those butterflies, flapping their soft little wings, putting out all the sparks of rage. He was like magic.

The door flew open and he barreled into the cottage like a tornado. His hair was damp and messy and his clothes were clean. Flashing a sexy grin, he picked me up off my feet and squeezed me tight.

"Hey, Cookie."

He smelled like heaven, and the way he could pick me up always made me feel giddy. I loved the way he spun me around, like I weighed nothing.

"Hey. How was your day?"

"Too long. How was yours?" He put me down. "Your nails are pretty. Did you have fun with my sister?"

"Yeah, we had a lot of fun."

"Awesome." He grabbed my hand and pulled me out the door, but paused just outside the cottage. "Oh. Do you want to have dinner with me?"

"Yeah, I'd love to."

"Good, because I'm so hungry I'm about to pass out. Don't worry about your clothes. You look hot. And we're just going to Ray's Diner because I think you'll love it and it's my favorite."

We drove to a diner in town. It looked cute from the outside with big windows and a bright red door. Cooper took my hand again as we went inside. He led me to a booth and we both took a seat.

An older woman wearing a red apron, her bleached blond hair in a bun, came to our table and handed us menus. Her name tag said *Jo*.

"There's my cutie pie," she said with a smile.

"Jo, you're looking especially gorgeous today," Cooper said. "Tell me, how's your life? Are they treating you well around here?"

"I can't complain. Can I get you anything to drink?"

"Water for me. Go ahead and bring me five or six glasses. Or maybe just a pitcher. I'm dehydrated as hell after being outside in the heat all day. Cookie, do you want something else? Jo, this is my Cookie, Amelia."

Jo turned to me with a smile. "What can I get you, sweetie?"

"Water for me, too."

"Do you need some time, or can I get your order going? We don't need Cooper dying on us before he gets fed." She winked at him.

"This is why I love you, Jo," Cooper said. "What are you thinking, Cookie? I'm eying their burgers. Bacon and extra cheese and their fries are the best."

I loved diner food, so the only tough thing was choosing from the five or six choices that sounded good. "I was actually thinking breakfast for dinner, if you do that?"

"We sure do," Jo said.

"Oh sure, that works too," Cooper said.

We ordered our meals—double bacon cheeseburger for Cooper and pancakes and eggs for me. Jo brought three pitchers of ice water and Cooper drank an entire one straight from the pitcher without stopping.

He put the pitcher down, then filled my glass with water from the second one.

"Cookie, I have the best news. Are you ready for this?"

"I think so."

"I talked to Ben, who knows Rob and Gayle from the ranch, remember them? Of course you do. They really liked you, and because the universe is awesome, they're looking to hire someone. Do you realize what that means?"

"I'm not sure."

"It means you don't have to go to L.A. to live with Daphne and the rock star in the tiny apartment. It means you can get the job at the McLaughlins' ranch and stay and your Cooper-moon doesn't have to end. You'll have to go to work and stuff, so it won't be a vacation anymore. But isn't that amazing?"

I stared at him, open mouthed, his words taking longer than usual to sink in. He talked fast, although I didn't usually have any trouble keeping up. But had he just said I should *stay*?

Tucking my hair behind my ear, I tried to process everything. Cooper tended to make me feel like I was caught in a whirlwind, and mostly I loved the sensation. He was wild and free and so much fun. But staying in Echo Creek was a possibility I hadn't really entertained. I'd resigned myself to the idea of going to L.A. with Daphne. That was the plan. Regroup at my parents' house, then get to L.A. as quickly as possible. From there... I wasn't quite sure.

But none of that involved Cooper. I'd been ignoring that part, pushing it to the back of my mind. It hurt more than it should—much more than I wanted it to. Because admitting how much it was going to hurt to leave him would mean I'd have to face *why*. And less than two weeks after being dumped in a wedding dress, I wasn't ready for that.

"I don't know, Cooper. Their ranch was beautiful, and you can tell they're good people who love their animals. You get a sense of that, you know? And I did get the sense that they do, which is wonderful and really important to me. So... yeah, that's a good thing. But this is really sudden. I've been planning to go to L.A. and this is such a shift. I didn't think this would even be a possibility, so I hadn't thought about it, and now I have to make a decision pretty fast, don't I? I mean, I was supposed to leave this weekend, and here it is Friday and you're saying maybe I should get a job and stay here and I don't really know what to think right now."

"If you're worried about where you'll live, don't be. You'll stay in the cottage at Salishan. I'll talk to Mom tonight, but I know she won't mind."

"That's really nice, but aren't we getting a little ahead of ourselves? Just because you heard they're hiring, doesn't mean they'll hire *me*."

"Sure they will. I already talked to them. I called Rob this afternoon and he thinks you'd be a great fit. I can take you over there tomorrow so you can talk to them yourself, but it's a slam dunk."

He'd already talked to them? That flare of anger fired up again. I was so tired of people making assumptions about what I wanted, like I couldn't make decisions about my own life. In the back of my head, a little voice was trying to tell me that Cooper's idea was pretty great. I would love to work on a ranch, and staying here would mean I wouldn't have to say goodbye—or face the pain that was going to cause.

But that spark of frustration was too hot.

"Why didn't you ask me before you talked to them? You didn't know if I'd want the job. You just assumed and suddenly you're making calls for me and telling me where I'm going to live, and cheese and rice, it's my wedding dress all over again. I was standing there in front of the mirror, looking at myself, and it wasn't me, Cooper. It was this big white dress and I hated it and my mom insisted it was the one. She'd already picked it out before I got there. And then I wore it and Daphne swore it was pretty, but I knew it wasn't, and it wasn't what I wanted and no one would listen to me."

I was babbling like a crazy girl and my voice sounded panicky, but I couldn't help it.

Cooper's intense expression relaxed, and he held up his hands, palms out. "I'm listening to you, Cookie. If this isn't what you want, I'm not here to make you do it. I just thought you might want another option. If Daphne and the rock star and L.A. are what you want—if that's where you're supposed to go—that's your call."

I took a shaky breath, trying to calm down.

He reached over and took my hand. Stroked his thumb across my skin. "I won't make you wear a dress you hate."

Looking up, I met his eyes. They were a vivid blue, his expression surprisingly soft. "You won't?"

"Never."

I nodded and a potent sense of relief washed over me. I didn't really understand it, but it took the tension out of my shoulders. Cooper kept stroking my hand and we sat in silence for long moments—which was unusual for both of us. He didn't even move when Jo brought our dinners and set them on the table. Just kept caressing my hand, his eyes on me.

"I'm sorry." I turned my hand over so I could squeeze his. "You're trying to do something nice for me and I snapped at you. Everything has been happening so fast, sometimes I don't know what to think. And Griffin tried to call me earlier and I guess it made me edgy, but that's not your fault and I shouldn't take it out on you."

Cooper sat up straighter. "Assgoblin called?"

"Yeah, he texted first and told me to answer my phone and I didn't. I don't want to talk to him."

"No shit." Cooper squeezed my hand, then let go to shove a handful of fries in his mouth. "Fuck that guy."

"Exactly. I'm going to think about it tonight. The job, I mean. But I need to be alone to do that because it's kind of hard to think when I'm with you. I'm pretty sure I have a really big crush on you, and you make me feel all these things, and oh my god, I just said that out loud." I clapped my hand over my mouth, mortified.

But... oh my god. It was true. I did have a crush on Cooper. Which was so weird because we'd been having sex for the last two weeks, and wasn't a crush supposed to come first, then sex?

A wide grin spread across Cooper's face. "Baby, I'm crushing on you hard."

I giggled behind my hand, my face flushing hot.

"I'll take you home after dinner and you do what you need to do, okay? I want to go see my nephew anyway, so I'll pay them a visit. If you decide you want to talk to Rob and Gayle, I can drive you out there tomorrow. And if not..."

His face fell, his expression tugging at my heart. "We'll just deal with that if it comes, I guess."

"Okay. That's fair. And Cooper?"

"Yeah?"

"Thank you."

He smiled again. "You bet, Cookie."

BACK AT THE COTTAGE, I ran a hot bath. I needed to regroup. I kind of regretted not asking Cooper to stay tonight—this bathtub was amazing and it would have been a lot of fun with him—but like I'd told him, he made it hard to think straight. I needed a little time.

My phone rang while I was still soaking in a tub full of hot water and bubbles—Daphne.

"Hey," I said. "I was going to call you in a little bit."

"I had a feeling. How are you? I haven't talked to you in a few days. Are you okay?"

"Yeah, I am."

"So have you talked to your parents yet? When do you think you'll head down?"

I took a deep breath. "Actually, I think there's going to be a change of plans."

"Oh yeah? What's up?"

"Well, it's a bit of a long story, but I found out about a job opportunity here," I said. "It's not a done deal, but it's at a horse ranch and the people are great and I think I have a really good shot at it."

"Wow... that's... okay, that's pretty cool."

"Yeah it is. It would be a great place to work, and I really like it here."

"How did you find out about it?"

I shifted a little and the suds moved in a slow wave. "Cooper took me riding there last weekend, and then he heard about the job from someone at work."

"Cooper? Are you still... you know, hanging out with him?"

"Yeah."

"Really?"

"Well, yeah. I told you, he's really fun."

"Sure, but don't you think it's a little soon to be dating someone new?"

"I guess, yeah, but we're not really dating. Not actually."

"You sure about that?"

"Yes. I'm sure."

She sighed. "He took you horseback riding?"

"Yeah."

"And does he take you out to dinner and things like that?"

"Yes."

"And you're sleeping with him?"

"Yes, but—"

"That's dating, weirdo," she said.

"Okay, but aren't there degrees of dating now? Like this isn't the old days where a boy would ask a girl's parents for permission to court her and that meant he wanted to marry her and then he'd come and sit with her on the porch while they had a chaperone, and he'd hope for a glimpse of her ankles. This is the modern era. I can hang out with Cooper and have fun with him and yes, even sleep with him— because god, Daphne, sex is basically the most amazing invention ever—and that's all it is. Two people who like each other who hang out and have fun and have amazing sex. Does that need a label? I'm not jumping into another relationship, and by another, I really just mean *a* relationship, because what I had with Griffin almost doesn't count, even though I was dumb enough to agree to marry him."

"Slow down, sweetie, you're babbling again."

"Sorry. I just mean, I'm fine with whatever Cooper and I are right now. And as much as I love you, moving to L.A. isn't really what I want. I like this option better."

"All right, I hear you," she said. "And it makes sense, in an Amelia sort of way. I just worry about you, that's all. You're vulnerable right now and I don't want a guy taking advantage of that."

"He's not like that, Daph."

"Plus, you have this beautiful future ahead of you. We just finished college, and there's a whole big world out there. Don't settle for the next thing that comes along just because he's hot and gives you great orgasms."

I laughed. "I know. I'm not settling in any sense of the word. I have no idea how long this will last—the job, or Cooper. And that's okay with me."

"I'm proud of you, sweetie," she said. "Just be careful. Pinky promise?"

"I will. Pinky promise."

FIFTEEN
AMELIA

FOR FOUR GLORIOUS WEEKS, everything was perfect.

Cooper had been right about the job at the McLaughlins' ranch being a slam dunk. They'd hired me on the spot and I'd started work the following Monday.

I'd arranged with Cooper's mom to stay in the Blackberry Cottage, and insisted on paying rent. The little cottage was perfect. Before my first day of work, Cooper had taken me out to my parents' house to pick up my car and move some of my stuff to Salishan. Conveniently for me, my parents had been out of town, so I'd been spared any lectures about my life choices.

I loved my job. Rob and Gayle were charming and sweet. One of my biggest responsibilities was teaching lessons in the youth program a few afternoons a week. The kids were curious and fun. Some were cautious, even scared, and I was excited to help them work through their fear and gain confidence. Others were a little too brave for their own good and needed to work on being safe with the animals. But I loved seeing their faces when they learned a skill or got up the courage to do something new.

Most of my free time was spent with Cooper. And I had no complaints about that. We played paintball again—sans wedding dress—and went river rafting. He took me on hikes through his vineyards, telling me all about his fields and his grapes. I could listen to him talk for hours.

I hung out at his place with Chase and Brynn, barbecuing dinner and watching movies. They marveled that Cooper would sit through an entire movie without getting up. Apparently, he was usually too restless to sit that long. But I loved to massage his fingers or play with his ear while we sat, and he was always perfectly relaxed.

We hung out with his brothers, too, although not as often. I met Roland and Zoe and baby Hudson. He was so adorable, and seeing Cooper hold a baby was basically the hottest thing in the history of ever.

Cooper talked Leo into coming to the cottage for movie night a few times. I didn't know what to think about Leo. Specifically, I didn't know what he thought about me. I was a little worried he didn't like me, but then I wondered if maybe he didn't like anyone. He didn't talk much, but he didn't talk to Cooper a lot, either, so I tried not to take it personally. His scars were alarming at first, but it didn't take long to get used to them. By the third time he'd come over, he seemed to be warming up to me a little more. He was friendlier, at least, which was progress.

My parents remained skeptical about my choice to stay at Salishan, so it wasn't too surprising when they called to say they were coming to town and wanted to meet me for dinner. What *was* surprising was that they called me from the road. I was still at work, and I was barely going to have time to go home and change before they wanted to meet.

Rob was fine with letting me leave a little early. I texted Cooper before I left, so he'd know I wouldn't be home when he got off work. He called while I was driving home.

"Hey, Cookie. What's going on? Your parents are coming?"

"Yeah, they called a little while ago," I said. "They're on their way. We're meeting at the Lodge, but I'm heading home now so I can shower first. I'm a mess."

"What time are you meeting them?"

"Five."

"Well, shit," he said. "I have at least two more hours of work to do out here. You okay doing this alone?"

"Yeah, I am. They'll probably try to tell me I should move home, but I'm prepared for that."

There was a noise through the phone that I couldn't quite place. Was he growling?

"I'm dreading it a little, but I haven't seen them since the wedding," I said. "It'll be fine."

"Okay. I'll text you later. And I've been fantasizing about fucking you all day. Fair warning."

I laughed. "Consider me warned."

I went home, showered, dried my hair, dabbed on a little makeup, and put on one of the dresses I'd picked out with Brynn. She and I had gotten manicures the other day, and mine were turquoise and purple ombre. They sparkled in the sun and matched my turquoise dress.

Pretty dress, sparkly nails, cute shoes. All in all, I felt pretty great. Ready to face my parents.

My dad had made reservations at the Lodge, so I walked next door to the big hotel. I checked my phone and had a message from my dad. They'd already been seated. I went into the restaurant and caught a glimpse of my mom. She held up her hand and I waved back, then stopped in my tracks.

They weren't alone. Seated at the table with my mother and father were Mr. and Mrs. Wentworth. Not only that, Griffin sat next to the last empty chair.

I gaped at them for a few seconds. This couldn't be happening. Griffin? That no-good, lying, cheating prick. The only—and I mean only—reason I didn't turn right around and leave was Griffin's parents. They were smiling at me with compassion in their eyes. They'd always been nice to me, and I didn't want to be rude.

"Well, this is a surprise," I said when I approached the table. I widened my eyes at my parents. "You didn't tell me this was a dinner party."

"That's my fault, Mimi," Griffin said. "I was afraid you wouldn't come otherwise."

I ground my teeth at that nickname. I'd never liked it and hearing it on his lips made me hate it ten times more. "It's *Amelia*, thank you."

Griffin cleared his throat.

"Amelia, please sit," Mom said.

It was very irritating that the open seat was next to Griffin—and that was obviously not a coincidence—but I didn't have much choice, so I went around to the other side of the table. Griffin stood and pulled the chair out for me. Maybe it was petty, but I didn't thank him.

An awkward silence settled over the table as we all perused the menus. Griffin's presence next to me made my skin crawl. How had I ever thought I was in love with him? His hair was slicked back and he wore a nice suit. He was objectively attractive, on the outside at least. But all I could see now was his betrayal. It made him hideous in my eyes.

The waiter came and took our orders. Dad gave me a

look when I ordered wine—a glass of Salishan Cabernet—
but I pretended not to notice.

"We have a few things to discuss," Mom said, finally
breaking the silence. "Amelia, since you've been away, there
have been developments that pertain to you."

"Have there?"

"Yes. Griffin has realized his errors in judgment."

It did not escape my notice that both of Griffin's parents
were glaring at him. They were clearly not happy with their
son. But what was this about? Was my mother trying to
apologize for him?

"That's fine, but I don't see how this is a development
that pertains to me."

"Of course it pertains to you," Dad said. "I'm sure
you're as anxious as we all are to put this unpleasantness
behind us."

"Mimi," Griffin said, then cleared his throat. "I mean,
Amelia. I realize I made mistakes, and I'm sorry. I hope you
can find it within yourself to forgive me."

The waiter brought our drinks and I took a quick sip of
my wine. It was taking all my self-control to keep from
babbling incoherently. My parents' eyes bored into me. Mr.
Wentworth looked angry, and his wife was pale. Griffin
kept inching his chair closer to mine, and I had the feeling
he was going to try to touch me.

All I could think about was that moment on what was
supposed to be my wedding day, when I'd realized Griffin
wasn't there. The shock and emptiness. The numbness that
followed.

I did not want to be here.

A subtle commotion near the restaurant entrance made
me look up. A man finished speaking with the hostess, then
walked straight for our table.

It was Cooper.

He was dressed in a faded gray Salishan Cellars t-shirt, a sweat-stained baseball cap and dusty jeans. His work boots were caked with dirt, but he walked with the confidence of a man in a well-tailored suit. I watched, open mouthed, as he grabbed an empty chair from the table next to us. He dragged it between me and Griffin, then unceremoniously scooted me over so he could wedge it in. With a wink at me, he turned his hat backwards and sat.

"Hey, Cookie. Sorry I'm late. What can I say, summers are busy. My babies need a lot of attention this time of year."

"Excuse me?" Mom asked. "Amelia, do you know this man?"

"Cooper Miles," he said, holding out his hand. Mom didn't take it. "I'm the head grower at Salishan Cellars."

"And how do you know my daughter?"

My eyes widened, and I made a little noise in my throat. Griffin stared at him, like he was too shocked to do anything else.

"That's an interesting story," Cooper said. "She was left here in a bit of a pickle, now wasn't she? She'd expected a wedding and a honeymoon, and didn't get either. When I found her, she was looking for something to do with her unexpected free time. Maybe try some new things. Have new experiences. And since I'm a nice guy, I was more than happy to help her with that."

"Indeed," Mom said. "How so?"

I was about to interrupt so Cooper didn't say what we'd actually done when we first met—and so many times since—but he kept talking.

"I suggested an internship in winemaking. My family has owned Salishan Cellars for generations. Wine runs in my blood. So I took our Amelia here under my wing." His eyes flicked to Griffin. "And I've been teaching her everything I know."

"Interesting," Mr. Wentworth said. "Have you been enjoying the experience, Amelia?"

"Um, yes," I managed to squeak out.

"She's an amazing student," Cooper said. "For a woman who had absolutely no experience when we met, she's come a long way. Really, she's an absolute natural."

"That's lovely, Amelia," Mrs. Wentworth said. "How exciting to learn a new skill."

"Oh, she's become very skilled," Cooper said. "In a wide variety of things."

Griffin's face reddened, and his jaw hitched.

"I'm happy to hear you've been doing something productive with your time," Mom said.

"Indeed she has." Cooper leaned back in his chair and put his arm over the back of mine. "I've gotten a lot out of it as well. You'd be surprised how much a student can teach you. Just when you think you're the expert. And you've been enjoying yourself, haven't you, Cookie?"

"Yeah, it's been a lot of fun," I said.

"You really need to stop calling her that," Griffin said, his voice low.

The corner of Cooper's mouth turned up. "I'm pretty sure you gave up the right to give a shit when you banged her cousin the night before your wedding."

A shocked silence settled over the table, but I beamed at him. He was dirty and ridiculous in his backward baseball cap and dusty boots.

And I was totally smitten.

"The thing is," Cooper continued, "most people would agree cheating is a hard-core deal breaker. Cheating the night before your wedding is worse. And cheating with a bridesmaid, who is also her cousin? Dude, you don't come back from that. I'm not sure what you're hoping to accomplish, but if you're here to try to talk her into taking you back, I have a feeling you're wasting your time. It's her call, so I'll let her speak for herself. But from an outside perspective, you seem like you're kind of nuts for even being here."

I knew my parents were probably about to blow a gasket, and who knew what Griffin's parents were thinking. I wasn't paying attention to any of them. My eyes were on Cooper.

He turned to me and ran a knuckle down my jaw. "What do you need, Cookie? You want to stay and have dinner? Or should we blow this Popsicle stand? I've got your back either way."

I smiled at Cooper, then turned to Mr. and Mrs. Wentworth. "It was very nice to see the two of you. I hope you enjoy your dinner. Mom and Dad, thanks for coming to see me. You look well, and I hope you have a pleasant drive home."

I didn't bother saying anything to Griffin. I stood, and Cooper followed.

"Amelia, if you walk out of here with him, there will be consequences," Dad said. "You won't see a dime."

Even though I wasn't touching Cooper, I could feel him tense up. I reached over and put a gentle hand on his arm. If Dad wanted to threaten to take my trust fund away, he was welcome to.

"I guess it's a good thing I have a job." I slipped my hand into Cooper's. "Have a nice evening, everyone."

Cooper led me around the table, then put his arm around my shoulders as we left the restaurant. I didn't bother looking back.

SIXTEEN
COOPER

CHASE and I sat out on our balcony, beers in hand. The sun sank below the mountain peaks, streaking the sky with color. I had a feeling we were in for some rain. It had been a dry summer so far, and there weren't any clouds to be seen. But I could feel it coming. Which was good. My babies needed it.

Amelia and Brynn had gone to the movies. Some chick flick, so I wasn't too broken up about missing it. Chase probably wished he was there. He tried to hide his love of chick flicks, but I was onto him.

I did miss Amelia, though.

"Dude, I need to have a talk with your wife," I said. "She already took you from me. Now she's making a play for my Cookie."

Chase took a swig of his beer. "She didn't take me, we still live together. And they're just having a girls' night. Plus this means you get me all to yourself, which effectively nullifies point number one."

"That's true, I do get you all to myself, which is fucking

awesome." I reached out with my bottle and he clinked his against it.

We'd grilled steaks for dinner. Felt a bit like old times. Except we weren't gearing up to go to a bar. Things were different, now. Chase had a wife, and I had Amelia. And that was all pretty cool.

I drummed my fingers against my leg and tapped my foot. The thing with my dad was weighing on me. Not just because he was fucking with my land and threatening my family. I knew shit and I couldn't tell anyone. I'd almost told Chase a few times. Moments like this when we were both quiet. I could just say it. I could tell him the truth. He wouldn't be able to do anything to help—not physically—but at least this shit wouldn't be festering inside me all the time.

But I didn't. Mostly because I didn't want to dump it on him.

"When do you think the girls will be home?" I asked.

Chase laughed. "Dude, you're such a clinger."

"What?" I shifted in my chair so I was facing him. "I am *not* a clinger. I'm the opposite of a clinger."

"Okay, so not usually with girls. But even you have to admit, when it comes to me or your family, you're a six-foot-three barnacle."

"That's a very weird image." Although he might have had a point. "Clinger, though? That's a serious accusation, Chase."

He shrugged. "With people you care about, you're clingy as fuck. It's not a bad thing."

I tapped my beer bottle, thinking about it for a second. It was dawning on me that he might be right. "Holy shit. Chase, I am a clinger. This is messed up. How did I not know this about myself?"

"I don't know." He stood. "Want another beer?"

"Shit yeah, I want another beer. Bring me two. I need to process this."

Chase went into the kitchen and came back with three beers. He handed me two and I put one down next to my chair, then opened the other one and took a long pull.

"What happened with Amelia's parents the other night?" he asked as he sat back down.

"Oh shit, bro, didn't I tell you?"

"Nope."

"Assgoblin and his parents were there."

"What the shit?"

"Yep. It's okay, I handled it. Actually, she handled it, I was just backup. He was a total douche, though. She's so much better off with me."

"That's true, man. She is." Chase tilted his head and scrutinized me for a moment. "Is she *with* you?"

"What?"

"She's a little more than the flavor of the week, or even the month, don't you think?"

"Yeah, so?"

"I've just noticed you're different with her. You've been different since you met her. Makes me wonder, has Cooper Miles taken the leap?"

I scrubbed my hand through my hair and took another drink. A feeling was growing inside of me, making my chest feel full and tight. It wasn't the first time. I'd felt this way a hundred times since I'd met Amelia. But now Chase was calling it out and on the verge of giving it a name.

And then it hit me. I dropped my bottle, spilling beer all over. I didn't even care. I stood from my chair, launching up like a rocket.

"Holy fuck, Chase. Oh my god. Do you realize what

this means?" I walked into the kitchen, but he didn't follow, so I went back out on the deck. "I am a clinger. I'm clingy as fuck. If I could carry Amelia around with me all day long, I'd totally do it. Sometimes I wish she was tiny so I could put her in my pocket and never be without her. I've never felt like this before. I've never cared about someone like I do her. When I found out her parents were coming to town, shit, I dropped everything so I could make it to that dinner. I wasn't even invited, but there was no way I was letting her go alone."

"Yeah."

"What's going on? What's happening to me?"

Chase was looking at me with a smirk. "You told me once that if you wanted to be someone's boyfriend, you'd be the best boyfriend on the planet. Remember that?"

"Yeah."

He shrugged. "I guess you were right."

"I'm her boyfriend, aren't I?"

"Yep."

"Jesus." I ran my hands through my hair again, turning in a circle. I paced through the apartment, over to the front door, and back outside again. Chase just watched, an amused smile on his face.

"She's my girlfriend," I said. "She's my girl, and I'm her guy, and oh my god, fuck yes. This is awesome. I want this. I should want this, right?"

"Yes, Cooper. It's okay. You should want this."

"Fucking awesome."

This realization was blowing my mind. It was like my world had suddenly expanded, opening into something bigger than I could have imagined.

"I know what I need to do." I dashed back into the apartment, beelining for my room.

"Coop, where are you going?"

I ripped the comforter and sheets off my bed, tossing it all to the floor. I threw a pillow behind me and Chase ducked.

"Dude, what the hell?"

"I gotta burn it."

It was over. Amelia was it for me, and I knew it. I knew it with everything in my soul. She wasn't just my girlfriend. I fucking loved her. I loved her so much I thought I might die, and this mattress had to go.

Chase watched me, open-mouthed, as I hoisted the bare mattress on its side and got it off the box spring and onto the floor. When I had it halfway out the door, he put his hands on the other side and pushed back.

"Whoa, what are you doing?"

"What does it look like I'm doing? I'm taking the mattress out to my truck so we can go burn it. If we hurry, we can get it set up before the girls come back. We're having a bonfire tonight, buddy."

"You know you can't unburn that, right?"

"Yeah, dumbass, I know. Why would I want to unburn it? This shit needs to be torched."

"Dude, Cooper, you've got to slow your roll, man."

"What? Why?"

"You just now realized she's more than a fling to you, and you're ready to burn your mattress? You haven't even talked to her about being exclusive or anything. And don't forget, she was about to marry another guy like a month ago."

"Almost two months ago."

"Okay, two months. My point stands. That's not a lot of time. You're going to scare her off."

I leaned the mattress against the wall, since Chase was

still in my way. "No, I'm not. Why would this scare her off?"

He sighed. "Coop, buddy. Think this through. We burned your mom's mattress because she was getting divorced. That's a big thing. We burned Zoe's because she got married. Same with mine. So you're going to explain the mattress thing to Amelia, and then tell her you're burning yours now? What's she going to think?"

"That I'm super into her and it's awesome."

"Okay, that's one option. Or, she's going to think you're moving way too fast and the next thing you know, she's asking for space."

"You're one to talk about moving too fast, dick," I said. "You married my sister less than a year after you started dating."

"Not the same. Brynn and I have known each other literally since she was born. You've known Amelia for less than two months, and you're not even official yet. Seriously, bro, you can't be thinking about marriage already."

"Who said marriage?" I asked. "I didn't say the m-word. I don't have a fucking ring. Jesus, Chase, get your facts straight before you give a guy shit."

"But you're ready to burn your mattress, which I think we've established is a sign of major commitment."

"Yeah, I'm a new man. Don't you get it? I just want her. All day, every day, forever."

"That's what marriage is, bro," he said. "Dude, I'm psyched that you like her this much, but this is nuts, even for you. And I'm telling you, she's not ready for this."

"How the fuck would you know that?" I asked. "Are you a mind reader now?"

"The only reason she's not married to another man is that he fucked it up," he said. "Give her a little time. I'd never argue fast is a bad thing, but when it's *this* fast? You gotta chill a little bit. At least make sure you two are on the same page."

"Clocks need to be in sync," I muttered to myself, recalling what Ben had told me. I didn't want Chase to be right. I wanted to do this now. Burn the mattress and tell Amelia I loved her and make sure she'd be mine forever. I didn't need to rush her into getting married. I wasn't in any hurry. But I wanted this done. I wanted to stand in front of the fire and watch my old life burn while I held my woman in my arms.

Except if Chase was right, I might be standing in front of the fire alone while Amelia caught a flight to L.A.

I took a few deep breaths, trying to calm down. My mind was racing, and I wasn't thinking straight. The irony of it all was, I needed Amelia right now. I needed her touch to slow me down, help me think.

Losing Amelia wasn't an option. I needed her. I loved her, and I wanted her, and if I had to, I'd get on my knees and beg her to stay with me. But maybe the answer was simpler. Maybe the answer was time.

Damn. I was not a patient guy.

Ben's voice echoed in my head again. *Slow down, Cooper.* I did this sometimes—got all manic and couldn't stop. It didn't always work out so well. My impulsiveness was mostly harmless. But there were times when it got me into a lot of trouble.

I didn't want that. Not with Amelia. I didn't want to get us into trouble before we really had a chance. Because there was one thing I knew with utter certainty. I couldn't fuck this up.

"Fine." My shoulders slumped as I pulled the mattress back into my room. "I won't burn it. *Yet.*"

Chase helped me get it back on the box spring, but I left the sheets and shit on the floor. I'd deal with them later. Without saying another word, I went back to the deck and sat down. Cracked open my other beer, ignoring the spilled one at my feet.

This wasn't sitting well with me. I knew Chase was just looking out for me—he'd never steer me wrong—but I was unsettled. Restless. I hoped Amelia would get back soon. I needed her. I was burning up from the inside, and she'd soothe the fire in my veins.

SEVENTEEN
COOPER

IT WAS two in the morning, and I was tired as hell, but I stood in the doorway of my bedroom, staring at the stupid mattress.

The damn thing was mocking me. I fucking hated that mattress. I'd been serious about burning it. Dead fucking serious. That piece of shit needed to go.

Seeing Amelia tonight had helped a little. When she came back from the movies with Brynn I'd tackled her onto the couch. I'd let her up once when she needed to go to the bathroom, but otherwise, I embraced my inner clinger. Because fuck it, she felt good and I loved being the guy who got to hold her.

Unfortunately, she had to be at work early in the morning, so she'd gone home. As much as I'd wanted to go with her—cling to her like the barnacle I apparently was—I didn't. I was suddenly worried about coming on too strong—about pushing her too hard. I bounced back and forth between wanting to smother her and assuming she loved it, and wanting to make sure I gave her space to figure things out for herself.

Chase did have a point about scaring her with the mattress thing. What was I going to say? Hey girl, in this family when we're ready to put our past behind us and move into a new phase of life, we have a big ass bonfire and burn our mattress. And guess what, we're burning mine tonight because after a couple of months I'm ready to flip the switch and be a committed, monogamous guy with you. Cool?

She probably wasn't ready for that. I hadn't given her enough time.

The irony of all this wasn't lost on me. Wasn't I supposed to be the one balking at commitment? I'd never been in a long-term relationship. Shouldn't I be freaking out about the enormity of my feelings for her? Clinging to my old life with everything I had? Shouldn't I be kicking and screaming as life tried to drag me away from my vow of perpetual singlehood?

And Amelia? She was made for this. Commitment was totally her thing.

Yet, here we were. I'd been like the Peter Pan of bachelorhood—resisted growing up for all it was worth. Because growing up was boring. It was what everyone else did. Why should I be like everyone else? Why not do what I want, and live my life, and be happy and to hell with what anyone thought of it?

Except that Amelia made me happy in a way nothing else ever had. Or ever would. I wasn't blind. I knew a good thing when it fell into my lap in a bar. Just because I'd never had it before didn't mean I couldn't recognize it for what it was. Amelia was everything. She was a fucking unicorn, and who in their right mind would let a unicorn go if he managed to catch one?

Not this guy.

I leaned against the doorframe and crossed my arms. This bed was not going to defeat me.

"Okay, here's the deal," I said. "We need to come to an arrangement that we can both live with. Yeah, I kind of tried to torch you tonight, but Chase talked me out of it. I guess you can thank him if you want. Whatever. Just stop being such a goddamn reminder of my fuck ups. Quiet down about it and let me sleep."

Nothing changed. It still sat there on the metal bed frame, silently taunting me.

"I get it. You saw a lot of action. Maybe you even liked it, you pervert. But that's over now. I'm with Amelia, and she's it. Your days of hosting meaningless sex with random women are over. I'm done. So can we just both shut up about it and move on?"

Nope. The mattress was most certainly not going to move on. Not because it was an asshole or had it in for me, but because it was what it was and it couldn't change. It couldn't stop being what I'd turned it into. A bed of hollow lust and self-indulgence.

"Fine."

I just needed to sleep. It wasn't going to infect me with its depravity if I slept on it. I wouldn't wake up with some random girl simply by sleeping there.

So why couldn't I lie down?

I paced back and forth, like a caged animal eying an electrified object I didn't understand. I knew that it hurt to touch it, but I didn't know how to neutralize it.

This was ridiculous. I'd just make the bed and go to sleep.

I grabbed the sheets off the floor. I told myself, again

and again, that there wasn't a single trace of another woman on these sheets. Not anymore. Everything was clean, and no part of my body would touch the actual mattress. Just the sheets and comforter, which all smelled like fabric softener.

Still couldn't do it.

Rolling my eyes in frustration, I dug through the closet for my sleeping bag. I opened it up and spread it out over the top of the bed. Maybe another layer would help.

But then I started thinking about the last time I went camping and... nope. Sleeping bag wasn't going to work either. In fact, this was probably worse, because at least the sheets had been washed.

Cringing, I tossed the sleeping bag into a corner.

Fuck.

This was ridiculous. Chase should have let me burn the stupid thing. Jesus, I was tired. My eyes were dry and gritty and my feet were starting to ache. I just wanted to fucking sleep.

I walked around the room for a few more minutes, trying to talk myself into lying down. But every time I got close to the bed, a coal of anger would flare to life in my chest. I didn't know what I was so angry at. Myself. Chase. My stupid bed. All I knew was I hated that mattress, and hell if I was ever going to touch it again, let alone sleep on it.

Eventually I gave up and went out to the living room to crash on the couch. Thank god Brynn had insisted we get a new one. The old couch was just as bad as my stupid mattress.

I sat up as I realized Zoe's water had broken on this couch. Granted, we'd cleaned it really well, and sat on it tons of times since then. And sure, maybe Chase and Brynn loved to make out on this couch, which was gross to watch. But that had nothing to do with me.

I got up again. Went out to the deck. The night air was chilly, but I put the back of one of the deck chairs down and tried to settle in. Still couldn't sleep.

My brain was a whirlwind of chaos. All those girls I'd brought home, without a second thought. Because life was hard and why not make it fun while you could? But there was such an emptiness to it that I hadn't felt before. Or maybe I just hadn't known better.

Had Chase gone through this when he'd fallen for my sister? Did love turn every guy into a fucking lunatic? It was sure as hell messing me up.

Because for the first time in my life, I wasn't in complete control. Even when I was doing crazy—and admittedly often ill-advised—shit, I was always in charge. Hanging off the side of the bridge over a river? No big deal, I knew what I was doing. Climbing onto the roof of the Big House to get Leo's cat when she got stuck? No worries. Meeting girls, throwing parties, fucking shit up with friends? None of that had ever scared me.

But this was different. Amelia had my heart, and she didn't even know it yet. And that was scary as fuck. I had no idea what she'd do with it. Not now, or when she discovered it was hers. Maybe she'd want to keep it. But what if she didn't? What if the timing was all wrong, and she couldn't handle it? What if she couldn't handle *me*?

Maybe I was just the fun guy she was using to get over being dumped on her wedding day. Maybe that was all she would ever need me to be. I didn't know.

By the time the sky glowed with the dawn, I still hadn't slept. I wasn't sure what I was doing when it came to Amelia, but all I could do was be me. I'd listen to Ben and think about timing. And I'd listen to Chase, because he'd made some sense. But at the end of the day, I was Cooper

Miles, and if that wasn't enough to make her fall hopelessly in love with me, nothing was.

EIGHTEEN
AMELIA

I WAS SERIOUSLY CONSIDERING whether or not to change my phone number. Griffin had texted me half a dozen times since he and my parents had been here the other day. I'd replied once, to tell him to stop messaging me, but he hadn't listened. He kept trying to say we needed to talk. But there wasn't anything I wanted to talk to him about.

Mrs. Wentworth had texted me the next day to say that she was sorry for how things had turned out but she was proud of me. That little message had meant the world to me. And it made me wonder, not for the first time, how Griffin had turned out to be such a jerk. His parents were nice people.

I didn't know what had happened between him and Portia. They'd probably been about to tell me at dinner the other night when Cooper showed up. It seemed likely that they'd already broken up, but I didn't know for sure. And I didn't really care. I'd stopped following them both on social media, and I hadn't even been tempted to check.

Putting them all out of my mind, I left my phone in the

kitchen and went to the bathroom to blow dry my hair. I'd showered after work, and Cooper was due to come over any minute.

There was a knock right as I was finishing. I came out to find him poking his head inside.

"Hey, Cookie."

"Hey."

He strutted in, puffing out his chest a little bit. "How was work?"

"It was good." Something on his shirt caught my eye. It was black with white lettering. "What does your shirt say?"

His smile widened, and he tugged on the hem. It read *World's Best Boyfriend* in big white letters.

"Boyfriend?" I asked, my heart fluttering. "Oh my god, Cooper. Is that shirt new? Did you wear it for me? Does this mean what I think it means? Are you my boyfriend?"

"Shit yeah, I'm your boyfriend." He paused, his body going still. His eyes were big and when he spoke again, his voice was uncharacteristically soft. "Or I'd like to be, if you want me."

I stared at his shirt, my mind reeling. He acted like my boyfriend. He held my hand and touched me. Hugged and kissed me. We hung out all the time. I'd been flipping *having sex* with him. It was fun—he was fun—but was I ready for this? Ready to admit this was not just a short-term fling to help me get over Griffin?

Maybe that's what it had been in the beginning. But it certainly wasn't anymore.

"Yes, I want you. I love your shirt and you're so cute and funny and this is kind of the first time I've really had a boyfriend. Even Griffin wasn't my boyfriend, although he was supposed to be, but he was really bad at it. And you're so good at it already. I mean, look at this shirt.

Except you've kind of been my boyfriend all along, haven't you?"

"More or less." He grabbed me and picked me up off my feet, kissing me as he set me down again. "It's a relief you said yes because I didn't bring a change of clothes or anything. And wearing this shirt if you'd rejected me would have been really awkward."

I slid my hands beneath it and ran them over the ridges of his abs. "You're saying if I said no, you'd take this off?"

"Cookie, if you want me to get naked, just say so." He yanked his shirt over his head and tossed it on the floor. Half a second later, he had his pants off. "Besides, we need to celebrate our new relationship status."

He backed me up into the bedroom, pulling off my clothes in between kisses. My body came to life instantly, my blood running hot for him. His expert hands popped the clasp on my bra and I shoved my panties down my legs.

His hands tangled in my hair as he kissed me. Cooper didn't just kiss. He kissed with *enthusiasm*. Like there was nothing else he'd rather be doing in this moment than lavishing my mouth with deep, wet kisses.

One hand moved down my back and over my hip. He slid it between my legs and groaned into my mouth.

"Jesus, Cookie, you're wet already. Such a dirty girl."

I loved it when he talked like this. I wasn't good at talking dirty, but Cooper's mouth was positively filthy.

"What does my dirty girl want?" he whispered in my ear, then licked my neck. "Does my girl want to get fucked?"

"Yes," I breathed.

He stroked my clit with his fingers while his other hand stayed fisted in my hair. "Fuck yeah, you do. You want me to fuck you good."

His fingers went lower, dipping inside me.

"I'm going to fuck you so hard, Cookie. I'm going to fuck you until neither of us can see straight."

I was already teetering on the edge of coming on his fingers, but he pulled them out and brought them to his mouth. With his eyes locked on mine, he sucked on his fingertips, then drew them out of his mouth with a smile.

"You taste so fucking good, baby. Get on the bed. I need my mouth on that pussy."

He shoved me down roughly, making me giggle. I wasn't a small girl, but he moved me around like it was nothing to him. His calloused hands roamed over my skin, caressing and squeezing while he licked and sucked and kissed. I'd spent my entire life feeling self-conscious about my curves. My not-flat tummy. My big boobs. My hips. Cooper's attention to all the contours of my body made me feel amazing. Sexy and beautiful. Desired.

After shoving me higher up the bed, he draped my thighs over his shoulders and settled between my legs.

"Life is short, so eat dessert first," he said, his mouth turning up in a smirk.

He went to work on me with his tongue, and from the first stroke, I was in paradise. My eyes rolled back as he licked and sucked. I'd never known anything could feel so good. His tongue lapped against my sensitive skin, making heat and tension pool in my core.

I slid my fingers through his hair. He didn't just kiss with enthusiasm. He did *everything* with enthusiasm. His fingers kneaded my thighs while he flicked my clit with gentle strokes. My legs trembled and my back arched. He moaned as he licked me, like he was enjoying this as much as I was.

"Baby, you taste so good, but I need to fuck you." Disentangling himself from my legs, he went for the nightstand drawer. He pulled out the box of condoms, but turned it upside down and shook it. "Shit. Empty. That's okay, I have one in my wallet."

His pants were in the other room, and I'd been thinking about bringing this up. "Cooper, now that this is... well, you know, now that you're my boyfriend, maybe we don't need those? I'm just saying, it's fine, I won't get pregnant because I get the shot, and it's so easy, I don't even have to think about it. I wasn't sure if I'd remember a pill every day, so this was a good option, and basically I'm saying if you want to, we could do this without a condom."

"Holy shit, Cookie, really?"

"Yeah. It's fine if you still want to use them, I don't mind. But if you're sure you're safe, would it be easier if you didn't need one?"

He nudged my legs apart and lowered himself on top of me. His eyes held mine as he brushed the hair back from my face. "Yeah, I'm safe. I've always used one. Are you sure? This is a big deal."

"I'm sure."

"Okay." Without breaking eye contact, he shifted his hips so just the tip of his cock pushed in. "Oh, fuck."

He slid in deeper, slowly. So slowly. Inch by thick, hard inch, until his full length was buried inside me.

"Fuck. Fuck, fuck, fuck, that feels so good I can't move oh my god."

I pulled his mouth to mine and rubbed the back of his neck while he kissed me. He held there, his cock filling me, for long moments.

"Your pussy feels so fucking good." He started to move, drawing his cock out, then in again. "Oh sweet Jesus."

The drag of his cock through my pussy felt unbelievable. I rolled my hips against him, seeking more, while my hands traced the hard planes of muscle on his back.

"Harder," I whispered.

"Fuck yes. Tell me."

"Harder, Cooper."

He gave me what I wanted, plunging in and out. His body flexed, his muscles tense, and he grunted with every thrust. I gave myself over to him, to the overwhelming sensation of his cock inside me.

"Baby, I could do this all night. I fucking love this pussy."

I lifted my arms overhead as he palmed one breast. He kissed down my neck to my chest and lapped his tongue across my nipple. Taking my hard peak in his mouth, he sucked gently before moving to the other side.

After a few more thrusts, he pulled out and flipped me over, grabbing my hips to guide me onto my knees.

"This ass is so magnificent," he said and smacked it lightly.

I squeaked as I sucked in a quick breath.

"Look at me."

I watched over my shoulder while he took his cock in one hand and held my hip with the other. He gave himself a few strokes, drawing his hand up and down his thick length.

"I want you to ask me for it."

His request took me by surprise. My pussy ached for him to be inside me again. To finish me and make me come.

"What?" I asked, almost breathless.

"Tell me what you want. I need to hear it, baby."

He kept stroking himself with one hand while he grabbed my ass with the other. The sight of his hand moving up and down his shaft was fascinating and desperately arousing.

"I want..."

"That's it, Cookie." He kept stroking, moving faster. "Tell me. Tell me before I come all over you."

"I want you to fuck me."

His mouth turned up in a mischievous grin as he grabbed my hips. "Fuck, yes, baby."

And then he was fucking me. Hard and fast and deep. His hands held me tight and his hips moved in a relentless rhythm. His groin slammed into me with every thrust, his grunts of pleasure filling my ears.

This angle was so intense, everything aligning. My muscles clenched around him, pulsing with need. The bed slammed against the wall, over and over, but he didn't let up.

"You feel so good, baby, I'm going to come. Do you feel it?"

His cock thickened and pulsed. "Yes."

"Let's come together. Are you with me?"

"Yes. Please. Oh my god, Cooper."

I couldn't get out another word. He drove his cock in and I shattered into a million pieces.

Deep waves of pleasure rolled through my body, over-whelming all my senses. His cock throbbed as he spilled his come inside me. I moaned and gasped as the orgasm went on, his climax spurring mine to new heights.

When we both finished, he turned me over and leaned in to kiss my lips. Soft, gentle caresses of his mouth on mine.

"Oh my god, Cookie. That was amazing."

I nodded, still breathless. "Yeah."

He slipped out of bed and came back with a washcloth, then peppered my tummy and thighs with kisses as he helped me clean up.

"Baby, I'm going to earn that shirt," he said, settling in

bed with me and wrapping me in his arms. "I'm going to be the best boyfriend you could ever have."

I giggled, floating in euphoria. "I know you will."

A few seconds later, he was fast asleep.

I sighed a contented breath and enjoyed the feel of his warm body. His arms around me. Today, there was no place I'd rather be.

NINETEEN

COOPER

I'D SPENT the night at Amelia's instead of going home, which meant I'd actually gotten some sleep. It felt good to be decently rested.

Harvest was coming soon. It had rained yesterday, but today was clear. I'd been out to the south vineyard earlier and things were looking good. I had some time to kill before dinner, so I wandered toward the Big House. Mom had invited us over to meet Grace's mom, Naomi, and our youngest brother, Elijah.

It was a big deal for everybody. Considering Naomi had been my dad's mistress, my mom was a fucking badass for making friends with her. But like Mom had said, they were both victims. Naomi had never known about Mom, or the rest of us. She'd just thought Dad had commitment issues.

We'd seen Grace a lot, which was good. Gracie was a cool chick, and she'd become good friends with Brynn. Both Brynn and my mom said it was important not to let Dad's shittiness hurt us anymore, and I agreed. Plus, our family was sweet, so why not let them be a part of it? I saw no downside.

I wondered what the littlest Miles dude was like. It was weird to think about having a little brother. I wasn't sure what to do with that. He was actually little, too—only seven. I was used to having my Brynncess, but this was different.

A streak of white fur caught my eye as I walked. Leo's cat, Gigz, darted across the path not far from me.

"What you got over there, Gigz? Chasing a squirrel?"

She stopped, like she knew I was talking to her, and looked at me, her bright green eyes flashing in the sun. Her tail twitched. She seemed to decide I wasn't worth wasting any more time on and sauntered off toward Leo's house.

Seeing Gigz reminded me of Leo. Which reminded me that I hadn't seen him recently.

My brother lived in the largest guest cottage on the property. It was set apart from the others—probably why he'd chosen it. I shoved my hands in my pockets and followed Gigz down the path toward his place. I'd see him at dinner later, but I was bored. Plus, it would be good for me and Leo to spend some more time together.

As I banged on the front door, Gigz rubbed against my leg.

Leo opened the door, tugging a sweatshirt down like he'd just put it on. "Yeah?"

Gigz darted inside, running between his legs.

"What's up?" I asked.

"Um, not much? Do you need something?"

The scars on Leo's face were partially covered by his shaggy beard, but you could see the damage if he turned. He'd brought in a tattoo artist to do ink all along his left arm and leg, obscuring the scar tissue with an intricate pattern.

I remembered all too well what my brother used to look like. But it wasn't his scars that made the difference now. Not to me, at least. It was his eyes. They used to be bright blue, like mine. Now they were dark and flat, more gray than blue.

"Nah, man, just figured I'd see what you were up to."

He moved aside as I went in, then shut the door behind me.

Leo's house was the sickest bachelor pad ever. Instead of a bunch of boring furniture, he had a big desk with multiple computer monitors and a badass office chair. I didn't know what he did with all that electronic shit— played a lot of online games or something—but his chair looked super comfortable.

Over where most people would have put a table and chairs, he had a home gym. Squat rack, bench, pull-up bar, weights. Say one thing for Leo Miles—he might not ever leave the winery grounds, but he took care of business. He was jacked as fuck underneath those long-sleeved shirts he always wore.

"This reminds me, I need to work out more," I said. "I've been hanging out with Amelia so much, I've been slacking. What are you doing? You busy?"

"No, I'm..." He shook his head. "If I say I'm busy, will you go away?"

"Too late, bro, now I know you're not. Getting in a workout?"

"Yeah, I was going to. Why are you here?"

"Do I need a reason? Can't I come see my brother? Speaking of brothers, have you seen Roland lately? It's like he and Zoe disappeared when their kid was born. What's that about?"

Leo shrugged. "They have a newborn. They probably don't sleep anymore."

"True, I guess. I wouldn't know. Cute kid, though."

"Sure."

"You're a grumpy asshole, aren't you?"

"You're a dick."

I grinned at him. "Awesome, now we're getting somewhere. Can I stay and work out with you? I totally need to get my fitness on."

"If I let you stay, are you going to talk the entire time, or will you just let me work out?"

"Do what you gotta do, bro. Just tell me to shut up if I get too chatty."

"Shut up."

I closed my mouth and put my hands up in a gesture of surrender. I could be quiet if I needed to be.

Leo went over to the bench press and put a forty-five on the bar. I started unfastening my jeans.

"Dude," he said. "What are you doing?"

"I can't work out in jeans."

"So you're just going to take them off?"

I glanced around the room, wondering what he was talking about. What else did he expect me to do? "Yeah."

"Did you bring something else to wear?"

"Do I look like I'm carrying a gym bag?"

"Jesus, Cooper." He walked down the hall and when he came back, he tossed a pair of light gray sweats at me. "I don't need to see you working out in your underwear."

I dropped my jeans and stepped out of them. "Awesome. Thanks, bro. This is probably a good thing because I'm wearing tightie-whities today. I didn't even remember I had these. I'm usually a boxer briefs guy."

"Shut up, Cooper."

"Oh, right. Sorry."

I changed into the sweats while Leo did a set. He moved out of the way so I could do mine. True to my word, I didn't say anything. It wasn't too hard. Lifting felt good and anything physical always calmed down my brain. I really hadn't been to the gym lately, and my body felt it. Even though my job was pretty physical, I had a lot of energy to burn all the time. Working out had always been a good outlet.

Leo was fucking strong. It was awesome to work out with him. Got my blood pumping and I pushed myself hard. We'd both worked up a good sweat by the time we were done.

He went into the kitchen and tossed me a water. "I have to give you credit, Coop. You got through that entire workout without saying a word. Did it hurt?"

I took a drink. "No, but it's going to hurt when we do legs tomorrow."

He scrutinized me for a second. "Fine. Legs tomorrow."

I resisted the urge to do a touchdown dance, but I was psyched. Hanging out with Leo was definitely an awesome idea. He needed some more Cooper in his life—might perk him up a little. Plus, although I had my Cookie, and she was fantastic, I didn't see Chase as often now that he was married. And Zoe was all wrapped up in being a mom. Maybe I needed some more Leo in my life, too.

"You coming to dinner at Mom's?" I asked.

"Yeah, I'll go." He nodded toward the sweats I was wearing. "You can just wear those over there if you want. I don't need them back."

"Bro, I can't wear these to dinner at Mom's." I gestured to the way they showed off my junk. "Light gray sweats? I'm not that much of a slut."

Leo just rolled his eyes.

Amelia was still at the ranch tonight, and even I was aware that this particular dinner might be a little much for my brand-new girlfriend. I walked over to Mom's house with Leo, and I think I set a new record. He only told me to shut up once.

Roland and Zoe were already there. Mom was standing with Roland, who held baby Hudson against his shoulder. Roland rocked back and forth on his feet, patting his kid on the back as he moved. Thankfully, Hudson was getting a lot cuter as he got older. He was cute as fuck, as a matter of fact. Big blue eyes, round cheeks, and brown hair that stuck straight up.

"Gimme that baby," I said, heading straight for Roland.

"I haven't even held him yet," Mom said.

I scooped him out of Roland's arms and propped him up over my shoulder. "That's your fault for being too slow, isn't it?"

"He just ate, so he might spit up on you," Zoe said.

"Do I look like I'm scared of a little baby spit-up?"

Roland took the cloth that had been on his shoulder and laid it over mine. "Here. This should catch it, although he's really good at missing the burp rag and getting it all over your clothes."

"Hey, slugger." I wandered away from Roland and Mom, walking Hudson around the room. He was so small, his little diapered butt fit in my hand. He was still pretty floppy, but the little dude was getting stronger. And he was more awake than I'd ever seen him. Big bright eyes, staring at the world like everything was new. Which, to be fair, it was. "You're the coolest little dude, do you know that, Huddy?"

"Oh my god," Zoe said. "Someone take a picture. Just don't send it to Cooper's friend, you'll make her ovaries explode."

"My *girlfriend*," I corrected.

"Wow," Zoe said, and I paused while my mom took five

hundred pictures of me and the baby. "Did Coop just say the g-word?"

"Yes. You obviously didn't read my shirt." I shifted Hudson so she could read it. I'd bought like ten different boyfriend shirts so I could wear one every day and not have to do laundry.

"*USDA Prime Boyfriend*." Zoe laughed. "That's cute."

"Amelia's a lucky girl," Mom said. "But give me my grandson."

I laughed and passed Hudson to my mom.

Brynn and Chase arrived, hanging on each other like they always did. I liked to complain about them being gross, but I actually loved seeing them so happy. And Chase made a point to come over and punch me in the arm, then tackle-hug me from behind, which was awesome.

A knock on the door heralded Grace, along with Naomi and Elijah. Seeing Grace next to her mom was a trip. She looked a bit like our dad, but she really resembled her mom. Naomi had dark blond hair, like her daughter, and they had the same upturned nose. She was pretty, and the smile lines around her eyes were the only indication she was Grace's mom, not her sister.

My younger brother peeked around from behind her as they walked in the door. I stared at him. He looked like a kid version of my dad. Same face shape, blue eyes, dark hair. He looked a lot like Roland and Leo, too. There was no doubt who this kid's father was.

My mom ruffled Elijah's hair, then hugged Grace and Naomi, which was awesome. Seeing them together felt like a big *fuck you* to my dad. I almost wanted to take a picture of them and text it to him.

Mom did all the intros, then started bringing out the enormous amount of food she'd cooked. We were a big crowd tonight, but it still looked like double what we'd need. Which was great news for me—leftovers. I chose a bottle of white and a red from mom's wine cabinet and poured glasses for everyone.

Dinner was slow. The food was good, of course. Naomi was pretty cool. We kept the subject away from Dad. She'd forewarned us that there was still a lot Elijah didn't know, so we knew to be careful of what we said.

I eyed the little dude. He looked bored. I was certainly bored, and if I was bored, a seven-year-old kid had to be bored.

"Psst." I tried to get his attention without interrupting everyone else.

He looked at me, then glanced around, like he was wondering if I meant him.

I nodded and jerked my thumb behind me, then mouthed, *want to go outside?*

He cracked a little smile and nodded.

I didn't want anyone to worry, so I got close to Mom and whispered in her ear. "I'm taking Eli outside."

She gestured to Naomi, I pointed to the door, and everyone seemed to be on the same page. Which was good. I didn't want her thinking I was trying to run off with her kid or anything.

I hustled him out to the front porch and shut the door behind us. He sat on the steps to put on his shoes.

"Want to go for a ride?" I asked. "I have a cool vehicle. It's kind of like a four-wheeler."

His eyes lit up. "Yeah."

"Awesome."

The utility vehicle was a short walk away, over by the work house. We climbed in and I drove us out past an empty field toward the closest of my vineyards.

"So Eli, what do you think of all these older brothers you have?" I asked. "Is it weird?"

He shrugged. "A little bit. The family who lives next door to me has a bunch of big boys like you. It's kind of like having brothers, so I'm used to it already."

"That's cool. They're nice to you and everything?"

"Yeah, of course they are," he said. "They taught me how to fish and catch frogs in the creek. And climb trees and play chess and all kinds of cool stuff."

"Good." I liked hearing that. I knew our dad hadn't been around for Elijah, and a boy needed at least one good man in his life. Not that our dad was a good man. But Ben had been that for me, and I was glad Eli had someone—or several someones—to fill that role.

I parked the utility vehicle and we jumped out. The sun was dropping behind the mountains, but the sky still glowed with evening light.

"Do you think I can stay out past bedtime?" he asked.

"I think we're definitely going to keep you out past bedtime." I ruffled his hair. We stood on the side of the gravel road next to the first row of grapevines. "Tell you what, you lead the way."

Elijah took off running and I followed. He darted in and out of the rows and pretty soon we were fake shooting at each other with finger guns, using the grapevines for cover. When we got to the creek, we splashed in the shallow water, then played a game of hide and seek.

We took another ride in the utility vehicle and I brought us back closer to the main grounds. There was something here I wanted him to see.

He got out and craned his neck upward, gaping at the huge oak tree. I'd spent countless hours of my childhood in those branches—with my brothers, or Chase. I'd taught Brynn how to climb it when she was big enough to reach.

The first branches were a little high for Eli, but I lifted him and helped him up. We climbed to a thick limb that stuck out over the path below, sitting side by side with our feet dangling.

I heard voices approach and pretty soon Roland and Zoe appeared on the path, heading toward us. He had his arm around her shoulders and she leaned into him. They paused just below us, and I held a finger to my lips, telling Eli to stay quiet. He nodded.

Roland brushed Zoe's hair back from her face while his other hand slid around her waist. They were both smiling as he moved in to kiss her. Eli made a grossed-out face, sticking his tongue out and scrunching his nose.

"Did you guys lose something?" I asked.

Zoe gasped and put a hand on her chest. Roland looked up at me like he might shoot daggers out of his eyes. "Cooper? What the hell?"

"I'm just trying to help you out, because it looks like you misplaced your baby. I'm not saying you guys are bad parents, but it didn't take very long for you to lose him. He is really small, though, so I guess there's that."

Elijah giggled, but then looked at me with serious eyes. "They didn't really lose him, right?"

"No, we didn't lose our baby," Zoe said. "He's sleeping on his grandma's lap."

"You do look naked without him," I said. "It's kind of weird."

"I feel naked without him," Zoe said. "What are you guys doing up there? Besides waiting to scare the crap out of me?"

"We weren't waiting for that," I said. "I just took an opportunity when one was presented to me."

"Do we have to get down now?" Elijah asked, his eyes darting between me and Roland. "I don't want to go inside yet."

"No way, pal," I said. "Roland looks like he's in charge, but he's really not."

"Who said anything about going inside?" Roland asked.

"We came out for a little break," Zoe said. "I love that kid so much I could die, but a girl needs some time off."

"I'm sorry, you guys were about to make out and I totally—" I paused, realizing I probably shouldn't say *cockblocked you* in front of the little Miles bro. "I interrupted you. Go ahead, kiss. We won't look."

I made a show of putting my hands over my eyes, and Elijah did the same. All was quiet for a moment, then I heard Zoe laugh softly. Then quiet again.

"Ew," Elijah said.

I leaned over. "Don't worry, buddy. You won't always think that's gross."

Grace and Brynn wandered up the path, arm in arm, laughing about something. Chase wasn't far behind. I was just about to ask where Leo was—although I figured if dinner had broken up, he'd probably gone home to his cave —when he appeared, walking slowly. His hands were in his pockets and he hesitated, like he wasn't sure if he was going to keep coming this way or turn around.

In my head, I cheered for him to keep going. *Come on, Leo. Just come hang out with us.*

He walked up the path, and I did a subtle fist pump.

Grace looked up and her eyes widened. "Elijah, how did you get up there?"

"I climbed."

"We should probably get our feet on the ground, big man," I said.

"Can you get down?" Grace asked.

"We've got him," Roland said. Chase came over and he and Roland reached up to help Elijah out of the tree.

When Eli was safely on the ground again, I climbed down.

Everyone started talking—and laughing—as we stood around beneath the big oak. A game of tag broke out between Roland, Brynn, and Elijah. Zoe and Grace stood close together, chatting. Smiling. Even Leo didn't isolate himself. He struck up a conversation with Chase.

"Hey!" a deep voice boomed. "Who's out there?"

Elijah ran over and ducked behind me, holding onto my shirt.

"Hey buddy, it's okay," I said, drawing him next to me. I raised my voice. "It's just Ben, here to ruin our fun."

"Ruin your fun," Ben scoffed as he approached. "I invented fun."

"He probably did," I said, leaning down toward Elijah. "He's really old."

"Watch who you're calling old there, son," Ben said. He picked up Brynn and hoisted her over his shoulder. "I think this calls for a bonfire."

Brynn squealed as he stomped off toward the clearing.

"Oh hell no," I said. "Come on, Eli, let's get him."

I crouched down so Eli could jump on my back.

"Let's go, Z-Miles," Chase said to Zoe, and she climbed on his back. "Race?"

"Hold up," Roland said, then motioned for Grace to jump on his back.

"Leo, go call it at the finish," I said, and Leo nodded and

jogged ahead. "We'll let Ben have the head start. He'll need it. Ready? Go!"

The three of us took off, running for the clearing. Elijah weighed next to nothing, even bouncing around on my back. Ben sped up, but the way he had Brynn wasn't good for running. I darted past him and made it to the clearing first. Leo slashed his arm through the air, as if he had a checkered flag.

"Elijah and Cooper take the gold," Leo said.

I put Eli down as Roland and Chase caught up with Grace and Zoe. Ben put Brynn down, but she was laughing so hard, Chase had to catch her to keep her from falling over. Elijah did a winner's dance while everyone clapped. Even Leo had a smile on his face.

I looked around and it hit me in that moment. This is what it always should have been. No grumpy father stomping around, ruining shit for everybody. All of us here, with Grace and Elijah. Chase. Even Ben. All of us, a family.

Holy shit, this was cool.

It felt like something was missing, and I realized it was Amelia. She would have had a blast with us out here tonight. Because she fit. She belonged.

And that was really cool, too.

TWENTY
AMELIA

TEN THIRTY IN THE MORNING, and Cooper was asleep in my bed like he was in a coma. He always slept like that lately. I wondered if something was wrong. Or maybe work was just busy, and he was extra tired. But he'd come over and pass out, not waking up for ten or twelve hours sometimes.

He was adorable when he was sleeping. So peaceful.

I'd been awake for a while, and it didn't seem like he was getting up any time soon. I left him to sleep while I showered and got dressed. I had a message from Daphne, so I went outside to sit in the sun and call her back.

"Hi, sweetie," she said when she answered.

"Hey. I miss you. How's California?"

"I miss you too. It's not bad. Hot, lately. How's your job?"

"I love it. The McLaughlins are amazing. They're so nice."

"Good," she said. "How are things with Cooper?"

I smiled. "Really great."

"God, Amelia, I can hear you smiling."

"You say that like it's a bad thing."

"No, it's good," she said. "At least, I hope it's good."

"It is good. We're official now. Together. Dating. Like, boyfriend-and-girlfriend official. Not just hanging out a lot and having fun. You know what I mean."

"Wow."

"Wow? Why do you sound so skeptical?"

"I'm not. If you're happy, I'm happy, but..."

"But what?"

"Are you sure you're ready for that? He's older than you, maybe he's looking to settle down. Your life is just beginning."

"Your life is just beginning too, and you're engaged," I said.

"Yeah, but Harrison and I have been together for three years. And he's going on tour soon. I'll be out seeing the country and having adventures."

"Daph, it's like you're forgetting I almost got married. You were supportive of that. Why are you so weird about me having a boyfriend now?"

She sighed. "The closer you got to that wedding, the more it seemed like it wasn't what you wanted. I didn't want to be negative, so I kept my mouth shut about it, and now I wish I hadn't. I thought you were moving too fast with Griffin, and I should have been honest with you. I feel like I failed you as a friend, and I don't want to do that again."

"But I'm not *marrying* Cooper."

"No, but you're tying yourself to one guy again. Aren't there things you want to do? Places you want to go? When things didn't work out with Griffin, I figured you'd cash in on that trust fund of yours and see the world."

I laughed. "I don't have the trust fund, Daph. I'm supposed to get married before I have access to it."

"Oh shit, I forgot about that. Still, let's be honest, we both know your parents would bankroll you if you wanted to take a trip around the world or something."

"Yeah, maybe. Although my dad threatened that I won't see a dime when I walked out on dinner." I'd told Daphne about my parents ambushing me with Griffin already.

"I doubt he meant it," she said. "You should take advantage of this time. Get out there and experience things."

"I've been experiencing lots of things," I said with laugh.

"Outside the bedroom," she said, her tone wry. "Orgasms are great, but you can't base your life choices on good sex."

"What about basing my life choices on insanely mind-blowing sex?"

"You're killing me, Amelia."

I laughed again. "I know, I know, I get it. Talk to me about you. When do you guys go on the road?"

"A couple of months," she said. "The label is still working out the details."

We chatted for a while longer and I managed to keep the subject off Cooper or the life experiences I was apparently missing by being with him. And what Daphne had said did make me think. It hadn't been long since I'd thought my life was going in one direction. Now it was going in another, but was it the direction I wanted?

Daphne had to go, and I heard Cooper moving around inside. I went in to say good morning. He came out of the bedroom dressed in nothing but boxer briefs, his toned body on full display. Broad chest, thick arms, defined abs. His underwear sat low on his hips, revealing the yummy trail of hair that went beneath them. And that tattoo. I didn't know any other guy who could rock a unicorn tattoo the way Cooper could. But it was so sexy on him.

With half-closed eyes, he shuffled over and slid his arms around my waist. He put his face against my neck and took a deep breath. "Morning, Cookie."

"Morning. You slept late."

"Tired." He took another deep breath, his nose against my skin. "Shower."

I laughed and squeezed him. He hugged me back, then shuffled off to the bathroom. If today was anything like usual, he'd be his usual energetic self by the time he finished his shower.

True to form, he came out running a towel over his head, his blue eyes bright again.

"Feel better?" I asked.

"Yeah. Thanks for letting me sleep in. Guess I needed it."

"Sure."

I followed him into the bedroom so I could watch him dress. He gave me a crooked grin while he tugged his underwear over his erection.

"It seems like it's always like that," I said, tilting my head to look at him. "Except for right after, you know. Is it always like that?"

"Around you, pretty much."

"But not when I'm not around?"

He glanced down at the bulge in his underwear. "He's much more likely to be on good behavior if you aren't in the vicinity. But even that's not a guarantee."

"Is it uncomfortable?"

"Sometimes." He grabbed himself and adjusted it, then got his jeans and started pulling them on. "It's all about positioning. If it gets hard when it's facing the wrong direction, I have to move things around."

I didn't know why I had such a fascination with his dick. Probably because I'd never had access to one before. I remembered a few of my friends in college talking about how guy parts weren't attractive, but I had no idea what they were talking about. Cooper's dick was both gorgeous and adorable. Obviously I loved what he did to me with it, but there was more to it than that. It was like having a new toy to play with.

"I bet that doesn't feel too good. Especially if you're wearing jeans."

"Yeah. You know what does feel good?" He stepped close, wrapping his arms around me, and kissed the tip of my nose. "You."

"Mm hmm," I murmured as his mouth moved to mine for a long, lazy kiss.

"I have an idea," he said, squeezing me against him, his eyes widening.

"What?"

"Let's go."

He didn't tell me what his idea was or where we were going. He did this all the time, and it was always something fun. We drove into town and stopped at the grocery store. Cooper got a cart and I followed him inside.

We walked through the store, and he grabbed things and tossed them into the cart.

"What else do we need?" he asked.

I glanced at what he'd added so far. Crackers, three kinds of cheese, a fresh baguette, and strawberries.

"Picnic?" I asked.

"Yeah. I want to take you out to one of my vineyards, but I'm hungry. So, picnic."

"I love your ideas."

He smiled. "Did we get marshmallows yet?"

"I don't think so. Why do we need marshmallows?"

"Why *don't* we need marshmallows?"

"Good point."

He flipped the cart around and we almost ran into a pair of girls coming down the aisle in the other direction. One had long blond hair, the other a cute brown pixie cut.

"Whoa, shit," Cooper said.

The brunette clutched her friend's arm, but the blonde smiled.

"Hey, Cooper."

"Oh, hey Jen." He sidestepped closer to me and slipped his hand into mine. "How's it going?"

Her eyes raked him up and down and she licked her lips. A potent flash of jealousy hit me, making my tummy ache. I did *not* like the way she was looking at Cooper.

"Pretty good. You?" she asked. "It's been a while."

"Yeah, I'm good. Sorry about the cart." He gave her a little chin tip. "See you."

"Bye."

The girls murmured something to each other as we walked away, but I couldn't make out what they were saying. Cooper pushed the cart with one hand while keeping mine clutched in the other—and he didn't look back, which helped ease the knot in the pit of my stomach. I felt silly for having such a reaction. He'd lived in this town his whole life. Running into someone he knew wasn't a big deal.

I took a deep breath, deciding to put them out of my mind. "So, marshmallows?"

"Yep. Right here." He'd led us right to them. He

grabbed two bags and tossed them in with our other groceries. "I think that's it. Need anything else?"

"Nope."

"Awesome. Have you ever played that game where you see how many marshmallows you can stick in your mouth and still say *fluffy bunny*?"

"No."

We walked up to the cashier and Cooper started unloading stuff from the cart. "Dude, I'm awesome at it. How many do you think you could fit?"

I thought about it for a second. "I'm not sure. I've never tried to get more than one in my mouth before."

The cashier started ringing up our items. She gave me a weird look and I almost asked Cooper if I had something in my teeth.

"Let's take bets. I'm going with five, if they're big. Small ones are no big deal, but jumbo size? We have to be realistic."

"That's a lot. I don't know if I have that kind of tongue dexterity."

"Sure you do, Cookie." He winked at me and the cashier cleared her throat.

I laughed. "I'm just afraid they'd start going down my throat and I'd choke—"

"Do you have a rewards card?" the cashier asked, her voice sharp.

"Uh, yeah." Cooper pulled a card out of his wallet and handed it to her, then raised his eyebrows at me. I shrugged. He swiped his debit card to pay, then put his wallet away.

The cashier gave us both another odd look as we grabbed our groceries and walked away.

"What had her panties in a bunch?" Cooper asked.

"No idea."

With our picnic all purchased, Cooper drove us back to Salishan. We parked his truck next to a large building set back away from the Big House. We got into his utility vehicle—sort of a cross between a four-wheeler and a small tractor—and drove out along a gravel road. It led through an empty field, over a small wood bridge that crossed a stream, and into one of their vineyards.

The sun was warm and the air fresh. He seemed to know where he was going and picked a spot to stop. We got out and set up our little picnic in an open area near the rows of grapevines.

"It's so beautiful out here."

He glanced around and took a slow, deep breath. "Yeah, it is. It's my favorite place."

"Growing up here must have been wonderful."

"It was pretty great. I can't say I had the perfect childhood, because my dad's a piece of shit, but other than that, it was awesome."

Other than what he'd told me when we'd gone horseback riding the first week I was here, he hadn't said much about his dad. He tended to change the subject when he came up. Not that I blamed him. My parents didn't seem terribly happy together—not that I would really know—but it was hard to imagine going through something so traumatic as finding out my dad had been hiding a series of affairs.

"What about you?" He leaned back against the trunk of the tree and adjusted his hat. "Where did you grow up?"

"Well, you saw my parents' house in Woodinville," I said. "They've lived there since I was little. Although I was always away at school. I went to boarding schools from the time I was six."

"Was that a good thing or a bad thing?"

I shrugged and licked strawberry juice off my fingers. "Both. My parents wanted me to go to the best schools, and most of their friends' kids went away to school, too. It seemed normal. And I went to camps and stuff in the summer. Horse camp was my favorite, of course, but Mom always signed me up for all sorts of things. Music camp, art camp, archery camp—"

"Archery? Tell me you know how to shoot a bow and arrow."

"I *do* know how to shoot a bow and arrow," I said. "I got pretty good at it, too."

"That's fucking awesome. I'm so turned on right now."

"The fact that I can use a bow and arrow turns you on?"

"Obviously."

I laughed. "How did you spend your summers? Wine camp?"

"Pretty much. I followed my grandpa around out here. Him or Ben. I played in the dirt and climbed trees and learned how to grow grapes."

"You say that like every little boy learns how to grow grapes."

He shrugged. "I've always loved growing shit. Mom says I started trying to plant my apple and watermelon seeds when I was a toddler. When I was about three, I planted a toy car in the garden behind our house. I was so disappointed when it didn't sprout into a toy car tree. I really thought I had it all figured out with that one."

"That's adorable."

He grinned. "I've always been cute."

"Did you always know you wanted to work for your family's winery?"

"Yep. This place is in my blood. I love it here, and I love what I do. What more could a guy want?"

I wondered what that felt like—to be so in love with a place, you knew you'd never leave. I'd never felt that way before.

"I guess that's what home feels like."

"Exactly," he said. "After my mom's divorce goes through, Brynn and Chase are going to break ground on a house out here. Well, not right here, but they have a spot picked out. Brynn doesn't know it yet, but I'm building mine right next door."

"Wow, a house?"

"Yeah. My apartment is fine, but I'll build something so I can settle down."

"It's hard to imagine you settling down," I said.

"Is it?" He shrugged and before I could answer, he'd jumped to his feet and held his hands out to help me up. "I have another idea. Let's go."

Leaving our picnic spread on the ground, we got back in the utility vehicle. The sun blazed hot overhead as he drove us down the dirt road. We crossed another road, and up ahead I could hear the sound of running water.

Cooper parked just before we got to a bridge spanning a river. The bridge was wide enough for the vehicle but looked like it was built more for foot traffic. Below, the slow-moving water was clear, sparkling in the sunlight.

He jumped out and stripped off his shirt, tossing it on the seat.

"What are we doing?"

"It's hot, so we're going for a swim." He kicked off his shoes and pulled down his shorts.

"How do we get down to the water?"

His mouth hooked in a grin. "We have to jump."

I grabbed the side of the utility vehicle, like if I didn't

hang on, I'd fall off the bridge I wasn't even on yet. "Jump? From the bridge?"

"Yep. It's fun as fuck. Don't worry, the current isn't strong here, and it's plenty deep. I've done it a million times."

"I don't know about this."

He pulled down his underwear and stood in the road, stark naked. I was momentarily too distracted by his semi-hard cock to think about the fact that he'd just suggested I jump off a bridge.

"But... what are you... why are you... what are we... you're naked."

"I don't want to get my clothes wet. Come on, Cookie. Strip."

"What? I'm not taking my clothes off out here."

He glanced around. "Why? There's no one around."

"What if someone comes? What if someone drives out here to do the same thing we're doing? What if it's a big group of high school kids and they're looking for a place to drink beer they got someone's older brother to buy and they come here and I'm totally naked and they see me?"

Cooper laughed and curled a finger, beckoning for me to come closer. "Come here, Cookie."

I released my death grip on the utility vehicle and went around to the other side.

"No one is out here." He held my eyes with his and rubbed his hands up and down my arms. "Just you and me. If jumping off the bridge scares you too much, I won't make you do it. But you can trust me. I won't put you in danger. And I really think you should try. It's so fun, I bet you do it once and climb right back up to do it again."

"I can't believe you're standing out here naked." I

paused, rethinking that. "Actually, I can believe you're standing out here naked."

He shrugged. "I like being naked. Naked is awesome. You can leave your clothes on if you want, but then you'll have wet clothes. Plus, I like it when you're naked."

"You're sure no one will see us?"

"Pretty sure, yeah."

I put my hands on my hips. "That's not very convincing."

"What's the worst that will happen? You get naked and someone shows up and I dive in front of you so no one else sees my Cookie. Besides, do you think they'll be looking at you with all this on display?" He raised his eyebrows, gesturing to himself.

I laughed, biting my lip because he was talking me into it. I wasn't sure what was more frightening. Jumping off a bridge or doing it naked in full daylight. I wasn't shy about Cooper seeing me without my clothes on. He always made me feel so good about my body. But I didn't want to mistakenly put myself on display for anyone else.

After taking a deep breath, I pulled my shirt over my head and put it on the seat. Cooper watched me with a sexy grin as I undressed. I put the rest of my clothes on the seat and tried to resist the urge to cover myself. I glanced around more than once, making sure we were really alone. I couldn't believe I was doing this.

"Ready?"

"I think so."

He took my hand and led me to the bridge. The sides weren't high, so we easily climbed over. I clung to the railing for dear life as I watched the water meander past below me.

"Don't overthink it," he said. "Just have fun."

Don't overthink it. Just have fun. That could have been

my motto since I'd started my Cooper-moon. It had worked out so far.

"Okay." Deep breath. "Let's do it."

"Holy shit, you're so fucking sexy and I'm getting the biggest adrenaline rush right now." He grabbed my hand, his eyes wild, a huge grin on his face. "Jump!"

My feet left the edge of the bridge and I screamed as the sensation of falling took over. The air rushed past and in no time at all, I hit the water feet first, gripping Cooper's hand like it was the only thing that could save me. I sucked in a quick breath at the shock of cold just before my head went under.

I came up gasping and laughing all at once, my head buzzing from the rush. Cooper grabbed me, pulling me against him, and kissed me all over my face.

"You were amazing," he said, then kissed me again.

"Oh my god, I did it!"

"Yeah, you did."

We drifted with the slow current, the water doing most of the work to take us to the bank. Cooper got out first, his naked body dripping wet. I ate up the sight of his toned physique, glistening in the sunlight. He helped me out and looked me up and down, biting his lip.

"We should do naked things all the time. This is fucking awesome."

I laughed. "Can we jump again?"

"Shit yeah, we can jump again."

A man's raspy voice came from somewhere to our left. "Hey! Who's out there?"

"Oops." Cooper grabbed my hand and we scrambled up the bank.

"You said no one would be around!"

"I said I was pretty sure no one would be around." He

turned to help me up the last of the incline. "There usually isn't."

"Who the hell is out here? Get off my property!"

Cooper laughed as he led me quickly back to the utility vehicle. Despite myself, I was laughing too. He tugged on his underwear, then jumped in. I got as far as my panties and held up my shirt to cover my boobs.

"Who was that?" I asked as we started to drive away.

"Murray Davis," he said. "He's actually a nice guy. Just grumpy."

I glanced back but I couldn't see anything through the haze of dust kicked up by the utility vehicle. "I thought we were still on your family's land."

"Nope. This is Murray's. The property line is up here."

"So not only did we just jump naked off a bridge, we were trespassing too?"

"I guess, yeah." He glanced at me with that mischievous grin. "But it was fun, wasn't it?"

And I had to admit, it was fun. But being with Cooper was like that. Everything was fun.

TWENTY-ONE

COOPER

AFTER OUR PICNIC and bridge-jumping adventure, Amelia and I went back to her place. We showered the river water off and played a round of *fluffy bunny*. Except we both forgot to count the number of marshmallows we had shoved in our mouths and wound up laughing and sticky.

It was still fun.

We cleaned up the marshmallow mess. I wiped my hands on a towel in the kitchen.

"Oh! I almost forgot," she said. "I got you something. Go wait in the bedroom and I'll get it."

"Awesome."

I went into the bedroom and lay down, putting my hands behind my head to relax against her pillow.

"Close your eyes," she said from the other room. "It's a surprise."

It was hard not to peek, but I loved surprises. I could hear the sound of tape ripping and then something that sounded like plastic.

"Oh my god, this is so cute," she said, her voice high and squeaky.

Now I was really curious. A cute surprise? Maybe it was hot lingerie. Or a sexy costume. How would I dress up my Cookie? She could rock one of those sexy maid costumes. Or maybe sexy nurse. Hell, she could dress up as a sexy anything and I'd be into it. I wondered if she wanted to role-play. That was something I'd never done before, but if she was into it, I was down.

She started to unfasten my pants and I must have opened my eyes. "Close your eyes!"

"Okay, sorry."

It was very hard to keep my eyes shut. She unbuttoned my pants, then lowered the zipper. I lifted my hips so she could slip my pants off. I bit my lower lip as she pulled down my underwear.

"This is already an awesome surprise," I said.

"Trust me. You're going to love it so much."

I was already semi-hard when she took my cock in her hand and started to stroke. She hadn't told me to open my eyes yet, so I waited, groaning at the feel of her hand on me.

"Almost ready. Keep your eyes closed a little bit longer."

She stopped stroking, but she was still doing something with my dick. It wasn't as nice as a handy, but it wasn't terrible either. The curiosity was killing me. What was she doing?

"Okay, you can look now."

I opened my eyes to find Amelia holding my dick at the base so it stood straight up. There was something on it—I wasn't totally bare—and it took me a second to realize it was a costume.

"Holy shit."

"Isn't it great?"

She'd dressed my dick up like a little cowboy—little

being a relative term; he was only little compared to the rest of me—complete with a vest and cowboy hat.

"Cookie! This is fucking awesome."

"Isn't it cute?" She wiggled it back and forth a little bit. "I love his hat."

"This is the coolest thing. I had no idea there were dick costumes. It's like Halloween, only a million times better. Where did you get this?"

"I found them online. I thought it would be fun."

"Shit yeah, it's fun. He looks badass."

I got up so I could admire myself in the mirror. Turning to the side, I adjusted my position so I could see the whole thing. Amelia stood next to me and reached down to pet the shaft, stroking it with her thumb.

"You know what they say: Save a horse, ride a cowboy."

"Baby, you can ride my cowboy any time you want."

She laughed, still giving my dick gentle strokes with her thumb and fingers. Whoever had made the costume knew what they were doing. I was getting harder, but the fabric stretched with me.

"I think he needs a name for when he's a cowboy," she said. "How about Clint?"

"Like Eastwood? I don't know, he's the man, but I'm not sure my awesome cowboy is a Clint. Seems too brooding and serious."

"That's a really good point. You're not brooding and serious."

"I know. Dick Holliday." I winked. "I'm your huckleberry."

She laughed again. "What about Boner Bill? You know, like Buffalo Bill, except Boner."

"That's a good one."

She kept caressing me absently and the more she did

that, the less I cared about what name she wanted to give my junk. "Cookie, at this point you can call him Bob for all I care, just as long as you take your fucking panties off. And I think Bob really wants to get naked, so maybe you could help him with that."

"Oh, I know—Wyatt," she said. "He can be Wyatt when he's a cowboy."

"Awesome. Wyatt really wants to fuck you, though."

"Aw, does he?" she asked, her voice a soft coo. "Wyatt, maybe you should take your hat off. It's not good manners to wear it inside."

"Sorry, Wyatt is kind of a dick."

She plucked the hat off the tip and let it drop to the floor.

"Wyatt, you're still wearing so many clothes." She lowered to her knees in front of me, nibbling on her bottom lip. "It's much too hot for this. Here, let me help you take this off."

I watched her, trying not to bounce with excitement, as she slipped the rest of the costume off my erection. Her eyes lifted to meet mine and she took the shaft in her hand. Leaning in, she let her tongue flick out to brush against the tip.

"Oh, Jesus."

She ran her tongue up my length, slowly, never breaking eye contact. I was enraptured, every muscle in my body tense with anticipation. She gave it a few more licks, then took the tip in her mouth. My hips jerked. Fuck, that felt good.

"You naughty girl," I said, threading my fingers through her hair.

I gently guided her, watching as my cock slid between her lips. She held the base with one hand and grabbed my ass with the other. I kept my thrusts shallow—I didn't want to hurt her—while she enthusiastically sucked my cock.

God, I loved her. Not because she was sucking me off and it felt so good I could barely contain myself. I loved her for being so fun and sweet and awesome to be with. For listening to me and understanding, even when I didn't understand myself.

"Amelia, this feels so fucking good," I said, my voice coming out growly and low. "I love watching you suck my cock."

She moaned around my dick, the vibration making me shudder. She moved faster, plunging down on me in a steady rhythm. I really wanted to get her clothes off and fuck the life out of her, but it was hard to think when she was blowing me. Especially when she was on her knees in front of me and I could watch my cock sliding in and out of her wet mouth. I was a visual guy, and the show was fucking fantastic.

Her hand grabbing my ass felt pretty good too. I grunted, fisting my hand tighter in her hair. Fuck, this was hot. She moved her hand again and holy shit, what was she doing with that finger? It slipped inside, just the tip, putting a little bit of pressure where I'd never known I needed it.

"Oh fuck, Cookie, I'm gonna come now if you don't stop, fuck, oh my god."

She didn't stop.

And then I was coming hard. So hard. My cock throbbed in her mouth, spilling hot spurts of come down her throat while the world went dark. I growled and grunted, leaning on the wall for support. My knees buckled as I finished, and I almost crumpled on top of her.

"What the fuck just happened?" I asked, staggering to the bed so I could collapse.

I lay on my back, trying to catch my breath. I'd never had an orgasm like that before. Had my sweet little virgin just given me a fingertip surprise? Holy shit. My mind was completely blown.

"How did you... where did you... oh my god, Cookie, I need a second... just give me a few... I mean holy fuck."

She laughed, then ducked into the bathroom. When she came back, she snuggled up next to me. "Did you like that?"

"Did I? I can't even think right now."

"I wanted to get better at blow jobs, so I did some research. Some of it was kind of mortifying, because I found a lot of porn. God, so much porn. But I also found some really helpful stuff. There's this blog by a woman named Nora, I think, called *Living Your Best Life*, and she has a ton of great articles. Some are all about womanhood and dating and that kind of thing, but her sex articles are amazing. She wrote this one on oral sex and it really resonated with me, you know? Like there's something so powerful about having that kind of influence over your boyfriend. I love making you feel good, it's so exhilarating. And I love Wyatt, too. Whether or not we're calling him Wyatt, he's my favorite."

"Fucking hell, Cookie, you're my favorite."

I almost said it, right then. I almost said, *I love you, Amelia*. She'd said *love* at least twice, although she'd been talking about blow jobs and my dick. Which was great, I was super happy that she loved those things—great news for me. But hearing her say that word made me think it, and think about how I really did love her. And how I hadn't said it yet.

But in a flash, I thought about what would happen if I said it and she couldn't say it back. The words died in my throat.

She was nestled against me and I realized she'd just

given me the most epic orgasm of my entire life, and so far—today at least—I hadn't given her even one. Goddammit, she wasn't even naked. That shit wasn't going to fly.

I rolled her over onto her back, pinning her to the bed. "Your turn."

And I made sure she was satisfied. Once. Twice. Three times. I ate her pussy and fucked her hard, giving her everything I had. I didn't stop until she was gasping for breath and calling my name. Until she was going out of her mind. Because if I couldn't tell her I loved her yet, I was sure as hell going to show her. And maybe some part of her, deep inside, would hear me and understand.

TWENTY-TWO
COOPER

EVER SINCE AMELIA had given me the epic blow job to end all blow jobs—god, I hoped she'd do it again—I'd been trying to analyze why it had been so freaking amazing. Had that little fingertip in my ass really done it for me? And Jesus, what did that mean? I'd never had a girl do that to me before and it was messing with my head a little that I'd enjoyed it so much.

The fact that Amelia had surprised me sexually was still a mind fuck, but a good one. Sex with her had been off the hook from day one, and it had only gotten better. And I was starting to realize why. Sex had always been fun for me. It felt good, and I liked doing it. Who didn't like having an orgasm?

But sex with Amelia was so much more than the end result. It was more than the physical pleasure. I'd never known it could be like that. Never realized how much it changed things when you *cared*.

Sex with a hot girl? Awesome. Sex with a hot girl you were in love with? There was nothing better. Not a single thing.

It was adorable that she wanted to learn something new to make me feel good. That meant more to me than I knew how to express to her. There was a lot I was having trouble saying lately. Which was not a normal thing for me. I usually said whatever came into my head the moment it arrived. But with her, I was taking my time. Slowing down. Thinking things through.

I hoped that was the right call. It wasn't easy, but I was trying. Hoping I'd know when our clocks were in sync. Hoping we'd get there.

But seriously, the fingertip thing? Kind of freaked me out.

Chase was in the kitchen, and Brynn wasn't home, so I figured I'd just come out and ask him.

"Chase, I have an issue."

"Again?" he asked. "What's wrong now?"

"Okay, I'm just going to be blunt and say it."

"As opposed to the rest of the time when you're so subtle?"

"I hear your sarcasm and I choose to ignore it," I said. "Seriously man, this is a thing. I have a thing."

"Okay, Coop, what's your thing?"

I took a deep breath and once I started talking, the words tumbled out, faster than I usually spoke—which was pretty fast. "Amelia gave me a blow job and it was fucking incredible and Jesus, Chase, she gave me a fingertip and it was so intense and I don't know what to do with that right now."

Chase blinked, like it was taking a second for him to get through what I'd said. Then a slow smile spread across his face. "Okay, I get you. Yeah, the fingertip is intense."

"Yes! Is that a thing? Chase, what does this mean? I've

done some freaky shit, but I've never had anything in the back door."

"Dude, it's cool. I promise, it's nothing to worry about. Most guys are afraid to try it, but they shouldn't be." He grabbed an apple out of the fridge and took a bite.

"Don't tell me who it was, because if it was Brynn, I really, *really* don't want to know, so leave out that detail. But I have to know, Chase. Give it to me straight, because I hear what you're saying, and I think you're implying that the answer is yes, but I need to ask. You've had the fingertip?"

"Yes," he said around his bite.

"And you liked it?"

"Oh fuck yes."

I let out a long breath. "That is such a relief. Seriously, I had no idea."

"I know, dude. I never would have thought. But holy shit."

He sat at the table, so I followed. I pulled a chair out, but leaned against the back of it instead of sitting down.

"Damn. It's too bad I can't ask for it again. I can't ask, right?"

"Hell no," Chase said. "There are lines. But if you liked it that much, she knows. She'll hook you up."

"You think?"

One side of his mouth turned up in a grin. "Yeah. I think so."

"Jesus, you're thinking about my sister right now, and oh my god, she and Amelia talked about this, didn't they? Cookie read an article or some shit and I bet she shared it with Brynn. Or Brynn showed it to her first, I don't know, and I don't want to know. You got the fingertip *recently*, didn't you? Don't fucking answer that."

Chase smiled the biggest shit-eating grin I'd ever seen on him.

"I hate you."

"No you don't," he said. "You love me, dick."

"Yeah, I do, but I also hate you. I'm leaving now."

I walked away before he could say anything else about my sister, or blow jobs, or fingertips. But secretly, I was kind of happy for him. It was obviously gross to think about my sister having sex, but another part of me wanted to give him a big-ass high five.

Life was confusing when your best friend married your sister.

Thinking about my Cookie made me want to see her. She was probably home from work by now. I was supposed to meet Leo to work out at his place, but I had time to pop over and squeeze her beforehand, so I drove back to Salishan. I parked outside the Big House, since I was going to her place, then Leo's.

I walked toward her cottage but stopped in my tracks. She stood in the doorway, talking to someone. A guy. A guy I knew, and the instant I saw him, I wanted to go ape-shit and punch him in his fucking face. It was assgoblin. Her ex.

What in the everloving fuck was that guy doing here?

I was about to march over there, grab him by his douchey polo shirt, and drag him out of here—I wanted him off my fucking land—when Ben stepped in front of me.

"Cooper, I need to talk to you."

"In a minute."

I started to step around him, but he put a strong hand on my shoulder. "Now. This can't wait."

There was something in his voice. An urgency. Almost a reprimand. The little boy in me remembered that voice. It wasn't something I could ignore.

"What's wrong?" I glanced around his shoulder at Amelia. She was letting assgoblin into her house. He walked inside, and she shut the door. I was about to lose my mind.

"Not here."

Only the force behind Ben's words kept me from pushing past him and busting down Amelia's door. I looked at his face and his eyes were serious. Hard, even.

Without another word, Ben turned, clearly expecting me to follow. I cast one more look toward Amelia's cottage. Trusting her was easy. I didn't trust the fucknugget she'd let in.

Cracking my knuckles, I reluctantly followed Ben.

He led me over to Leo's place, and I started to worry.

"Ben, what's going on, man? Is Mom okay? Where's Brynn? Did something happen to Huddy? Should I call Zoe? What's up?"

"We'll talk inside."

Leo opened the door before Ben could knock. He fixed me with a hard stare, crossing his arms as I walked past him, and shut the door behind us.

"You guys are freaking me out. What's going on? Did something happen?" Why did they both look so angry?

"We know about your dad," Ben said.

I froze, my normally jittery body going still. It was like he'd sucked the air from my lungs. I couldn't get a breath.

"You need to explain yourself, Cooper," Leo said, his voice dangerously low. "Now."

"Fuck." I rubbed the back of my neck and started pacing around the room. Gigz darted past me, jumping onto Leo's desk to get out of my way. "Goddammit. Okay. Here's the thing. Dad wants money, right? That's why he's holding out on the divorce and threatening to take all our land. So he came to me after Brynn's wedding and said he had a plan and if I helped him, he'd agree to Mom's settlement offer and give her the divorce. He'd fucking go away."

"And you agreed to it?" Leo asked.

"What was I supposed to do? His plan is fucking stupid, but that's not my problem. So he's growing a bunch of weed. Is it really that big of a deal? I make sure he can plant and harvest his crop, he takes it, does his deal, Mom gets divorced, everyone is happy."

"He's not growing cannabis," Ben said.

"What?"

"Is that what he told you?" Leo asked.

"Yeah, it's the plan. I've been out there, he's growing weed. It's not even illegal anymore. I mean, he's not growing it legally, so that's an issue, but come on. Is it really worth getting all pissed about?"

Ben and Leo looked at each other.

"Cooper, listen to me," Ben said. "This is important. He told you he was growing cannabis?"

"Yeah."

"That's it? That's all he said?"

"Yes. I don't get why he thinks this is going to make him an ass-load of cash. I guess he's growing some rare strain, I don't know. But that's not my problem."

"He's not growing weed," Leo said. "He's growing opium poppies."

I stared at Leo, the shock of his words beating at my brain. "What? No, I've been out there. I've seen it."

"Did you walk through the fields, or did you just look from the perimeter?" Ben asked.

"The perimeter, I guess. I didn't even want to be out there. You guys, if you think I was happy about this, I'm fucking not. But what do you mean, he's growing opium?"

"He must have set it up to fool you." Leo brought up aerial photos on one of his computer screens. Drone photos of the once-empty field. "There's a small cannabis crop all around the perimeter. But that's not the bulk of what he's growing. The entire middle is opium."

"When Leo found it, I went out there to confirm," Ben said. "It's definitely opium."

I raked my hands through my hair and paced across the length of the room again. I had no idea how they knew I'd been involved. Saw me. Heard me. Fucking sorcery mind-reading magic bullshit. I didn't really want to know. "Jesus."

"Do you have any idea what you've done?" Leo asked. "You've put our entire family at risk. If the feds find this, they'll raid our property. They'll confiscate everything, and we might never get it back. Mom and Dad are still legally married, and with you complicit in this, they'd have everything they need to take it all. Not to mention throw your ass in prison."

"No." I was muttering to myself like I'd lost it. "No, no, no, no. It wasn't supposed to be dangerous. It was just a little weed. Who fucking cares? He'd make some money and go away and leave us the hell alone. Why didn't he fucking tell me? *Opium?* Dude, that's how they make heroin. That's fucked up."

"No shit," Leo said. "And your dumb ass let him do it."

"I was trying to protect you," I said. "I'd do anything to protect this land and everyone on it. I've been carrying this shit around for months while it ate at me from the inside. But if this was what I had to do to get rid of him, then fine, I'd do it."

"This is bad, Cooper," Leo said. "This is really fucking bad."

I knew that. I didn't need Leo rubbing my face in it. But

I held back from squaring off with him. This was my screw-up, not his.

"Does Roland know?" I asked.

"Not yet," Ben said. "We didn't tell anyone else."

"Yet," Leo said, the word snapping off between his teeth.

"You don't have to be a dick about it."

"Boys," Ben said.

"I'm not the one who put our entire family in danger," Leo said, stepping toward me.

Ben moved between us. "Boys. Enough. He didn't know, Leo. We knew he wouldn't have helped your father if he did, and he's confirmed that."

Leo crossed his arms and stepped back.

"What do we do?" I asked. "Tell me what you need me to do, and I'll do it. Do you want me to turn myself in?"

"No," Ben said, putting a hand on my shoulder. "No, we're going to avoid that if we can. I have an old friend who's with the DEA. I already talked to him, completely off the record. I didn't give him a lot of details, mostly theoretical questions. But he said if we had something going on out here, he'd help. It wouldn't be you they're after, Coop. It'd be your father, and the people he's working with."

"Okay. So what does that mean?"

"It means we'd cooperate with him to take these guys down," Ben said. "And that probably means you have to keep your dad from finding out."

More secrets and lies. But I had no qualms about lying to my father, and the thought of setting him up to go down was enormously satisfying. That fucker needed to pay for what he was doing to my family.

"I'm in," I said. "I'll do whatever it takes."

"Good," Ben said. "Let me talk to him. And keep this discreet. Don't tell anyone. Does your girlfriend know?"

"No."

"Thank god," Leo said.

"Hey, we can trust Amelia," I said. "Don't—"

"Cooper," Ben said, stepping in front of me again. "He's not accusing her of anything. But we need to keep this to as few people as possible."

"Should we talk to Roland?" Leo asked.

"Jesus, don't burden him with this," I said. "He has a kid now. He can't be involved. I don't want to expose him to this shit."

"We'll wait to tell Roland," Ben said. "Unless something changes and he needs to know."

"Fuck." I raked my hands through my hair again. I couldn't believe I'd let this happen. I'd put my entire family in danger.

"We're going to deal with this," Ben said. "We'll fix it and make sure everyone is safe. Got it?"

"Yeah." I had to get out of there. Leo's place was always so fucking dark. I was about to start climbing the walls. "Look, I gotta go. Talk to me when you know more. I'll cooperate, I'll do whatever. I just... I gotta go."

I left, feeling like I was going to crawl out of my skin. Panicky rage filled my mind, clouding my vision. I wanted the solace of Amelia. Her arms around me, her skin against mine. Her scent filling me. But her fucking ex was with her.

With my last shred of decent judgment, I turned away from the path to her cottage and toward the utility vehicle. I had just enough presence of mind to know I wanted to avoid prison, and if I went to Amelia's now, I'd probably wind up murdering her ex.

But aside from that, I was not in my right mind. I wasn't

okay. I'd let my father pull one over on me and the consequences could be devastating. I'd invited danger onto my family's land. Put my family in peril. Hell, I'd even put Amelia in peril. Suddenly, my entire life felt like an enormous disaster, and I wasn't sure there was going to be a way out of it.

TWENTY-THREE
AMELIA

IT WAS odd that Cooper knocked and didn't immediately come barreling inside. The door wasn't locked, so I wondered what he was waiting for. Who knew with him. Maybe he was holding something heavy. I had no idea what that could be, but Cooper was unpredictable like that.

I brushed my hair back from my shoulders and answered the door. My mouth popped open and I made a squeaky noise in my throat. Because the man standing in my doorway was not Cooper. It was Griffin.

"Are you serious?" I asked. "Please tell me you're not serious. Why are you here?"

"Because we need to talk, Mimi," he said, and I rolled my eyes. "Sorry. I meant Amelia. It's hard to remember. I've been calling you Mimi since we were thirteen. You used to like it."

"I'm not thirteen anymore, Griff," I said. "I'm not a little girl who'll follow you around like a lost puppy."

"Come on, I never saw you that way." His expression softened. "Can I please come inside? I just want to talk."

Since I'd walked out on Griffin—and our parents—at

dinner a few weeks ago, my anger over what he'd done to me had dissipated. I didn't like him. There was no way I wanted him in my life, even as friends. But maybe I could make peace with him. Let him say what he wanted so we could both move on.

"Fine."

I stepped aside then shut the door behind him.

"The place is cute," he said, turning in a slow circle.

"Thanks. It's mostly not my stuff. The Miles family keeps these for guests. I'm just renting it for a while."

I gestured toward the couch, but decided not to offer him any refreshments. My mother would have had a fit over my lack of manners, but I didn't want him staying any longer than necessary. I sat down in the chair, as far from him as I could get.

"Well? You said you came here to talk. Now's your chance."

He took a deep breath. "I guess I should start by saying I'm sorry. I kind of freaked out the night before our wedding. Everything moved really fast and it was like all of a sudden, I was about to get married. Shit got real, you know?"

"Getting married was your idea. It's not like I pressured you into it. You asked me, pretty much out of the blue."

"Yeah, I know. But even you have to admit, it all happened really fast. I proposed and then the parents jumped all over it."

"That's true."

"Anyway, my point is, I know I made a mistake. I got overwhelmed."

"You slept with my cousin because you were overwhelmed?" I asked. "That's not a very good response. I was overwhelmed, too, but I didn't bang one of your groomsmen."

"I said it was a mistake. I'm trying to acknowledge that."

"That's fine, it's acknowledged. I'm glad you realize it."

He leaned back. "I just wish we could go back to the way things used to be."

I almost said, *me too*, but then I stopped. Because what *used to be* did I want to go back to? "What do you mean?"

"We were good together," he said. "There's a reason we were friends for so long."

"Yeah, because I was a flipping doormat."

"No you weren't."

I sighed. I didn't like to admit it—made me feel pretty stupid—but it was true. "Yes, I was. I let you walk all over me. We weren't good together, Griff. We had fun sometimes, sure. But we only hung out when you were in between girlfriends. I was your fallback. I was just a consolation if you didn't have something better going on. And the worst part is, I knew it. I didn't think of it like that at the time, but I always felt it. And I still let you come back into my life, over and over again."

"You were never a consolation," he said. "You were my best friend."

"Was I, though? That's what I always told people, too. I kept a picture of you in my room next to my bed. *Who's that guy*, people would ask. *Oh, he's my best friend Griffin*, I'd say with stars in my eyes. It's no wonder I never had a boyfriend."

"You had boyfriends, didn't you?"

"A best friend would know that. But don't pretend like you didn't know. You were well aware I didn't date anyone. Cheese and rice, Griffin, the couple of times I got close with a guy, I told you about it and suddenly there you were, hanging around all the time. I don't think that was a coincidence."

"What are you talking about?"

"You liked me being available," I said. "I thought of you as this super cool guy who might one day notice me in a new way. But you weren't. You just used me as someone to make you feel better when you were single. You'd ignore me for months, then swoop into my life every once in a while and fuck up my shit."

Griffin's eyes went wide, probably because of my language. I'd uttered a swear word probably twice in my life, and I'd just dropped two in one sentence. But sometimes no other words would do.

"That's not how it was, Mimi. I mean, Amelia."

"Whatever. It doesn't matter now."

"No, it does matter." He sat up and scooted to the edge of the couch. "It matters a lot. I want to fix this."

"Fix what? Our friendship? I think we're past that now. And I don't really need a friend who just wants me when he doesn't have anything else going on."

"Not just our friendship."

The anger I'd felt when he'd first left me started to heat up, simmering in the pit of my stomach. "How's Portia?"

"Amelia—"

"No, tell me. Does she know you're here? Or are you thinking about cheating on her with me this time? Maybe mix it up a little. Try to score with your ex-fiancée while your wife is off getting a third boob job?"

He shook his head and sighed. "No. I'm not with her anymore."

"Divorced already? I thought only celebrities had those kind of quickie marriages."

"We had it annulled," he said. "Very soon afterward. I said I made a mistake."

"Mistake isn't even the word. Sleeping with Portia the night before your wedding was a mistake. Marrying her was a blunder of epic proportions."

He grimaced. "I know."

There was a terrible person inside of me who really wanted to know the details. I wrestled with it for a few seconds. The angel on my shoulder reminded me it wasn't necessary for me to know what had happened between them. The devil wanted the gossip.

The little devil was a lot louder.

"What happened?"

"Like I said, I was overwhelmed. I made a mistake, and then instead of trying to fix what I'd done, I kept making bigger mistakes. I realized right away that Portia and I would never work, and I felt terrible for what I'd done to you. At that point, I didn't know what to do. Things were falling apart. And Portia... I don't know. She obviously thought I was made of money."

"Portia's a trust fund kid. What is she worried about?"

"Not really. She acts like she has a big bank account, but she's really looking for a sugar daddy."

"Sounds like you two were a match made in heaven."

He furrowed his brow. "Not really. I wasn't interested in living the rest of my life with a gold digger. I thought she had her own... Anyway, it doesn't matter."

"No, you thought she had her own what? Her own money?"

"Yeah."

I narrowed my eyes at him. "You thought she had a big trust fund, didn't you? Wait a second, you're a trust fund kid, too. Why are you worried about her money?"

"My parents are making that... difficult."

"Since when?"

He leaned back against the couch cushions and looked away. "Since earlier this year."

"I knew it. You slimy little worm, that's why you wanted to marry me. I bet you thought you got the balance when you graduated college, but your parents told you that wasn't the case. They were sick of you whoring around with all your bimbo girlfriends, so they told you to settle down and get married first, didn't they?"

"Well..." He sputtered a few times, like he was trying to talk, but couldn't figure out what to say.

I didn't bother letting him keep trying. "And you thought hey, if I have to get married to get my money, who can I rope into marrying me? Oh! How about someone else with a trust fund? Maybe some pushover who'll fall for my crap. I know the perfect girl. Amelia!"

"That's not what happened."

"We'll be rich little assholes living off our parents' money together in some fancy house we didn't earn. And I'll just have side chicks, and she's so dumb she'll never even know. That sounds like a great life. I can see why you thought it was a good plan."

"Are you being sarcastic right now?" he asked. "Because I can't tell."

"Of course I'm being flipping sarcastic right now. What a crappy thing to do to someone. You didn't love me. I have no idea if you even liked me, or if you just liked how I made you feel when you were lonely and bored. I can't believe I let you do that to me."

"Amelia, you're overreacting. It's not about the money. I know you emptied the honeymoon account, and I haven't even said a word about it. Because I want to fix this. We really were good together. I see that now. We both had our fun. I had a fling, and you had one too. But now it's time to get serious about life. Move on."

"A fling? Cooper's my boyfriend. He's not a fling."

He sighed, a patronizing exhale that made me want to punch him in the face. "Yeah, I'm sure he is. But like I said, it's time to get serious."

"I am serious. I'm serious about you leaving. Now."

"You're not kicking me out."

"Yes, I am. Go, Griffin. Go back to your parents—who are really nice, by the way, and I have no idea what they did to make you turn into such a flipping jerk."

"God, Amelia, when did you get so mean?"

I crossed my arms, standing my ground. "When you stood me up on our wedding day, asshole."

He gaped at me, his eyes wide. "Okay, then. I guess I shouldn't have come."

I waited, my arms still crossed, while he got up and went for the door. I didn't say a word when he paused, like he was hoping I'd tell him not to leave. He opened the door and hesitated again, his back to me. Like he couldn't believe I was letting him go.

He took one more step, clearing the doorway, and I rushed over to shut the door behind him.

My heart was pounding and my cheeks warm. I'd known Griffin was a jerk—a nice guy wouldn't do what he'd done to me. But seeing him like this—seeing him with clear eyes—made me realize exactly how lucky I was. I'd almost married that guy. And I'd never been more grateful that he'd left me at the altar than I was in that moment.

TWENTY-FOUR
AMELIA

COOPER STILL WASN'T ANSWERING his texts.

I'd been trying to get a hold of him since Griffin had left. It had been over an hour, and still nothing. Cooper was supposed to come over—we had plans tonight—but I hadn't heard a word. No texts, no calls. He hadn't burst in through the door, a wide grin on his face, excited about the new fun thing he had planned.

Something was wrong. I didn't know how I knew, but I was sure of it. Maybe he'd seen Griffin. Would that make him angry? Was he mad at me for talking to my ex? It didn't seem like Cooper to get angry without waiting for an explanation. If he was upset about Griffin being here, I could easily explain, and everything would be fine. Was he going to give me the chance?

It was entirely possible his phone was just dead, and he was busy out in the vineyards. But something inside told me there was more going on. My instincts were screaming at me to find him.

I walked outside and found his truck, but didn't see

him. So I went over to the Big House to find out if anyone there had seen or heard from him recently.

Brynn was working in the tasting room. She was busy, with a group seated at the bar and more guests at the tables. She smiled when she saw me and motioned for me to go around to the back. I waited for a few minutes before she had a chance to break away.

"Hey," she said. "Sorry, I'm super busy tonight. What's up?"

"Have you seen Cooper recently?"

"No. Why? Is something wrong?"

"I don't know. He might just be working later than he planned. But he was supposed to come over and I haven't heard from him. And he's not answering his texts."

"For a guy who will mass text you with eight hundred memes when he's bored, he can be notoriously bad at checking his phone. He's probably just still out in one of the vineyards."

"Yeah, you're probably right."

"I have to get back, but text me if you don't find him soon and I'll send Chase out."

"Thanks."

She gave me a quick hug, then went back to work.

I left and walked back toward the work house where his truck was parked. One of the utility vehicles was parked nearby. For a second, I contemplated taking it. But if he was out in the vineyards, I had no idea how to find him. There were acres upon acres of land stretching out across the hills. He could be anywhere out there, and I'd just wind up lost.

Movement caught the corner of my eye. Cooper's brother Leo came out of the work house, shutting and locking the door behind him.

"Hey Leo." I took a few quick steps toward him. "Have you seen Cooper?"

He turned his face slightly, angling the scarred side away from me. "Not in the last hour, but I saw him earlier."

"Do you have any idea where he might be? I thought he was coming over, but he hasn't, and his truck is here, so he must be around, but he's not answering my texts and it's probably stupid but I'm worried that something is wrong. Leo, oh my god, my ex was here, and I talked to him, and what if Cooper saw and he's mad at me and now he won't talk to me?"

"Okay, slow down," he said. "He's probably just in one of the vineyards."

"I know, that's what I keep telling myself. But I feel like something is wrong. Does that ever happen to you? You just know something is off, and you think you might even know the reason, but you're not sure and it starts eating you up inside?"

"I guess," he said, looking at me with a furrowed brow. His eyes darted to the utility vehicle, then back to me. "Do you want me to take you out there?"

"That would be amazing, would you?"

"Sure."

I got into the utility vehicle next to him, feeling better already. Leo would know where to find him. We drove away from the main area of the winery, down a gravel road. He turned, taking us through one of the vineyards. The vines grew in rows on either side, stretching as far as I could see. But still no Cooper.

"We'll try another area," Leo said, turning the vehicle around.

"Thanks. Sorry about this. I'm sure you have better things to do than chase your brother around."

He shrugged. "It's fine. Wouldn't be the first time I had to go hunt him down. Probably won't be the last. If we don't find him, I'll call Chase. Somehow Chase always knows where he is. But those two are weird as hell."

I laughed. "They are pretty funny."

The road curved and as we turned the corner, the other utility vehicle came into view. I didn't see Cooper, but he couldn't be far.

Leo parked behind him. "Do you want me to wait?"

"That's okay. He'll come back for this at some point, right?"

"He should. You have your phone on you?"

"Yeah."

He held out his hand. "Can I put in my number? That way you can text me if he doesn't show. I don't want you out here alone when it gets dark."

I gave him my phone so he could add his number. His sleeve slid down, revealing some of the tattoos on his arm. The skin was mottled with scar tissue, but the tattoos were intricate and beautifully done.

"Thank you."

"You're welcome. Listen, I know Cooper is usually the human version of a puppy—only with more energy—but I think he has a lot on his mind right now."

"Okay. Thanks, Leo."

He left and I checked Cooper's utility vehicle. He'd left his phone on the seat. That explained why he hadn't been answering me. But where was he?

I walked out between the rows of vines, guessing at the direction. I didn't want to go too far and get lost. But I didn't want to sit around and wait for him to come back to his vehicle, either. I kept the road on my left and wandered a little, hoping I'd run into him.

Bees buzzed in the waning sunlight, flitting through the vines, and the breeze rustled the leaves. It was cooler today than it had been. Still sunny, but not blazing hot. Even still, a trickle of sweat dripped down my back as I walked. I hoped I'd find him soon.

And then I heard his voice.

I followed the low but familiar murmur, slowing when I saw him. He was wandering up the row, gently fingering the leaves as he went. Talking to his grapes.

There was tension in his body. I could feel it from where I was standing. His voice was calm and quiet, but I could see the storm raging beneath the surface by the way he moved. Something was indeed wrong.

My heart beat faster, dread filling the pit of my stomach. Was he upset with me? Were we about to have our first fight? I was almost afraid to say anything. But I hadn't come all the way out here to leave without speaking to him.

"Cooper?"

He turned around, and instead of rushing to grab me and lift me off my feet, he stayed where he was. "Hey."

"Is everything okay? I thought you were coming over, and you didn't answer my texts, so Leo brought me out here."

"No, not really. I don't know."

"You're not okay?"

He shoved his hands in his pockets. He was too still. Almost motionless.

"Griffin was here," I said. "Is that why?"

"I didn't like seeing that. I saw him go inside with you, and I had to go deal with something else, and I have to be honest, Cookie, it's fucking with my head a little."

"You don't think... I mean, you can't think something happened. Can you? I would never. He wanted to talk to me and I figured if I let him say what he wanted to say, we could both put everything behind us for once and for all."

"You let him in."

"But I didn't even offer him anything to drink."

"Does that make a difference?" he asked. "So you didn't sit and have tea or some shit. I thought you were done with him. I thought you moved on."

"I am moving on," I said. "It's kind of a process. I almost married him a couple of months ago. And when that happened, he just left and didn't talk to me. And then I saw him at dinner, but our parents were there, and I walked out with you. We never had a chance to get any real closure."

"Closure. Okay, I get it."

I could tell he didn't get it. He either didn't understand why I'd needed to have that one final conversation with Griffin, or he actually thought I had let something happen. I wasn't sure which hurt more.

"Cooper, I promised you."

He looked up. "What?"

"I promised you the night we met that I'd never take him back. I didn't break my promise. I didn't even let him hug me. I let him say what he wanted to say, but it was just a bunch of excuses. He was a crappy friend and I let him be a crappy friend. And he would have been a crappy husband, too. So I'm glad he left me the way he did. He didn't leave any room for me to be confused or wonder if I should give him another chance. I'm done with him. I've *been* done with him. And I'm so sorry I gave you any reason to worry."

Cooper took a deep breath, then came over and wrapped his arms around me. Gratefully, I leaned into his chest. He smelled like fresh air and soil. I ran my hand up to the back of his neck and rubbed it while he held me. Then traced my hand to his ear so I could caress his earlobe between my thumb and fingers. The tension melted out of him and he took deep breaths, his face against my neck.

"Damn it, Cookie, I'm sorry. I trust you. It just bothered me, and I have all this other stuff on my mind. It's just work stuff, it's not something you need to worry about. But I let it all get to me, and I wanted you. I wanted this, and I couldn't because he was there and I didn't want to add murder charges to my list of problems. So I came out here."

"I'm sorry." I kept rubbing his ear while his gentle nuzzles against my neck turned to kisses.

He kissed me a few times, then pulled away. "We should get back."

"Sure, okay."

He took my hand and led me to the utility vehicle. And although I didn't think he was still worried about Griffin, there was still something wrong. Something he wasn't telling me.

TWENTY-FIVE
COOPER

MY FEET WERE FREEZING. I was still tired—I really needed more sleep—but my awareness of my cold feet was waking me up. That and my sore neck. I tried to adjust my position, but there were only so many options for sleeping in a bathtub.

The door opened, and I cracked one eye. Brynn stopped, halfway in, and started to shriek before clapping a hand over her mouth.

"Cooper, what the hell are you doing in the bathtub?"

"Trying to sleep."

She pulled the sides of her robe closer together. "Why are you sleeping in here?"

I shifted, but the bathtub wasn't very comfortable no matter what I did. "I have to sleep somewhere."

I didn't even want to talk about my bed. Fucking mattress. I hadn't slept on it once since the night Chase talked me out of burning it. When I had to sleep at home, I tried various places. My bedroom floor. The couch. Bathtub. One of the deck chairs. I ended up in a different place every night, usually after moving five or six times. It was exhausting. I slept like the dead when I stayed over at Amelia's. Her bed was currently my favorite place on the planet.

"You have a bed."

"Can't sleep there." I pulled the blanket over my shoulder and turned on my side so my back was to Brynn.

"Why can't you... never mind. Are you okay?"

"Yeah."

I heard Chase's voice, asking Brynn what I was doing in the bathroom.

"He's sleeping, I guess?"

"Oh, okay," Chase said.

Chase got me.

"Well, can you get up soon? I need the bathroom."

My neck was sore anyway, so I abandoned the last shred of hope that I might go back to sleep and got up. "Fine."

I spent the first part of the day dragging ass. The gallon of coffee I drank helped, as did a quick lunch with my mom. She looked great. The more time she spent without my asshole father around, the better she looked. She was vibrant, her eyes shining with life. It was fucking fantastic to see her like this. I knew she was stressed about the divorce and Dad's threats to Salishan. We all were. But she still looked better than she had in years.

Shortly after lunch, I got a text from Ben. It was just an address. No explanation, but I didn't need one. I knew exactly what this was about.

My stomach was in knots as I drove out to the location, a warehouse not far from Chase's shop. Ben had told me I could trust this DEA guy, but for all I knew, I was about to get arrested. Although if they wanted to arrest me, they could have done it already. It wasn't like I was hard to find.

The parking lot was empty except for a blue SUV. I

parked behind it, and a man got out, dressed in street clothes—button-down shirt and gray slacks.

"Mr. Miles?" he asked when I got out of my truck.

"Cooper."

"Agent Rawlins." He held out a hand, so I shook it. "Thanks for meeting me."

"Sure."

"Ben told me what he knew, so I have an idea of what's going on."

"Look, I didn't know what my dad was into when I agreed to help him. I thought if I cooperated, he'd grow his crop, harvest it, and get out. We wouldn't have to deal with him anymore. I didn't know what he was really planting out there."

"I understand. We're not after you. Ultimately, we're not even after your father. We're trying to get to the people he's working with."

"Yeah, well, if you take my father down in the process, you won't hear any complaints from us."

"That's likely," he said.

"I just need to know that my family and their land will be safe. I'll do what I have to do. But no matter what happens to me, I need to know they'll be okay."

"If you cooperate with our investigation, I'll do everything in my power to make sure that's the case."

"Okay," I said. "Tell me what you need me to do."

MY MEETING with Agent Rawlins didn't last long. Under different circumstances the whole thing might have been pretty fucking cool. Secret meetings with a DEA agent and plans to catch bad guys. But the reality wasn't so awesome.

Rawlins couldn't guarantee anything, which meant there was still the risk of losing our land. Working with him was our best bet, but what if something went wrong? Or someone got hurt? I'd never forgive myself.

There wasn't a lot for me to do at this point, other than string my dad along so he didn't get suspicious. I hated that I had to let my dad's people onto our property. I didn't want these assholes anywhere near my family, and I really didn't want Amelia involved. It was hard to keep this from her, but the less she knew the better. In fact, it made me nervous to have her living in the Blackberry Cottage. I'd have felt better if she stayed with me, but I wasn't sure how to bring it up without telling her what was going on.

But maybe I could just ask her to move in without giving any reason other than wanting her to. It would be the truth. I'd have loved to have her with me all the time. The nights I spent without her were never as good as when we were together—and that wasn't just because I couldn't bring myself to sleep in my bed. She was my favorite.

Plus she calmed my shit down. She was my peace, and I loved that about her.

I needed that now. I had a lot to do back at Salishan, but I could swing a detour out to the McLaughlin's ranch to squeeze my Cookie. It would be worth it. I texted her to make sure I could stop by, then headed in her direction.

She met me out at my truck, all smiles and sunshine.

"Hey, you."

I pulled her close and clung to her like a koala. "How do you smell so good after working with horses all day? You still smell like birthday cake."

"Birthday cake?"

"Yeah." I leaned in and smelled her hair. "With sprinkles."

She laughed. Putting her hands on my chest, she leaned back. "What does your shirt say?"

I moved back and stretched it out so she could see my latest boyfriend t-shirt. It read *If you think I'm cute, you should see my girlfriend.*

"Aw, I love this," she said.

"Thanks, baby."

Seeing Amelia was time well spent. She only had about ten minutes to spare, but I was glad I'd stopped. We hung out at my truck and made out a little.

Reluctantly, I let her go back to work and I drove back to Salishan. I felt better. Things had been a little tense between us after assgoblin had been here, but we were good now. And even that felt good. It hadn't been an epic fight or anything dramatic. But it was the first time we'd been through something un-fun, and we'd made it.

I pulled into the winery and my chest tightened with fear. A fire truck and ambulance were parked outside the work house, their lights flashing. I hopped out of my truck and hauled ass over there to see what was going on.

Inside, I found a cluster of paramedics loading Ben onto a stretcher. His neck was in a brace and his body strapped down. A crowd of guests stood nearby and one of our employees was busy herding them out. They must have been on a tour.

I caught sight of my mom on the other side of the stretcher. She was speaking to Ben in a quiet voice, her forehead creased with worry.

"What the hell happened?" I wasn't asking anyone in particular, but Roland appeared at my side, seemingly out of nowhere.

"He was up on a ladder. Leo was in here helping him. Right as the tour showed up, Ben slipped and fell."

"Jesus. And you had to call 911?"

"Mom did," Roland said. "He tried to talk her out of it, but there's concern about a neck or back injury. They're taking him in to get checked out as a precaution."

"Fuck. Where's Leo?"

Roland cleared his throat. "He, um... he left. It's good he was here. He kind of broke Ben's fall. Probably kept it from being worse. But there were a lot of people in here when it happened."

Oh shit. Leo avoided guests like the plague. Or like a guy with half his body—including his face—covered in scar tissue.

"Was it bad?" I asked.

"There was a lot of staring. I think he heard some comments. I got here right after, and... yeah."

I ran my hands through my hair. Fuck, this was bad. Mom got in the ambulance with Ben.

"Why don't you follow the ambulance. Mom will need a ride home. I'll go talk to Leo."

"You sure?" he asked.

"Yeah."

Roland patted my shoulder. "Just... stay calm, okay? And give him some time before you go over there."

"Yeah, I've got it."

He looked at me like he wasn't sure he believed me. But he left, pulling out his phone while he walked. Probably calling Zoe.

I did give Leo some time, but not much. I waited about ten minutes, then went in search of Miles brother number two.

He was at his place—I could hear his TV or something on his computer—but he wouldn't answer the door. I knocked again, louder this time.

"Leo. Come on, man. Let me in."

He opened the door a few inches. "Can't you take a hint? I'm busy."

"Are you okay? They took Ben to the hospital, dude. Did he fall on you? Are you hurt or anything?"

"I'm fine, and I know. Roland gave me a heads up. He'll call me when he gets there and they know if Ben's okay."

"Why are you talking to me through a crack in the door? Just fucking let me in for a minute."

Leo groaned, but stepped aside so I could come in.

"Are you sure you're okay?" I asked.

He walked over to his desk and sat heavily in his chair. "Yes, I'm fine."

Leo wasn't fine. He was never fine, and it ate at me that I didn't know what to do to help him.

Gigz jumped up onto the kitchen counter and knocked over a glass. It crashed to the floor, spilling something everywhere.

"Shit. Damn it, Gigz." Leo got up and went into the kitchen to clean up the mess.

He'd bumped the mouse when he stood, and a video played on the screen. It was security footage—looked like the aftermath of Ben's accident. There was Ben on the ground, and Leo next to him, checking him out.

It started again, playing the same clip in a loop. Ben on the ground. Leo crouching beside him. Why was he watching this over and over?

And then I noticed what else was in the frame. The guests.

A man had just fallen, and was clearly hurt, but Roland had been right—some of the guests were gesturing at Leo. At his scarred face and arm. Even I could see it, on the grainy security video.

Leo came back in and clicked the mouse, turning off the looped video.

"Dude, why are you doing that to yourself?" I asked.

"I was just checking it for insurance purposes."

I raised my eyebrows. That was a weak excuse. He wasn't even watching the portion where Ben fell.

"You know what, Ben's the one who got hurt," he said. "If you need to feel useful, go to the hospital. You can have fun flirting with all the nurses."

"I was just making sure you were all right."

He sat and turned his chair, putting his back to me.

"Okay. I guess Roland has it covered," I said. "I'll see you later."

Leo didn't say anything as I left. I felt like shit. He shouldn't have been there when Ben fell. If I hadn't stopped to see Amelia, I might have been there. Ben still could have been hurt, but at least Leo wouldn't have been put on display like that. I knew how much he hated people looking at him.

I hated feeling helpless. Hated that my brother was a mess and there wasn't anything I could do about it. Hated that I hadn't been there. That our family was in trouble and it was partially my fault.

The weight of it all sat heavy on my shoulders.

TWENTY-SIX
AMELIA

RIDING classes were done for today. I finished brushing Skip, one of the horses we used for youth classes. He was such a gentle soul. It seemed as if he knew his riders were small. He never tried to assert his dominance or take advantage of their inexperience, which made him perfect for children.

"There we go, sweet boy," I said, running my hand across his shiny coat.

When I came out, Lola caught my eye. She was in her stall, but I could tell by her eyes that she was restless. We didn't use Lola for youth classes. She was too spirited for young riders. She was too spirited for a lot of adult riders, in fact. But I loved that sassy girl.

"Hey, beautiful," I said as I approached. "You look like you need some exercise. Should we go outside?"

She nodded, her head bobbing up and down, as if she understood what I was saying.

I let her nuzzle my hand, then opened her stall. "Let's go, Lola. We'll take a ride."

After getting her saddled up, I led her outside and

mounted. She only took one step back as I swung up into the saddle. Cooperating with me, but making sure I knew she could change her mind.

I patted her neck. "Yeah, I feel you, sweet girl. Let's get some of that energy out, shall we?"

Taking the reins, I clicked my tongue and nudged her forward. She followed the fence line that led to a trail. I'd take her through a patch of woods out to another field where I could let her run a bit.

I always marveled at the power beneath me when I rode a horse. They were so sturdy and strong. There had been times in my life when I'd preferred the company of horses over people. Many times, in fact. Being tall and chubby as a girl had made me a target. I'd never fit in with the popular girls. Always felt insecure about how I looked, and how my clothes fit. Always a bit of an outsider.

Horses never made me feel self-conscious or inadequate. I'd never lost my cool and babbled nonsense to a horse. Even when I was dealing with a challenging animal, I felt sure of myself.

My parents hadn't exactly been the loving or nurturing types. They were distant, at best, always putting me in someone else's care. Nannies when I was young. Boarding schools when I got older. But the one thing they'd done for me that I would always appreciate was to instill a love of horses. From the horses we'd owned to the coaches and riding classes they'd paid for, they'd given me this. I was grateful for that.

Lola and I walked until we'd crossed through the patch of woods that bordered the ranch. On the other side was a wide-open field. The grass was kept short by grazing, a big expanse of open space where we could bring the horses and really see what they could do.

Using the pressure of my legs, I urged Lola forward. She felt my commands and responded, picking up her pace to a trot. The wind whipped my ponytail as it rushed by. I could feel Lola's tension—her desire to run. I leaned into her stride and let her have it.

As she broke into a gallop, euphoria swept through me, lighting me up. Running this beautiful animal was one of my favorite things. She was so wild. So free. We raced across the field, her hooves pounding into the ground. The rhythm reverberated through my body, exhilaration making me giddy.

We turned in a wide circle. I felt like she needed to open up more, so I urged her on. She went faster, hooves pounding, her powerful muscles flexing.

When she'd seemed to have her fill, I slowed her down to a canter and then eventually a trot. She was warm and sweaty, her nostrils flaring. I breathed deeply, enjoying the high I got from riding.

"Good girl, Lola. How'd that feel?"

We trotted a while longer, then I slowed her to a walk. Her energy felt different—satisfied. She seemed content and happy after a bit of exercise. I rode her back to the stable and got her squared away in her stall. I put her gear away and made sure she had what she needed, then checked on a few of the other horses.

Rob came in, wearing his usual easy smile. "Hey, Amelia. If you're finished up in here, can we chat with you for a bit?"

"Sure." I brushed my hands together while I followed him out. We walked over to the front porch where Gayle had lemonade waiting for us.

I sat at the little round table and Gayle passed me a

glass. Something about the way they looked at each other made me nervous. This felt serious.

"Is everything okay?"

"Yes, everything is fine," Gayle said. "There's just something Rob and I have been talking about and we've decided it's time to discuss it with you."

"All right."

"We aren't getting any younger," she said. "We love what we do here, but it's harder for us to keep up with everything than it was a few years ago."

"I wake up so stiff in the morning it takes me twenty minutes just to get out of bed," Rob said with a laugh.

Gayle gave him a warm smile. "Neither of our children were interested in staying on and working with us. They have their own lives and families. Careers. So as much as we'd have loved to keep the ranch in the family, we've known for a long time that wasn't an option."

"Oh no," I said. "Are you about to tell me you're closing? I hope not because that would be so sad."

"No, nothing like that," she said. "We're not quite ready to throw in the towel. But we have been talking about retirement. We're a year or two away from that at minimum, but we want to plan ahead."

"That's a relief. Planning ahead makes a lot of sense."

"That it does. And that's where you come in," Rob said.

"Oh?"

"We were wondering how you'd feel about taking on more responsibility around here, specifically with an eye for taking over when it's time for us to retire."

"Obviously you haven't been here long," she said. "But you're a natural with the horses. We saw that the first time you came here for a ride. You learn fast, you're smart and educated. We'd teach you everything you need to know and make sure you're ready before we pack it in. But we've been hoping to find someone we trust so we don't have to close, and we think that someone is you."

I stared at them, unable to find words. This was so unexpected, I didn't know what to think. Stay here and take over the ranch? I hadn't even dreamed of that as a possibility. This was just a job to get me by while I... while I what? While I hung out with Cooper in my free time? Was it just an excuse to stay in Echo Creek so I could be near him? Or was it more than that?

"Wow. I'm sorry, I just didn't see this coming. It's amazing, but it's a lot to take in."

"You take your time and think about it," she said. "This is a big decision. We don't need you to give us an answer right now."

"Things will be quiet around here for a few weeks, what with the break in the youth program now that school is starting," he said. "We can take that time to show you more of what it takes to run the ranch, from the business side. That will help you decide if this might be something you'd like to do. No rush."

"I'm so touched that you think I could do this," I said. "I'll definitely think about it."

"Good," she said, her eyes crinkling with her bright smile. "That's all we ask."

I chatted with Gayle and Rob over lemonade, but my thoughts were a whirlwind. When I left, I hoped the drive home would help clear my mind. But as I drove back toward town, my confusion only grew.

Working for the McLaughlins had been a great experience. I loved them, and their ranch was beautiful. The chance to work with horses was practically a dream come true.

But this was so sudden. Taking on a business, even if it was a year or two from now, was a huge responsibility. Was I ready for that kind of commitment? I didn't want to say yes to their offer if I wasn't absolutely sure this was right for me. It wouldn't be fair to them. But if I said no, would they want me to stay? Or would they need to hire someone new in the hopes that they'd find another person who was the right fit?

This was a big, fat reminder that I'd crash-landed in Echo Creek after my wedding went bust, and I'd basically never left. Was this where I was supposed to be—where I wanted to be—or simply where life had dumped me?

It was overwhelming. Things kept happening so fast. Even though they were good things, I couldn't help but feel like I was careening down a winding road and someone else was driving. I needed to get behind the wheel so I could be sure I was going in the right direction.

Right when I pulled into Salishan, my phone rang. Cooper.

"Hey," I said. "I just got back from work."

"Okay. So, Ben fell while he was working on some machinery and had to go to the hospital."

"Oh my god, that's terrible. Did he break anything?"

"I don't think so, but I'm waiting to hear from Roland. Last I heard, they were taking x-rays to be sure, but they didn't think he had any back or neck injuries. That was the big worry."

"How scary."

"No shit."

His voice was subdued. This had really scared him.

"Are you okay?" I asked.

"Yeah. It's been a long day. I need my Cookie. Want to get dinner?"

"I'd love to."

"I need a shower, so I'm going to run home. Is an hour enough time for you? I need like ten minutes, but I know girls need more. I mean, you can skip all the girly shit and come as you are, it's fine with me. But if you want some time, that's cool."

"An hour is great."

"Okay, Cookie. I'll see you in an hour."

TWENTY-SEVEN

AMELIA

COOPER PICKED me up and we went to Ray's for dinner. When the waitress came to take our order, she asked if we wanted something from the breakfast or dinner menus. I blurted out dinner while Cooper said breakfast.

We had a nice dinner—the food was good. Roland called to let Cooper know that Ben was being released from the hospital. No serious injuries, but he'd be bruised and sore. Some of Cooper's tension seemed to ease after that phone call, and I was relieved to hear Ben was going to be okay.

It was still early when we left Ray's, so we decided to go to Mountainside Tavern for a drink. I walked in with my hand clasped in Cooper's and glanced at the bar. I'd been sitting on one of those stools—in my wedding dress—the night we'd met. It seemed so surreal now. So much had changed in such a short time.

We took a seat in a booth opposite the pool tables. Music played, and the hum of conversation filled the air. It was busy—typical for a Friday night. Cooper went to the bar and brought back drinks—a beer for him and a white wine for me.

I hadn't told Cooper about the McLaughlins' offer yet. I was still letting it sink in. But I knew he'd want to know.

"So, Rob and Gayle talked to me today. They're wondering if I might be interested in taking over the ranch in a couple of years so they can retire."

His eyes widened, and a big smile crossed his face. "Seriously?"

I nodded. "Yeah. Isn't that crazy?"

"It's fucking awesome."

"Yeah. It's a little overwhelming."

"If you're worried about whether or not you can handle it, don't be," he said. "I'm totally positive you'd rock this. You're amazing. This is an awesome opportunity."

"Thanks. I told them I'd think about it."

"What's there to think about?" he asked. "Sounds perfect to me."

"I know, I just need to give it some thought. It's a big decision."

"What are you worried about?"

"I don't know, I'm just saying it's a big deal."

"Okay." He took a drink of his beer.

I wanted to change the subject. I felt like if I kept discussing it with Cooper, he'd have me signing a contract with the McLaughlins by the end of the night. Normally I loved his enthusiasm, but I was feeling off-balance, like I was about to get caught in his tornado. I wanted to keep my feet on the ground.

A group of three girls saved me the trouble of coming up with something else to say. They paused as they walked by our table and one smiled at Cooper.

"Hi, Coop. How's it going?" Her eyes darted to me once, then back to him.

I got that familiar ache in my tummy, my blood running hot with jealousy.

"Hey, Emily," Cooper said, his voice nonchalant. "I'm good."

"Cool." She eyed him for a second.

One of her friends rolled her eyes and grabbed her arm. "C'mon, Em."

Emily looked at me again, then back to Cooper. "Well, it was good seeing you. Call me sometime when you're not busy."

"Take care," he said.

As they walked away, Emily's friend leaned in, but I could still hear her. "That was bold. He's not even alone."

"He'll call," Emily said. "Trust me."

Cooper ignored them and went back to his beer.

"Who was that?" I asked.

"Who, her?" He glanced over his shoulder. "Just a girl I used to hang out with sometimes."

She'd given Cooper that look—the same look I'd seen other girls give him. I had a sinking feeling I knew why, and it wasn't simply because she found him attractive.

"When you say she's a girl you used to hang out with, what does that mean? Did you two date? Was she your girlfriend?"

He shrugged. "No, not really. I've never really had a girlfriend. Not like you."

"Wait, what?" There was no way that was true. "You've never? Come on, that can't be right."

"Nope. Well, okay, I dated the same girl in high school for a little while. Maybe six months? I don't remember."

"But you haven't been single since then?"

He opened his mouth, but paused, his eyes intent on my face. "No, not quite that either. I mean, yeah, I've been single mostly. I guess you'd say I've had casual things with girls. Nothing long-term or committed or whatever."

"So she was someone you had a casual thing with?" I asked, gesturing in the direction the girls had gone.

Cooper rubbed the back of his neck. "I mean, yeah, but do you want to talk about all that?"

"Yeah, I kind of do want to talk about it."

I knew Cooper's sexual experience exceeded mine. Of course it did. But by how much? I hadn't given it a lot of thought. I'd assumed he'd had several girlfriends before me. But that wasn't what he was saying.

"What do you want to know?" he asked.

I swallowed hard. "How many?"

"You want to know how many girls I've been with?" He looked away. "Jesus, Cookie. Why?"

"Because I need to know."

He fidgeted, adjusting his hat and moving in his seat. "I don't know."

I stared at him for a long moment. That was not what I'd thought he'd say. "You don't know? How can you not know?"

"Because I didn't put a notch on my headboard every time I was with someone," he said. "I've never kept track."

"But if you don't know, that has to mean it's a lot. Not just a lot, but *a lot*. At what point do you lose track? After ten? Twenty? Fifty? How can it all be so meaningless to you that you don't even know who they were?"

"No, it wasn't like that," he said. "I never hurt anyone. I never meant to, at least. I was honest. I didn't hang out with girls who wanted more from me."

"Then what was it like? I don't understand how that works."

He sighed and looked away again. "I don't know. I was just having a good time. If I met someone who wanted to have a good time with me, then we did. That's all."

"Did you ever sleep with the same girl twice?"

"Sure, if she wanted to."

"But there were so many, you don't remember."

"Yeah, but it's not a big deal. That's not who I am anymore."

"Well, it feels like a big deal to me. I didn't realize. I mean, this is a huge thing about you that I didn't know. I guess I should have figured it out, it's pretty obvious now and I feel kind of stupid for not getting it. That's why you were so easy to pick up in the bar the night we met. You did that all the time. I wasn't anything special, just your fun for the night."

"Cookie, no."

My cheeks were hot, and I fanned myself with my hand. "I'm feeling really out of control and confused. This is a lot to process."

He sat back and tapped the table with his fingertips. "I'm sorry this is overwhelming. I didn't think it was a big thing. What do you want me to say about the night we met? That within five minutes of knowing you, I'd already realized you were different? You wanted me, remember?"

"I know, and that's not what I mean. You didn't know we'd be together this long when we met, and neither did I. I didn't know anything, and that's the problem. I still feel like that. I have to make all these big decisions, but now I'm sitting here wondering what else I don't know about you."

He was practically squirming in his chair, his face angled away, like he didn't want to look me in the eyes.

"I feel like I'm on a roller coaster," I said. "Bob and Gayle are thinking about retirement, and you're talking about building a house and settling down, and there are all these girls, and I need to figure this out."

"Figure what out?"

"My life. Only a couple of months ago I thought I was getting married. You have to understand, that was a whirlwind, too. Griffin proposed, and our parents sprang into action. Before I knew it, there was a date, and a venue and a dress and flowers, and I hadn't chosen any of it. They'd just told me what was happening. I swear, it was like they knew Griffin was going to mess it up, so they were in a rush to get us married. And then that blew up, and I'm glad it did, but nothing has slowed down since then. I stayed here and the next thing I knew, I had a job and a boyfriend. A boyfriend who knows what he wants and where he wants to be. You don't have any doubts about where you're supposed to end up. And I love that for you, but I don't know if all this is what I want, or just what's fallen into my lap. I don't want to wake up one day and realize I never made any of the choices that got me to where I am."

"What are you saying?"

I took a deep breath. "I just need a little time alone. Can you take me home?"

"Sure, yeah."

We got up and went out to his truck. My thoughts were in total chaos. I couldn't get my head wrapped around everything. Cooper was upset—I could see it in his eyes—and the last thing I wanted to do was hurt him. But it was so hard to think clearly when he was around. I needed some quiet—some space to get my head together.

He dropped me off and I went inside. Looked around at

the blackberry curtains and throw pillows. It was all so cute, but none of it was mine. Did I really belong here? When had my Cooper-moon turned into so much more? Was I ready for any of this?

I really didn't know.

TWENTY-EIGHT

COOPER

I SPENT the night moving from my bedroom floor to the couch to the deck chair. I couldn't sleep anywhere. I didn't sleep well at home under the best of circumstances, but after last night, my brain wouldn't shut off.

I was losing Amelia. I'd felt it in the bar when we left. Felt her slipping away, inch by inch, as I drove her home. By the time I'd dropped her off at Salishan, the gap between us felt huge. And I had no idea what to do about it.

Eventually I gave up on sleep. I went out to the south vineyard in the pre-dawn haze, just to walk. Up and down the rows of vines, moving my legs. Unable to keep still, even for a second. Despite the lack of sleep, my body was buzzing with energy. Waiting for Amelia to text me. Dreading what she was going to say.

She finally did, asking me if I'd come over. I replied that I'd be there soon.

With my heart in my throat and too much adrenaline coursing through my veins, I went to the Blackberry Cottage.

"Hi," Amelia said when she opened the door. She stepped aside. "Come in."

I wanted to do what I always did. Grab her and pick her up. Spin her around and kiss her all the way down. But everything about her body language told me not to. She was distant and closed off—a *no* vibe if I'd ever seen one. So I respected her space and shoved my hands in my pockets so they'd behave.

"I need to talk to you," she said.

"Okay, sure."

"Do you want to sit down?"

I shook my head. Sitting down wasn't an option.

"Okay." She tucked her hair behind her ear. "I was up all night thinking about everything. Not just you. Everything in my life. Living here and working at the ranch. And I decided I need to do what I'd planned to do in the first place. I need to go stay with Daphne in L.A. for a while."

Her words punched me in the gut. I kept my eyes locked on the floor and resisted the urge to grab my stomach and gasp for breath. "Why?"

"I need to figure out my life. And I can't do it here."

"What is there to figure out? If you like it here, and you like me, then why would you go?"

"Because I've spent my entire life letting things happen to me. Letting other people make my decisions."

"You're not letting anyone make your decisions now, are you?"

"No, but I didn't mean to wind up here, either. It just sort of happened. Ever since Griffin proposed, it's like my life has been on fast forward. And all I've been doing is trying to keep up. I haven't ever stopped to ask myself what I want. One minute I was studying for midterms, thinking about what I was going to do after graduation. And then the next, I was engaged to a guy I'd had a crush on since I was thirteen. Then it felt like I blinked and I was standing behind all those guests in a dress I hated, realizing it had all been a lie. So I wasn't getting married at all, and then I was sitting in a bar with a hot guy, deciding to be reckless. Now, here I am, a whirlwind of changes later, and I'm wondering how I got here. I'm facing all these huge decisions about my life and I don't even know where to begin."

She paused, like she was waiting for me to reply, but I couldn't.

"You have a home and a future here. You're sure about it, and I think that's great. But you also have a past that's going to haunt any woman who's with you."

"Jesus, Cookie, my past doesn't have anything to do with you."

"Maybe not, but we can't go anywhere in this town without running into someone you've slept with."

"That's not true."

"Close enough. That's a lot to ask a girl to deal with, Cooper, especially so soon."

I shoved my hands deeper in my pockets. I didn't know what to say to that.

"I don't know what I want right now. And honestly, I'm scared. I'm scared out of my mind. I want to do what's right for me, and I'm afraid I don't know how." She stopped and took a deep breath, like she was trying to stop herself from babbling. "I'm not asking you to wait. I can't do that to you. It wouldn't be fair to make you sit around here while I figure things out."

"So what are you saying?"

"I'm saying I'm going to go. And I don't know what comes next or what's going to happen. But you're free to do what you want."

I stared at her, willing her to keep talking. To get to the punch line. To the part where she told me she'd thought that leaving was best, but she'd changed her mind because she couldn't leave me.

But she didn't.

"You're breaking up with me, aren't you?"

Her eyes glistened with tears as she nodded. "I'm sorry, Cooper. I care about you so much and I don't want to hurt you. But things have been moving so fast. Being with you feels so good, but it's like the good you feel when you're going down the drop on a huge roller coaster. It's exhilarating. But I have to stop. I have to get off the ride so I can figure out my life."

"Is this because of those girls last night? I know that freaked you out, but honestly, Cookie, you don't have anything to worry about."

"Maybe not now, but how long am I going to be fun for you? If you just move from girl to girl, from one fun thing to the next, what happens when I'm not fun anymore? Where's that going to leave me? When things seem too good to be true, that usually means they are. And it definitely seems too good to be true that you'd suddenly decide to change for me. I've been down that road, and I ended up dumped on my wedding day."

"So that's it? You have one bad experience with a shitbag of a guy, and I have to pay for it?"

"No, I just have to face reality. If I'm going to settle down somewhere, it needs to be because I choose to. For *me*. Not because I stumbled into it and stayed for a guy who may or may not be around in a few months. I don't want to be one of those girls you run into and blow off with a chin tip, like you never cared."

I couldn't stand still anymore. Raking my hands through

my hair, I started pacing. "Fuck, Amelia. That's not what you are to me. Is that what you think? I'm just fucking around, like you're my latest toy?"

"I don't know. That's certainly how it started. And that's all any other girl has ever been to you. What am I supposed to do with that? Base my future on it? That's what I'm trying to tell you. I need to decide what I'm doing with my life, not just run around having fun with you until the fun wears off and I'm left all alone wondering what happened."

"That's not going to happen," I said. "I wouldn't do that to you. You're not one of those girls, and you never will be."

She looked at me with sad eyes filled with tears. "Maybe not. I hope you won't think of me like that."

For a second, I held back. I didn't want to steamroll over her with my Cooper-ness. But then the dam broke.

"Fuck this. No. I'm not going to get tired of you, and I'm not going to leave you. You're not just some girl to me. You're everything. I fucking love you and I've wanted to say it a million times and didn't, mostly because people kept telling me to slow down. But I don't know how to slow down. I'm terrible at it. I don't want to slow down. I want you all the time. I want you to move in with me and help me plan the house I want to build for us. I want you to take the job with the McLaughlins because it's awesome and perfect and it means you'll stay. I know I've been with a lot of girls before you, but that doesn't mean I can't change. People can change if they want to. And I do. I have."

She covered her mouth with her hand, tears starting to spill. "Cooper, don't."

"No, you have to listen. We're fucking awesome together. Don't overthink it."

"Just have fun?"

"Yes. I mean, no. It's not just fun. Fuck, I'm terrible at this too. I didn't think I was terrible at anything. This will work, Cookie. If you're worried about—"

"Cooper, stop."

I quit talking mid-sentence.

"I have to do this. I can't think when I'm with you. It's like my brain turns to mush. And right now, I'm confused and so overwhelmed. I have to get off the roller coaster."

Holy fuck. She really was leaving.

I staggered backward a few steps, feeling like my chest had caved in. "So you're... when?"

"Today."

I nodded because what else could I do? She was leaving because she had to, and there was even a part of me that understood. I hated it, but I understood.

"Will you text me when you get there?"

"Yes."

I nodded again, then went for the door. The walls were closing in, ready to crush me. I had to get outside. This was all too much. I couldn't handle all these fucking feelings. They were too big.

THE DAY WENT by in a blur. I walked out to the north vineyard—the farthest from the main grounds. Didn't even take the utility vehicle. Just my legs. I wandered through my grapes, trying to get calm. Slow down. But I couldn't. My brain was on fire, my blood coursing with adrenaline. By the time I came back, I was exhausted, dehydrated, and hungry.

And still pretty fucking broken.

I had an unanswered text from my mom, inviting me

and Amelia over to the house for dinner. I didn't reply, just walked over there on aching feet.

My family was gathered around Mom's dinner table when I stumbled in the door. Roland and Zoe with baby Hudson sleeping in Zoe's arms. Brynncess and Chase, snuggled up close on the bench. Leo, with his hair hanging over his face. Mom with her hair pulled back and a glass of wine in her hand. And two empty place settings. One for me, and one for my Cookie.

Who wasn't my Cookie anymore.

I was pretty sure I was going to die. I staggered toward the couch but didn't make it that far. Clutching my chest, I collapsed onto the ground.

"Cooper!" Mom was at my side in an instant. She knelt beside me and touched my forehead. "Cooper, what happened? Are you hurt?"

"I think I'm dying." It felt like my heart had stopped beating. I couldn't have much time left. "I'm sorry, Mom. I'm the one who broke Grandma's tea pot. The one with the blue flowers on it. I let Leo take the blame, but you should know the truth before I go."

"I knew it was you," Leo said.

"Didn't that happen when you were like ten?" Brynn asked.

Mom brushed my hair back from my forehead. "Cooper, what's wrong?"

I dug my fingers into my chest. Fuck, it hurt so much. "I'm dying."

"Why are you dying?"

"Mom, will you stop indulging him?" Roland said. "This is just like that time we went to Disneyland and had to leave early because Leo got sick."

"Am I ever going to live that down?" Leo asked. "It wasn't my fault I got strep throat."

"I know, I'm just saying, Cooper lost it."

Mom shook her head. "Cooper, honey, if there's really something wrong, tell me. If not, come have some dinner."

"Amelia left. She broke up with me and she left."

The hint of humor in her expression disappeared and the room went silent.

"Oh honey," she said.

I closed my eyes. Saying it out loud hurt a million times more than just thinking it. It made it real.

"Do you want to talk about it?" she asked.

"No. Yes. I don't know."

"Why don't you at least get up on the couch," she said.

I draped my arm over my forehead, but didn't answer. I wasn't ready to move yet. A few seconds later, I heard footsteps, then felt something next to me. I blinked my eyes open to find Chase lying on the floor beside me.

"Hey, bro."

"Hey."

"What are they doing?" Roland asked.

"Shh, just let Chase help," Zoe said. "He speaks Cooper."

"Do you need CPR?" Chase asked. "I'll do it if I have to, but it's going to make your sister really jealous and probably make the rest of your family wonder if the gay rumors are true."

"You do still live with me," I said. "It's very suspicious."

"That's what I'm saying. So I'm hoping you don't need CPR. Zoe would take a video and once something's on the internet, it's forever."

"He's right, I would," Zoe said. "Actually, do it, Chase. I'd pay to see that."

I lifted my head slightly. I wanted to make a snappy comeback, but I didn't have it in me, so I let my head drop back to the floor.

Zoe handed Huddy to Roland and came over to lie down on my other side. I had to admit, having two of my favorites lying on the floor with me kind of helped. It wasn't going to heal the gaping hole in my chest where my heart used to be, but it made me feel a little bit better.

"God, this family is so weird," Leo muttered.

"What happened, goofball?" Zoe asked. "Are we sure this is a real crisis, or a Cooper crisis?"

"It's real. She broke up with me and went to live with her bestie in L.A."

"No shit?" Chase asked. "She's gone?"

"Left today."

Zoe clasped my hand and squeezed. "I'm sorry, Coop. Did she say why?"

"Because I'm a slut."

Someone spit out whatever they'd been drinking—either Roland or Leo. Or maybe Brynn. I wasn't sure.

"Because *what*?" Zoe asked.

"That's not the only reason. She's overwhelmed, and things were moving fast, which yeah, I get that. It wasn't that long ago that she almost got married, and she just kind of stayed here with me because I kept talking her into it. She was supposed to go to L.A. to figure out her life right after her wedding didn't happen, and I didn't want her to, so I convinced her to stay for a Cooper-moon, but I guess maybe I should have let her go because now she's confused about what she wants and she can't think when I'm around because I'm like a roller coaster."

"It sucks, man, but it's all pretty understandable, if you think about it," Chase said.

"You understood all that?" Leo asked.

People kept talking, but I stopped listening. My mind suddenly cleared, a single thought overwhelming everything else. I jumped up and ran out the door, leaving their questions behind.

I couldn't fix things with Amelia. Not tonight, at least. I didn't know if there was anything I could do to change her mind. But there was one thing I could do, and should have done a long time ago. And no one was stopping me this time.

CHASE AND BRYNN followed me back to our apartment, but didn't say a word as I stripped my mattress bare. Silently, Chase helped me load it into my truck. He bearhugged me before I got in, then stood in the parking lot, watching me leave. I hadn't asked him to come, and because Chase knew me better than anyone, he didn't follow. He knew this wasn't a party. This was something I had to do, and I wanted to do it alone.

I hauled the mattress out to where we'd had our other bonfires. Propped it up and splashed some gas on it. Then I stepped back and tossed a lit match. Watched it go up in flames.

The fire caught quickly. I pulled up a folding chair and sat, staring into the flames. Sparks blew into the night air, winking out against the backdrop of the darkening sky.

This was it. Amelia was gone, and I had no idea if she was ever coming back. There was a part of me that wanted to book a flight to L.A., get my ass down there, and drag her back with me. Make her see that she should be here. That yes, maybe things had moved fast, but fast wasn't bad. Fast was fun, and if *I* knew we were perfect for each other, and nothing else mattered, how could she not see it too?

But I knew that was the wrong thing to do. I hadn't been sure about holding back with her—about waiting to burn this stupid mattress, or slowing down so I didn't scare her off. Those things had made some sense at the time, but I hadn't been totally on board. This, I knew. I knew it deep down in my gut. I couldn't Cooper my way through this. Couldn't burst in on her like the tornado I was and sweep her off to live the life I wanted for her.

She had to make that call. She had to decide. Which meant I had to wait. And waiting was the worst.

Footsteps approached behind me.

"Hey, Coop."

I looked up to find Ben holding a six-pack. "Are you supposed to be up?"

He dragged a chair next to me and gingerly lowered himself down. "Yeah, it's all right. I'm sore as hell, and the doctors told me to take it easy. But I'm okay."

"How did you know I was out here?"

"Saw the smoke from my place," he said. Ben's house was up the side of the mountain, not far from here. The views from his place were incredible. He opened a beer and handed it to me. "Figured I'd join you. But I didn't think you'd be alone."

I took a long pull of my beer. "Yeah. My life fucking fell apart today."

"That bad?"

"Amelia broke up with me and left."

It seemed like my words echoed against the night, bouncing back to reverberate in my head. I wasn't as manic as I'd been at my mom's house. The frenetic energy coursing through me had been replaced by a hollow ache. This fucking hurt, and it hurt *deep*.

"I'm sorry to hear that."

We sat in silence for a few minutes, drinking our beers. My head buzzed from the alcohol almost immediately. I hadn't eaten anything all day.

Ben put his beer down. "Can I ask you something?"

"Sure."

"Why burn the mattress?"

It was a good question. If she was gone, why bother? Why not just go out and get drunk and forget about her? Pick up some girl and lose myself between her legs. Maybe I should just say fuck it and be the guy Amelia was afraid I was.

But I wasn't that guy anymore.

I wasn't going to try to be someone else—I couldn't stop being whatever it was that made me Cooper Miles—but I was ready to say goodbye to that part of my life. Forever. The thought of casual sex with someone I didn't care about sounded fucking awful. Which was weird, but also not surprising. Now that I'd experienced love, nothing else would ever be enough.

And I wouldn't do that to Amelia. She might have left me, but my heart was still hers.

"Because it's time."

"Good," Ben said. "I'm proud of you."

"Thanks."

"What happened?"

I took another drink, then explained as best as I could, in slower, more coherent sentences than when I'd babbled about it at my mom's. Ben listened, nodding occasionally. When I finished, he handed me another beer.

"I think you're doing the right thing," he said. "I know

you're probably itching to go down there and toss her over your shoulder like a caveman."

"Fuck, man, you have no idea. I almost bought a plane ticket like five times today. I'm still having to talk myself out of it."

"It's not always easy to know the right thing to do. Sometimes we just have to do our best and hope things work out."

"Yeah, I guess so. I just wonder if I already played my part in her life. Maybe all she needed me to be was the fun guy who helped her get through a rough time."

"Maybe."

"You know what's messed up? I don't regret it. If that's what she needed, I'm glad it was me. I'm glad I could do that for her, even if I didn't get to keep her." My voice broke on the last word and a single tear slipped down my cheek. I cleared my throat and swiped the tear away with the back of my hand before Ben could see it. If he noticed, he didn't say anything.

"I think that's what love is," he said after a moment. "It's wanting the other person to be happy, no matter what it costs you."

Something in his voice cut through my self-pity. He wasn't just talking about me.

I blurted out the question before I could hold the words back. "Are you in love with my mom?"

Ben froze, his entire body going still, his beer halfway to his mouth. Very slowly, he turned to look at me. "Do I need to worry about what you'll do if I say yes?"

"No." I set my bottle down in the dirt, screwing it a few turns so it wouldn't tip over. "Guess I can't blame you for asking that after how much of a dick I was to Chase. I'm not proud of that."

"I know you're not."

"So are you?"

He took a deep breath. "Yes."

The word hung in the air between us, silently echoing into the night.

"Awesome," I said, my voice soft.

"I don't know if it is."

"Why not?" I twisted in my chair to look at him. "My dad's been gone for a year and a half. It was over between them years ago, she just needed the courage to get rid of the fucker."

"I know. Believe me, I'm well of aware of every day that's passed since she told him to leave."

"Then why not make a move?"

"Our clocks aren't in sync, Coop," he said. "Until the divorce goes through, she's still married."

"Only technically," I said. "And only because my father's an asshole. It should have been done a long time ago."

"I know it should, but I have to live with what is, not what should have been. A lot of things should have been different, as far as I'm concerned. She should have left him years ago, but she didn't."

"You've always loved her, haven't you?" I asked. It was occurring to me that I was either much dumber than I'd ever thought, or I was blind. Had Ben stayed at Salishan all these years because of my mom?

He took a drink of his beer and stared into the fire in silence for a long moment before answering. "Yes. I have loved her for a very, very long time."

"Shit, man."

"Shit is right," he said.

The heat of the fire beat at me and I scooted my chair back so it wouldn't singe my leg hair. "You should tell her."

He shook his head. "Maybe someday, if the timing is right. But I don't know if it'll matter. I don't know if she'd ever love me back."

I wanted to tell him that of course she would. It's what I would have blurted out, once. Because Ben was fucking awesome, and what woman wouldn't love him? But I'd learned that sometimes love was a lot more complicated than that.

"I guess I can't answer that for her. But I'll tell you one thing." I looked him straight in the eyes. "When you decide the timing is right, I'll have your back. We all will, man. You won't have any resistance from us. That I can tell you for sure."

He smiled, but even in the low light, I could see the sadness in his eyes. "Thanks, Coop. I appreciate that."

"Love sucks," I said. "I want to say that things were better before, but that's the weirdest part. I can't even say that. I feel like shit right now, and I still wouldn't trade it all in. I still wouldn't go back to how things were before her. Jesus, Ben, even if she never comes back, I don't think I'll regret it. Is that normal?"

"Yeah, it's probably normal."

"Fuck."

"I'm clearly no expert," he said. "But I think that if things are going to work out with you two, this is what you both need. This is how you sync up your clocks."

"So you're saying if she decides to come back, it'll be because she's ready?"

"Yep. And if she doesn't, it's for the best. For both of you. Because it'll mean it wouldn't ever have been right."

I crossed my arms, scowling. I didn't want him to be right about that. "I guess."

"I remember hearing your mom say once that raising you was like trying to contain a river. The water's going to flow no matter what. The best you can do is give it a little guidance here and there and hope it doesn't sweep you out to sea."

"Sounds like something Mom would say."

"Yeah. My biggest worry for you—aside from the obvious fear you'd father a pack of illegitimate children—has always been that you'd wind up with someone who tried to dam the river."

I nodded and rubbed the back of my neck. Somewhere in the back of my mind, I'd always been afraid of that too.

"Amelia didn't. She rode that river like she already knew every ebb and flow. Sometimes she probably had to hold on for dear life, but that's life on the water for you. It scared her a bit. But you don't have that kind of connection with someone, that fast, and not have it touch your soul. If I was a betting man, I'd say you touched hers, and you touched it deep down."

I rubbed my chest again, wondering if I'd ever get rid of this ache. This emptiness. Fuck, this hurt. "So what do I do? Wait?"

"Yep. You wait."

"Fuck. I hate waiting."

"So do I, Cooper. So do I."

I picked up my beer and finished it off. Then we had another while the mattress burned down. I was pretty fucking drunk by the time the fire was down to coals. Drinking on an empty stomach would do that to a guy.

"You want to crash at my place tonight, or should I take you to your mom's?" Ben asked.

"I can't go home, can I? I don't have a fucking bed." I laughed my ass off at that, even though it wasn't all that funny. "I'm fine. Mom's. Whatever."

I stood and stumbled to the side. Ben steadied me with a hand on my arm. "Careful, there."

"I got it, I got it. Maybe I'll just sleep right here."

My knees started to buckle, but Ben held my arm tight. "Come on, big guy. My truck's over here. Let's get you to bed."

"I probably should have eaten today."

He chuckled as we walked, his hand still on my arm. "Yeah, you probably should have."

Chase was on Mom's front porch. I didn't know if he'd been waiting for me, or if he was just randomly hanging out at my mom's house.

"I've got him," Chase said, draping one of my arms around his shoulders. "Thanks, Ben."

"Night, Chase."

"Chasey, you do love me," I said.

"Yep. Come on, keep your feet moving. You're fucking heavy, dude."

He dumped me in one of the extra beds, then made me drink a glass of water before he'd let me sleep. I reached for my phone to text Amelia—maybe all that stuff about waiting and giving her space was bullshit—but someone had taken my phone. Assholes.

But they weren't really. I'd never felt worse in my entire life—not even the time we had to leave Disneyland early— but at least my people had my back. I passed out, my head swimming, my heart cold and empty, my thoughts on Amelia.

THIRTY

AMELIA

L.A. WAS HOT, the air hazy with smog. I sat in one of the little bistro chairs on the tiny concrete patio outside Daphne and Harrison's apartment, fanning myself with a magazine. Staring at the dingy morning sky.

Their apartment was small, but Daphne had made it adorable. She'd hung framed album covers by their favorite bands next to cute things she'd picked up at farmer's markets. It was colorful and sweet with a little edge, just like Daphne.

She came out and handed me an iced tea before taking the other seat. "I'm off this afternoon. Maybe we should go get our nails done. It might cheer you up."

I spread my fingers, looking at my chipping nail polish. "Yeah, that would be nice."

I'd been here for four days, and things were certainly quieter than they had been at Salishan. Harrison was busy recording all day, and Daphne worked afternoons and evenings at a local bar. It had given me a lot of time to myself to think.

But I was miserable.

I missed the fresh mountain air. The way the sun slid down behind the peaks in the evening. I missed the bees buzzing around all the flowers Cooper had planted for his sister outside the cottage. The pine trees and fields of grass. I missed Rob and Gayle and the horses. I'd asked for some time to consider their offer, and they'd been so gracious about it.

More than anything else, I missed Cooper.

I missed him so much I ached with the pain of it. I kept wondering if that feeling would start to fade. If the distance between us would ease his hold on my heart. If he didn't come bursting in through the door, a huge smile on his face, maybe I wouldn't need him so much. Maybe my head would clear, and I'd know what I was supposed to do.

But all the distance did was hurt.

"I almost hate to ask this, but have you talked to your parents?" Daphne asked.

"Yeah, I called. They're on vacation in Hawaii. Honestly, I don't know what to think about my conversation with them."

"What happened?"

"Well, you know that tongue clicking thing my mom does when she's irritated? She did it the entire time I explained where I was. And then Dad asked about a transfer that was made to my trust fund the day of my wedding."

Daphne laughed. "The honeymoon money?"

"Yeah. I told him what it was. Mom started to gripe about it, but Dad actually laughed. I can't remember the last time I heard the man laugh."

"I don't think I've ever heard him laugh."

"It doesn't happen very often. Anyway, he asked me why I hadn't made any withdrawals from the trust and wanted to know if I needed the account number again. First, I said I thought they cut me off. He tried to backpedal and say he hadn't meant it. Then I said I thought I had to be married to have access to it, and I'm not married, so..."

"Is that really a thing?"

"Yeah, it's called a conditional trust. I guess the point is to make sure your kid is a responsible adult before you give them access to a bunch of money. I don't know how marriage is supposed to guarantee someone is a responsible adult, but whatever."

"Rich people are so weird."

"I know. Anyway, he asked me where I ever got that idea, and I said Mom told me, and then they both got really quiet."

Daphne's eyes widened. "Oh my god. Are you telling me your mom lied to you about your trust fund?"

I nodded. "She did. Around the time we graduated high school, she told me that they had a trust fund set up for me and they'd use some of it to pay for college. And she distinctly said that I'd have access to the balance after I got married. But apparently marriage wasn't one of the conditions. Graduating from college was."

"So you have it now? How much is it? No, you don't have to tell me, we never talk about money. Actually, please tell me, I'm dying to know."

"It's just over five million dollars."

"What the fuck?"

"I know. It's so weird. I was always grateful they paid for my college and everything, but that money has never felt like it belonged to me. I didn't earn it."

"No, you're just a lucky bitch."

"Yeah, in some ways. I mean, my parents aren't evil or

anything, but my mom is horribly critical, and they encouraged me to marry a jackass to further their social standing."

"True. And they basically missed out on your entire childhood because they paid other people to raise you."

"Yep."

"That's actually really shitty. I wouldn't trade my family for five million dollars. I'm sorry, sweetie."

"It's okay. There's nothing to be sorry about. My parents are who they are. My mom knows how to push all my buttons, and we're never going to be close. It's just something I have to learn to accept."

"Is she still mad at you for walking out on dinner when they surprised you with the Wentworths?"

"She still mentions it every time we talk, like it's this big crisis. She's paranoid the Wentworths are holding a grudge, even though I sent her screenshots of the very nice text Mrs. Wentworth sent me to show they weren't insulted."

She shook her head. "Your mom is something else."

"Yeah."

"So I guess... yay that you're rich now?"

"It's weird, isn't it? I should be super happy about this. I can do anything I want now. I know I grew up super privileged, and this is an advantage so few people will ever get. But it's not making me happy. It's just adding to the pressure to make the right life choices. Like I can't squander this."

"You won't. You've never been like that. Honestly, it's a lot of why we became friends. You were never like those other rich kids. You didn't expect things in life, and you've always been grateful for the good things you have. I love that about you."

"Thanks. I could do some good with the money. That's what I really want." My thoughts kept straying to the

McLaughlins' ranch. To the improvements I could make. Build a bigger stable. Make room for rescue horses.

"Of course you will. By the way, in case I haven't said this already, you can stay here as long as you want. I know we're a little tight on living space, but Harrison and I are both so busy, we're hardly ever here. I guess you can afford a swanky hotel or something, but sometimes a girl needs her BFF."

"Thanks, Daph. I appreciate that."

"You're welcome. And, you know, if you want to use your suddenly improved financial status to spring for takeout once in a while, we won't say no." She winked at me.

I laughed. "That's all you want? You're a cheap date."

"I really am."

I put the magazine down and stood. My body was restless with too much pent-up energy. There wasn't much room to move, but I paced around the patio.

"I miss him, Daphne. I know you don't want to hear me say that, but I do."

"Of course you do. It's only been a few days. But you did the right thing. You need to get your head on straight."

"Yeah, I know I do. But I feel so terrible."

"Don't feel guilty for taking time for you, sweetie."

I kept pacing and Daphne's eyes followed me as I walked back and forth. "But this isn't just *taking time*. I broke up with him. I basically murdered his soul."

"No, you didn't. Now you're being dramatic."

"You weren't there. You didn't see the look on his face. Cooper is always happy. He's wild and crazy and funny. And I stripped that all away. He looked like a lost puppy stuck outside in the rain."

I hated that I'd hurt him. That wasn't what I'd wanted

to do. I'd just needed things to slow down, to get my feet on the ground. And asking him to wait for me would have been selfish and bratty. Cooper was... Cooper. I doubted he ever went very long without a girl in his life in some capacity. Maybe he had already hooked up with one of those girls we'd run into. The thought made me sick to my stomach.

"Would it have been better if you'd stayed? Come on, Amelia, you're twenty-two. You graduated college a few months ago, and you just found out you have enough money to do basically whatever you want. The entire world is at your feet. Don't get hung up on some guy."

"He's not *some guy*."

"Isn't he, though? You picked him up in a bar to have crazy sex the night you got dumped."

"I know that's how it started, but he's not just some random guy I had sex with. Although, god Daphne, I suddenly understand the existence of the entire sex toy industry. It's only been a few days, and I'm crawling out of my skin. How do you deal with it when you have to be away from Harrison for more than like eight hours?"

"Hours?" She blinked at me a few times, her face clouded with confusion. "We don't like being apart, but when we have to, we just deal with it. See, this is what I'm worried about with you. I'm sure it's great for him to have such an amazing dick that you're craving it after a few days, but that's not the basis for a long-term relationship."

I took my hair in my hands and twisted it up on my head to get it off my neck. "But that's the thing, I'm not just craving his dick. It's amazing, but it's not just that. I couldn't fix this feeling by going out and banging some other guy, no matter what kind of dick he had."

"You sure? Harrison has this friend—"

"No," I snapped. "No, that's not what I need. Not even a little bit."

"Look, I'm not suggesting you need to go ho it up to get over Cooper. I'm just saying, you're going to meet other guys."

My shoulders slumped, and I let my hair drop. "I don't want to meet other guys."

And that was the truth. My body craved release, but it wasn't just sex I wanted. It wasn't Cooper's man parts—impressive as they were—that made me hot for him. I was craving *him*. All of him. His smile and the way his face lit up whenever he saw me. His arms around me, lifting me off my feet. His crazy ideas, and the way he made me feel so free.

The way he understood me, even when I talked too fast, or babbled nonsense. He never made fun of me or made me feel invisible. With him, I'd felt wanted. Needed.

I was starting to wonder what had been so bad about being on the roller coaster.

"Oh my god, Amelia, I love you, but will you sit down? You haven't stopped moving for more than five minutes since you got here."

"Sorry, I'm just restless." I sat back down and took a sip of iced tea. "Daphne, what would Harrison say if you bought him a dick costume?"

"A what?"

"A dick costume."

She looked at me like I was crazy. "Is that a real thing?"

"Yeah. Like a little outfit to dress it up, just for fun."

"Um, I think he'd ask what was wrong with me."

I blew out a breath. I couldn't imagine having the courage to explore and play with anyone else the way I did with Cooper. He didn't care about what other people thought, or what was expected. He didn't do things because you were supposed to. He lived life on his own terms. That was part of his chaos, but so much of his charm. He'd made life fun.

But I felt like I'd done everything wrong. I'd slept with Cooper before I even knew him—gave my virginity to a stranger. And then stayed, because staying had been a lot more fun than facing reality. But then my Cooper-moon had turned into something else. And I hadn't been prepared.

"Cooper told me he loved me," I said, my voice quiet.

"Whoa. Wait, are you serious? You didn't tell me that part. When?"

"When I told him I was leaving. He said he'd wanted to tell me a million times, but he'd been holding back so he wouldn't scare me away."

"Do you think he meant it?" she asked, her voice suddenly quiet too.

I met her eyes and nodded.

"Holy shit, Amelia. Do you love him back?"

My heartbeat sped up, blood rushing to my cheeks. I opened my mouth to answer when my phone rang. My eyes darted to the screen and I gasped, putting a hand on my chest. It was Brynn.

Grabbing the phone, I fumbled it, almost letting it drop to the concrete patio. It bounced between my hands and I flew out of my chair as soon as I had a grip on it. I swiped to answer.

"Hello?"

"Amelia?" Brynn asked. "I'm so sorry to bug you, but we have a situation up here."

THIRTY-ONE
COOPER

I WAS UP BEFORE SUNRISE, after tossing and turning all night. In an effort to get some rest, I'd bought a blow-up air mattress and a new sleeping bag. But I was still too restless. The sleep deprivation probably wasn't good for me, but there didn't seem to be anything I could do about it. I'd tried sleeping at my mom's. Beneath the stars in the south vineyard. I'd even spent a night on Roland and Zoe's couch, but ended up walking a fussy Hudson around the house so they could sleep, since I'd been awake anyway.

With the sky still full of stars, I left home and went over to the winery. The grounds were silent, only a slight breeze whispering in the air. I took one of the utility vehicles out to my vineyards. I needed the solace of my plants, the grounding my family's land gave me. I didn't have anything else left cling to.

The other utility vehicle was parked on the outskirts of the south vineyard. There was only one person who'd be out here at this time of night. Leo.

I found him sitting on the ground near the edge of the vineyard, looking out over the hills. He was only about five feet away from the edge of our property. An old fence, its wood weathered gray, marked the boundary on this side. Beyond were several acres of unused land—what had once been a pear orchard, but had fallen into disuse. Tall grasses grew between the trunks of the pear trees, and blackberries crept in toward the fence.

It wasn't the fence that kept Leo inside. Nor was it the creek or the mountain range or the trees. Whatever plagued Leo lived in his mind and body. He'd brought it back with him when he'd been discharged, and so far, he hadn't conquered it.

"Morning." I sat on the ground next to him.

"Is it?"

"Almost. Are you up early, or late?"

"Late," he said. "Haven't slept yet."

"I didn't either."

We sat in silence for a while, the chilly air making my skin prickle. I wanted to say something to make things right with my brother, but for once I was at a loss for words. I'd done damage to my family and as hard as I'd been trying to fix it, I didn't know if it would be enough.

This land meant everything to me, but it meant *more* than everything to Leo. He couldn't leave. If something forced him, I didn't know what would happen. How he would handle it. *If* he could handle it. Although maybe I just wasn't giving him enough credit.

"I don't want to talk about it," he said out of the blue.

"About what?"

He nodded toward the fence. "You're wondering if I could climb over the fence. Step outside."

I had been wondering that. "Yeah."

"I don't know."

"I'll do it with you," I said. "When you're ready, I mean.

I'm not saying it has to be now. But when the time comes, I'll be there if you want me to be. Even if it's one step."

"Thanks, Coop." He stood and brushed the dirt off his jeans. "I'm going to go get a few hours of sleep. Do you want to come over and work out later?"

I grinned a little, the first time I'd smiled since Amelia had left. "Yeah, I need it."

"Me too. I'll see you later."

Leo left and I sat on the cold ground for a while, watching the sky turn pink and orange with the sunrise. My chest still ached from missing Amelia—I didn't think that was ever going to go away—but at least Leo and I were cool.

Despite everything, I still had work to do. We were days away from harvest, so I focused on work. I lost myself in being busy. Pushed away my thoughts of Amelia, and what she was doing. Tried not to worry about her or wonder if she was okay.

But I wondered, in the back of my mind, if she was missing me too.

I drove in from the fields for an early lunch. But when I got there, I noticed two county sheriff's cars parked outside the Big House.

A spike of adrenaline hit me. Something was wrong. I broke into a run, fear coursing through my body. Why were police here? What did they want?

I was pretty sure I knew the answer.

The handful of guests in the lobby turned to look when I burst in through the front door. Lindsey, one of our employees, stood behind the counter, her expression worried. She flicked her eyes upstairs.

I took the stairs two at a time. Roland came out of one of the offices, his face dark with anger. I was about to ask what the fuck was happening when two deputies came out, one on either side of my mom.

The one on the left held Mom's arm, leading her toward the stairs. I gaped at them, momentarily frozen. Mom met my eyes, her forehead creased with worry.

"Don't, Cooper," she said. "It's going to be fine."

"No," I said. "No, no, no, you can't take her."

"Roland, get him," she said.

In an instant, Roland stood in front of me, his hand on my chest. "Stay put, Coop. Don't make this worse."

"No," I said again. "You're going to just stand here and let this happen?"

"They're just taking her in for questioning," Roland said.

"What the fuck is happening right now? Why are they taking Mom?"

"Stay calm. Let's go over to the house. Where's Leo?"

I stepped back so Roland would get his hands off me. The cops were leading Mom down the stairs. Instinct made me try to push around Roland—I had to get to my mom—but he held me back again.

"Focus, Cooper. Have you seen Leo?"

I barely understood his question. My thoughts were moving too fast. Mom. Cops were taking my mom and it was my fault. I'd let this happen. "What? Leo? I don't know. He went home to sleep."

"He's not answering his phone."

They were down the stairs, out of my sight. I couldn't just stand here.

"Whoa, slow down." Roland put his arms around my chest and planted his feet. I'd tried to bolt down the stairs, and I hadn't even realized I'd moved. "Let's go to the house. We'll figure this out, okay?"

Somehow, I found myself at Mom's house. I didn't remember the walk over, just had a vague notion that Roland had kept a death grip on my arm. Someone was behind us, standing on the porch. Was that another deputy? Why was he here?

Roland led me inside, then went into the kitchen. I could hear him making phone calls, but I couldn't process what he was saying.

I was like a wolf caught in a trap, ready to chew my own leg off. I paced around the house, running my hands through my hair, my heart racing. Every nerve ending felt open and raw, my body buzzing with too much adrenaline. I glanced out the window, and sure enough, the deputy was still out there, like he was guarding our front porch.

Zoe arrived with baby Hudson. She tried to talk to me, her voice calm, the way she spoke softly to her son when he was crying. I paced. Chase and Brynn showed up, asking questions as soon as they walked in the door. Where was Mom? What happened? Why did the police need to talk to her? What did they say? What did Roland know? Why was there a deputy outside? I kept pacing.

I heard bits and pieces, none of it really sinking in.

"...no, she wasn't arrested..."

"...I don't know, they wouldn't tell me..."

"...he's not answering his phone..."

"...we have until closing..."

"...if we cooperate..."

"...here to make sure..."

"Someone needs to go get Leo." Roland's voice caught my attention. "I don't know how we're going to do this, but we have to be gone by closing."

I stopped, whipping my head around. "What did you say?"

"We have to vacate the grounds. Everyone."

"Why?"

He sighed and pinched the bridge of his nose. "The sheriff's department is going to search the property. They're giving us the courtesy of waiting until the winery closes and the guests leave. That's why there's a deputy on the porch— or were you too busy wandering around the house to notice?"

"Search the property? What the fuck?"

"I don't know," Roland barked. "I don't know what the fuck they're talking about. They took Mom in for questioning and now they're coming to search the property, but they're not telling us why or what they're looking for."

Oh fuck. Leo. "No. No, they can't. They can't make us leave. Fuck this, Roland, this isn't happening."

"It *is* happening, and if you'd slow the hell down, maybe you'd hear what I've been saying."

"This is my fault." I didn't stop moving, but everyone else seemed to.

"What?" Roland asked. "How can this be your fault?"

Fuck. I had to tell them.

"Focus, Cooper," Roland said. "How is this your fault?"

"It's Dad. Fuck, Roland, it's Dad and I helped him. I didn't want to but I did, and I didn't tell anyone, and now they have Mom."

"Helped Dad what?"

"He's growing drugs out on the north end. There's acreage out there where no one goes. He had this stupid fucking plan and he told me if I helped, he'd give Mom her divorce and leave our land alone. But he lied to me, because of course he fucking lied."

"Lied about what?" Zoe asked. "Coop, buddy, you're not making any sense."

I raked my fingers through my hair and did a lap through the kitchen. I couldn't stop. My veins were filled with fire, burning me from the inside. I was trying to explain, but everything was coming out garbled. My brain was moving faster than my mouth. I couldn't keep up.

"Dad. Wanted money. Thought he'd use our land to grow illegal shit. Told me it was cannabis. He was going to sell it, then walk away."

"Okay, we're with you," Zoe said. "Keep going."

"I made sure his guys had access. Told them what they needed to know about the soil. Irrigation. All of it. Made arrangements for him. He lied about what it was. He's not growing cannabis out there. He's growing fucking opium."

"Oh, god," someone said. Maybe several someones. I couldn't tell.

"I swear to god, I didn't know. He was going to take everything. Make us sell. This way he wouldn't. He'd accept Mom's settlement offer and sign the fucking papers and it would be over."

"Fuck," Roland muttered. "Does anyone else know?"

"Yes," I said, stopping dead in my tracks, my eyes wide. "Yes, Leo knows. And Ben. They found out. I told them everything, but the fewer people who knew, the better, so I didn't tell you. Where's my phone? I need to call Agent Rawlins."

I patted my pockets and looked around. Had I put it down? I couldn't remember.

"Wait, who's Agent Rawlins?" Roland asked.

"DEA. Where's my phone?"

"Why do you know a DEA agent?"

I blew out a frustrated breath. "Ben knows him. He called him when he found out what Dad was doing.

They're investigating. Trying to get the guys Dad is working with."

"Is anyone following this?" Roland asked.

"Coop, are you saying you've been cooperating with a DEA investigation?" Chase asked.

"Yes, Jesus, that's what I just said. Where's my phone?"

"If there's already an investigation in progress, why is the local sheriff's office involved?" Zoe asked. "Are they working with the DEA or something?"

"I don't know." I found my phone on the floor in the hallway and paced back to the living room while I tried to find Agent Rawlins' number. "This wasn't supposed to happen. We weren't supposed to get in trouble. Rawlins said he'd keep this from happening."

I found his number and called. It rang. Once, twice. I walked, feeling like I could climb the walls. Three times. Voicemail. "Fuck." I waited, listening to his voicemail greeting. "Rawlins, it's Cooper Miles. Dude, we have a problem. The cops took my mom and they're coming to search the property and they want us to leave and fuck man, we can't leave, this can't be happening. Call me back, for the love of god."

"That's one way to do it," Roland said.

The front door flew open and Ben barreled in. "What happened? Where is she?"

"They took her in for questioning," Roland said. "She's not under arrest."

Ben clenched and unclenched his fists. The last time I'd seen him look this unhinged had been when my dad had showed up on Brynn's wedding day. His eyes were wild, his salt-and-pepper hair unkempt. Even his beard looked more rugged than usual.

"Cooper, how did this happen?" Ben asked.

I threw my hands up in the air. "Fuck if I know. I tried to call Rawlins and he didn't answer."

"You don't think Dad would turn us in and try to make Mom take the blame, do you?" Brynn asked.

"At this point, I wouldn't put anything past him," Roland said. "But that's a hard sell. Cooper knows the truth. Coop, does Mom know anything about this?"

"No."

"I bet they don't keep her long," Roland said. "But they're coming to search the property. We have to be out by closing."

"That's not good," Ben said. He took a few breaths, seeming to get himself under control. "What can I do?"

"Run over to Leo's," Roland said. "We haven't been able to reach him."

"Is Deputy Asshole out there going to let me by?" Ben asked. "He almost didn't let me come in."

"I'll tell him what you're doing," Roland said.

It hit me in a flash. "I know what we need to do. Burn it. I'll go out there right now and fucking burn it all."

"No, Cooper!"

I didn't know who said it. Maybe they all did. All I did know was Chase was there, his arms holding me back, before I could reach the front door.

"Let go!"

"You're not helping," he said. "Calm the fuck down."

I couldn't calm down. I stopped trying to push against Chase's hold, but calming down wasn't going to happen. This was such a clusterfuck I had no idea what to do. They'd taken my mom. They were going to make us leave our land. And when they got here, they were going to find opium poppies growing out there.

We were going to lose everything. I'd already lost Amelia, and now I was going to lose everything else.

I started pacing again, my head swimming. Jesus, I was tired. My body ached from the lack of sleep and my head was pounding. At some point, Zoe tugged on my arm and led me to the couch. I sat, but only for a second. Sitting wasn't going to work.

"Coop, maybe you should go lie down," Chase said.

"Great plan. Everything is falling apart, so I'll go take a nap. Awesome."

Ben came back with Leo, and the look on his face as Roland explained the situation made me want to die. He didn't say a word. Just went over to the dining table and sat, his eyes vacant with shock.

The passage of time felt meaningless. Roland made phone calls. He tried to explain to the deputy outside that they needed to call the DEA—they didn't need to search the property—but he didn't listen. Ben tried to reach Rawlins. Still no answer.

I checked my phone every few minutes, but I wasn't even sure what I was looking for anymore. A call back from Rawlins? A text from Mom saying she needed a ride home? A message from Amelia?

Probably all of the above.

I was aware of more snippets of conversation as my family tried to make a plan. Talked about options for Leo. His stress beat at me, like the heat from one of our bonfires. It stoked the flame of my manic energy. I tried to leave again —I still thought burning the fucking field was a good idea— but Chase stopped me. I wanted to burn it all. Or go down to the sheriff's office and get my mom the fuck out of there. But every time I got near the front door, someone was there to block my way.

I couldn't slow down enough to fucking think. I needed to stop and figure this out. Come up with an idea that would help, but I was too far gone. Somewhere in the back of my mind, I was aware that I was making things worse. My family needed to focus on the problem, and they had to keep my ass from starting a forest fire.

But I couldn't stop. I was losing everything, and I'd never felt so helpless in my entire life.

THIRTY-TWO
AMELIA

IT WAS AMAZING what money could do.

I'd never been comfortable with being wealthy. Today, however, I was nothing but grateful. After Brynn's phone call, I raced to the airport. There were no open seats on the flights to Seattle—not at any price, not even for emergencies. After a frustrating conversation with a ticketing agent, I decided to get reckless. I walked through the airport holding a sign I'd made on a piece of paper, offering five thousand dollars to anyone willing to give up their seat on a flight to Seattle.

Thirty minutes later, I was on a plane.

After landing in Seattle, I rented a car. The two-and-a-half-hour drive to Echo Creek felt like twelve. My back and shoulders were tense, and I gripped the steering wheel, my knuckles going white.

I had to get to Cooper.

Brynn had only given me a brief account of what was happening. Something about cops, and their mom being taken in, and a search of the property. But one thing she'd said had made me beg Daphne to take me to the airport.

Cooper's falling apart.

I had no idea if he knew I was coming, or what he'd say when he saw me. I might be making a bad situation worse. He might hate me for leaving. He might tell me to go. By the time I got there, he might not be alone, and the thought of walking in on him with another girl there to comfort him made me want to throw up. This might be the worst mistake I'd ever made in my entire life.

But I was still going. I had to risk it.

I pulled up in front of Cooper's mom's house, feeling like I could barely breathe. My throat was tight, my chest hurt, and my stomach churned with anxiety. A bubble of useless words sat on the tip of my tongue, ready to spew forth and make a fool of me.

I went up the porch stairs, but a sheriff's deputy stopped me.

"Can I help you?" he asked.

"I'm here to see Cooper," I said.

The front door opened, and Brynn poked her head out. "Oh my god, it is you. She's my brother's girlfriend. Can you please let her in?"

I almost corrected her to say *ex-girlfriend*, because that was technically correct, but I couldn't bring myself to say it. That sounded so awful, and I hoped, with everything I had, that in a few minutes, I'd be able to fix that.

"Go ahead," the deputy said.

"Thank you." Brynn grabbed my arm and hauled me inside, closing the door behind me. "Thank god you're here."

"Where is he?"

She stepped aside. Cooper came around the corner from the kitchen and halted, his body freezing still. His hair was a mess, his hollow eyes ringed with dark circles. He looked like he hadn't slept in a week. His shoulders slumped, and he swayed slightly on his feet.

The room went quiet. His whole family was here—except his mom—and from the corner of my eye, I could see them all silently retreat into another room.

Cooper stared at me, not saying a word.

I swallowed hard. "I don't know if you want to see me, but Brynn called and told me what happened, and I had to come."

"Amelia?"

I nodded, taking a few tentative steps toward him. "I'm so sorry about your mom. I don't know what's going on, but I'm sure it will be okay somehow."

He rubbed his eyes. "Are you really here, or am I seeing things? Because I'm not sure what's real and what's not right now."

"I'm here."

My heart felt like it might burst, and tears stung my eyes. I moved closer, approaching him like an injured wild animal, slow and careful. I reached out a hand to touch his face, but he grabbed my wrist.

"Don't," he said, his voice full of anguish. "Don't touch me if you're going to leave. I can't take that again."

"No, I won't leave," I whispered, moving in closer. "Cooper, I love you."

His whole body shuddered as he loosened his grip on my wrist. I gently cupped his cheek and slid my hand across his rough jaw to his neck.

He leaned down, resting his forehead against mine. "Say it again."

"I love you. I love you so much. I don't know if you can forgive me for leaving, but I had to come back. I'm so sorry."

His arms wrapped around me, crushing me against him.

He buried his face in my neck and took a deep, trembling breath. I held him tight, tears breaking free from the corners of my eyes, wetting his shirt.

"I love you," I whispered, running my hands up and down his back. "I love you, I love you, I love you."

His knees buckled. We took a few steps to the side, arms still wrapped around each other, and fell onto the couch. He curled himself around me, his face still against my neck.

I kept murmuring. "I love you. I'm sorry. I love you."

In a rush, the tension in his body released and he shook with sobs. He cried, his arms clutching me so tightly I almost couldn't breathe. I held onto him, rubbing his back, pressing my cheek against his feverish head.

"I love you, Cooper. I love you and I'm so sorry."

It only lasted a minute. His deep sobs became shallow, shaky breaths. I slid my fingers through his hair and rubbed slow circles across his back as his breathing evened and his body relaxed.

I sniffed, letting the last of my tears fall. My heart was shattered into a million pieces for him. But I was here, holding him, pinned down by the weight of his exhausted body. He hadn't told me to leave, and I was going to take that and run with it.

Gradually, his family crept back into the room. Brynn tilted her head to look at his face.

"Oh my god, you got him to sleep," she whispered. "I don't think he's slept for a few days."

"Are you serious?" I asked.

She nodded. "He was holding it together until the police took Mom. Then he kind of lost it. We've been trying to calm him down all day. Thank you for coming."

I brushed away another tear. "I'm so glad you called."

Roland came out, walking fast. "Mom just called. They're releasing her."

"Oh thank god," Brynn said.

Ben made for the front door. "I'll go pick her up."

No one argued with him. He left, and everyone else came in and settled on the couch and chairs. Leo went to the large dining table, and I wondered if he was purposely keeping distance between himself and everyone else. He looked as bad as Cooper—maybe worse. Chase took a sleeping baby Hudson from Zoe and nestled him in his arms. Zoe declared she was taking the opportunity for a quick shower and went upstairs.

"Can you tell me what happened?" I asked Brynn.

Brynn explained, and I stared at her in silent disbelief. Cooper secretly helping his father. Growing drugs on their land. Then Leo and Ben finding out, and bringing in the DEA. And this morning, all hell breaking loose. Their mom being taken in for questioning.

Cooper had been dealing with all of this and I'd never had any idea. I didn't blame him for keeping it from me. He'd hid it from his entire family. In a way, I was glad it was out in the open now. At least he wasn't carrying this burden alone.

He'd never have to again. No matter what happened, I'd be by his side.

He slept on while we waited for Ben to come back with their mom. I stroked his hair and held him, hoping he could feel the comfort of my hands, even in his sleep.

Ben came back, leading Mrs. Miles in with an arm around her shoulders. She leaned against him, like she needed him for support. The tension in the house eased. She looked tired, but the first thing she did was assure everyone that she was fine. She hugged her kids and gave me a warm smile.

"Has everyone had dinner?" Mrs. Miles asked.

"Mom, stop," Brynn said. "You don't have to take care of everyone. We're in a crisis here."

"I'll run out if you need anything," Ben said.

"Thank you. I'm just not sure what to do. I figured if people were hungry, that's at least a problem I can solve."

"Has anyone heard from this Agent Rawlins?" Roland asked. "We don't have much time."

"Not yet," Ben said. "Did anyone check Cooper's phone?"

Brynn picked up a phone off the coffee table and looked at the screen. "No calls or texts."

"Damn it," Roland said. "If the DEA is supposed to be conducting an investigation, the sheriff's office must be pissing all over their jurisdiction right now."

I perked up at that. DEA? Sheriff's office? I had an idea, but I needed my phone and I couldn't exactly move under Cooper's weight. "Can someone please hand me my purse? I think I might be able to help, but I don't want to wake him."

Mrs. Miles cast a worried glance at the full-grown man passed out in my lap.

"I think he'll be okay, he just needs sleep," I said. Brynn handed me my purse and I dug out my phone. I went through the contacts in my phone, hoping I still had Mrs. Creighton's number. I found it and hit call. I hadn't talked to her in over a year, so I hoped she'd answer.

"Hello?"

"Mrs. Creighton? This is Amelia Hale."

"Amelia, so nice to hear from you. How have you been?"

"I'm fine. How's Braden?"

"He's doing great. He misses you. He still asks about you at least once a week."

"That's so sweet. I miss him too," I said. "Listen, I know it's been a while since we've spoken, but I need your help."

"Of course, Amelia. What can I do? Are you all right?"

"Yes, but some very good friends of mine are in a crisis."

"How can I help?"

"I think the easiest thing to do is let you talk to them. Can I put you on the phone with someone? His name is Roland Miles."

"Please do."

I held the phone out to Roland. "It's Leslie Creighton."

He stared at me, his mouth slightly open. "Leslie Creighton, the state attorney general?"

I nodded.

He took the phone and put it to his ear. "Ms. Creighton? Yes, hi, I'm Roland Miles." He walked into the other room.

"How do you know the attorney general?" Ben asked.

"I used to give her son Braden horseback riding lessons. He has some learning disabilities and behavioral issues, so she had a really hard time finding someone who would work with him. But he just needed some space to move and be himself. Horses don't judge, you know? So it was a perfect fit for him."

We waited while Roland spoke with Mrs. Creighton in the other room. After about ten minutes, he came back in. "She's going to make a few calls, but she said not to worry about vacating. If the DEA is already investigating, the sheriff's office will back off. She just needs to get the right people talking to each other."

"We don't have to leave?" Mrs. Miles asked.

He shook his head. "We don't have to leave."

I let out a long breath, so relieved for them. Mrs. Miles hugged her son, then hugged Brynn. I glanced over at the table. Leo sat with his head in his hands. My heart hurt for him. I knew he never left the property. He must have been terrified.

"Thank you, Amelia," Mrs. Miles said. "Thank you so much. For everything."

I shrugged. "I didn't really do much. But you're welcome."

Her eyes flicked to Cooper, then back to me. "You did a lot more than you realize."

With Ben's help, Mrs. Miles and Brynn got out some food for everyone. Leo slipped out, although I didn't think anyone else saw him leave. And through it all, Cooper slept on. I held him, caressing his hair and rubbing his ear, hoping when he finally woke up, he'd still be happy to see me. Hoping he'd still love me. Hoping I'd be enough.

THIRTY-THREE
COOPER

MY HEAD SWAM with confusion as I woke. Where was I? Was this a bed? My eyes were still heavy with sleep, but I forced them open and glanced around. Was this Mom's house?

Holy shit. Amelia.

She was asleep next to me, her hands tucked beneath her cheek. My heart felt like it might burst apart in my chest as the memory of her soft voice in my ear ran through my mind, like a song on repeat.

I love you, Cooper. I love you, I love you, I love you.

Oh my god, it had been real.

The previous day came back to me in bits and pieces. What the fuck had I done? I'd lost it. From the time I'd seen my mom taken away by police, I'd been a fucking disaster. Frantic and out of control. Great. Just what my family had needed—me being a lunatic in the middle of a crisis. I had a lot of work to do to make this right.

But just the sight of my Cookie, sleeping so peacefully next to me, kept the storm from breaking. I didn't fly out of bed to go wake people up so I could find out what was going on. I had vague memories of my mom being home. Somewhere in the back of my mind, I knew she was safe. And above all else, I needed to do what I'd failed at so miserably yesterday. I needed to stay calm.

With Amelia here, it was easy.

I breathed in the scent of her, letting it fill my lungs. Touched her face with my fingertips just to feel the softness of her skin.

She stirred, slowly opening her eyes.

"Morning."

"Hi." She reached for me, but hesitated, her eyes clouded with doubt.

I hooked my arm around her waist and hauled her against me. My lips found hers and she was like a cold drink after a long, hot day in the vineyard. Sweet, soothing relief. I touched her cheek and kissed her softly while our legs tangled together beneath the covers.

"I missed you," she said when I pulled away. "I missed you every second and I'm so sorry I left. I'm so sorry I wasn't here."

"Shh." I kissed the tip of her nose. "It's okay. You did what you had to do. But maybe we could go back to that part where you said you loved me, because Cookie, I really liked hearing that."

"I love you. Oh my god, I love you like crazy."

"I love you, too." I kissed her again. And again. And once more, because even though there was more to say, kissing her felt really fucking good. Finally, I pulled away. "I want to keep doing this, but I think we should probably talk."

"Yeah, I think so."

We shifted a little, moving apart a few inches, but she kept her legs twined with mine.

"I know I'm a lot to handle," I said. "I just get excited about stuff. And I got really excited about you. I realized I loved you and god, Cookie, it blew my mind. And I know I don't exactly have a great history with women, but I'm telling you, I'm going to be the best boyfriend ever. You don't ever have to worry that I'll get bored or that you won't be enough. You're everything. You're amazing and beautiful and sweet and fun and you get me. I'm never going to stop wanting you. We'll be in our nineties with white hair and wrinkles and I'll still kiss you and grab your ass and tell you you're hot and love the shit out of you every single day."

She laughed softly. "Promise?"

"Hell yeah, I promise. And I'm not asking you to make decisions about the rest of your life right this second. We don't need to plan a quickie wedding and lock this down. I told you, Cookie. I'll never make you wear a dress you hate."

"Oh, Cooper."

"I just want to love you. That's all."

"That's all I need." She touched my face and slid her fingers through my hair. "I realized when I was in L.A. that maybe things have been crazy, but I like crazy. And maybe we're not a likely pair, and maybe we did this all out of order, and maybe it's really fast to fall in love. But neither of us are very good at fitting the mold. So why not embrace who I am, and who you are, and go with it? Why not give us a chance, because you were right, we are really good together. We're great together."

"We really are."

"And my life here was unfolding into something amazing. I love working with the McLaughlins, and I love this town, and the winery. I love it all. I was worried I was missing something. Like it was all too perfect to be true. And Daphne meant well, but she kept saying she didn't understand how I could settle down here so fast. Didn't I want to travel and have adventures? And I do, but I want to have those adventures with you."

"Baby, if you want to have adventures, you've come to the right place. That's my jam. Plus, you know I travel for work sometimes."

"Do you?"

"Sure. We source our grapes from different regions, so I go check out their operations and coordinate with other growers. And there's always more for me to learn. I was thinking about touring some vineyards in Italy next year, talking with their growers."

"Oh my god, that sounds amazing."

"Will you come with me? To be honest, I'm not actually going to give you a choice about that. If I'm going to be gone for a few weeks, I don't think I can live without you that long, so you'll just have to come. But we can pretend since I'm trying not to make your decisions for you."

She laughed. "Of course I will. You can make that decision for me. I don't want to be without you either, anyway."

I kissed her forehead. "Good."

"Um, Cooper?" She nibbled her bottom lip. "There's something else I need to tell you."

The worry in her voice sent a hint of nervousness into my stomach. "Yeah?"

"So, you probably guessed, because you saw their house, and it's really big and everything, but my parents are very wealthy. And it's always been kind of weird to come from that, but it sort of is what it is, you know? And the thing is, they set up a trust fund for me, and I didn't think I'd get it because, well that's a long story, but it turns out I did and now I have it and it's a lot of money, so what I'm trying to tell you is that I have five million dollars. Except for the money I spent to get here yesterday, that is."

I blinked at her, dumbstruck. "Wait, what did you just say?"

"I'm rich now?"

Why that struck me as hilarious, I wasn't sure, but I burst out laughing. Maybe it was the fact that it made her so nervous to tell me. Or maybe it was the adorable way she looked at me like she was hoping it wouldn't change anything between us.

"Are you telling me I have a sugar mama? Fuck yes, that's awesome." I pulled her closer and kissed her forehead again. "Cookie, that's amazing. For you. I mean, sure, if you want to buy me cool presents, like more dick costumes, that's awesome and all. But that's yours. It doesn't change anything for me. Except now I'm going to call you sugar mama sometimes."

She snuggled against me. "Okay. But I like Cookie better. God, Cooper, you realize what we found, don't you? I think some people search for this and never get lucky enough to find it. And we did. We got lucky."

"Hopefully I'm getting lucky later." I winked.

"Oh! That reminds me." She twisted around and reached for her phone on the bedside table. "I was bored last night after things calmed down, and I couldn't move because you were sleeping on me. I wasn't sure what was going to happen today, but I figured I'd be optimistic and buy you a let's-be-boyfriend-and-girlfriend-again present."

"Sweet, I love presents."

She smiled as she swiped her thumb across her phone screen. "I know. And you're really going to love this one.

Normally I'd wait and surprise you when it arrives, but I'm too excited."

I took another deep breath, savoring her scent. I couldn't get enough.

"See?"

She held up her phone to show me. There was a picture of a plastic dick dressed in a costume.

"Another dick costume? Oh my god, Cookie!"

"Yes! Do you see what it is? A farmer!" Her voice got all high-pitched and squealy.

"Holy shit. *I'm* a farmer."

She wiggled against me. "That's why it's so perfect. I saw this one and obviously had to order it."

"I love it. My dick is going to look fucking adorable in this."

"Isn't he? I can't wait. It'll be here next week."

"Thanks, baby." I drew her close again and kissed her forehead. "What happened last night? How did we get in here?"

"You don't remember?" She put her phone back on the table. "You sort of half woke up and were trying to ask about your mom. She told you she was fine and you just needed to go to bed. Then you started mumbling something about your mattress, but I didn't know what you meant. Ben and Chase helped you in here. I followed, but I wasn't sure if I should stay. I mean, I said I love you and you seemed like you were happy I was back, but I didn't know what would happen when you woke up this morning. But you pulled me into bed and wouldn't let go of me, so I just stayed and snuggled with you until I fell asleep."

I tucked her head below my chin. "Thank you for coming back. God, I needed you so much."

"I'm sorry I wasn't here when things were difficult."

"It's okay. I'm just glad you're here now." I kissed her head again. My dick was achingly hard for her, but now probably wasn't the time. "I fucked up yesterday, Cookie. I'd really love to lie in bed with you all day, because you feel like heaven, but I should probably get up and go figure out how much trouble I'm in for being such a nutjob."

"I don't think they're mad at you." She scooted closer, dragging her leg up the outside of mine beneath the covers. "And it's still so early. I'm sure no one's up."

I groaned. "Oh god, you feel so good."

Her mouth came to mine and she nibbled on my bottom lip. "We should be naked."

"Naked is my favorite."

She laughed softly into my mouth. "I know."

We stripped off our clothes beneath the covers. As soon as I was inside her, I felt whole again. I held there, not moving, reveling in the sensation of our bodies connecting. Of the pieces of us joining together. It was some deep shit, and I couldn't get over how good it felt.

"God, I love you."

She caressed the back of my neck. "I love you, too. Oh my god, I love you and I'm so glad you love me back."

"It's pretty cool, isn't it?"

"Yeah." She rubbed my neck again, then shifted her hips beneath me. "But can you love me harder because I'm dying for this."

What my Cookie wanted, my Cookie got. I fucked her hard, losing myself in the feel of her skin. In her pussy and her mouth. In her scent and the way she touched me. Held me. Loved me. I lost myself in her.

And she was everything.

Neither of us lasted long. We were both keyed up,

aching for release. And we found it in each other. Nothing had ever felt better.

Afterward, we nestled beneath the covers, our bodies close. I held her tight, so fucking grateful she was here. That she was mine. And I was never letting her go again.

THIRTY-FOUR
COOPER

EVENTUALLY, I did have to get up. As amazing as it felt to lie in bed with Amelia, I had shit to deal with. Like I'd told her, I'd fucked up yesterday. I had to get to fixing things.

I had a text from Agent Rawlins, saying he'd call me at eight. I also had a text from Roland, telling me to come to Leo's when I was up.

Mom was at Leo's when I got there. She looked tired, but good, considering what she'd been through yesterday. Roland and Leo raised their eyebrows at me, and I knew exactly what they were thinking.

I put my hands up in surrender. "It's okay. I'm chill."

Roland looked me up and down, then nodded.

"I owe everyone a huge apology," I said. "I lost my cool yesterday and I made a bad situation worse. I'm sorry I didn't keep it together."

Leo surprised me by speaking up first. "It's okay, Coop. You're not the only one who lost it a little bit yesterday. You were just noisier about it."

"You all right?" I asked.

"Yeah."

Mom came over and stepped into my open arms for a hug. I squeezed her and kissed the top of her head.

"Did you get some sleep?" she asked.

"Yeah, did you?"

She took a deep breath. "Some."

"I guess Roland and Leo probably filled you in on what's going on." I'd been an idiot to think I could pull this off without Mom finding out. And a bigger idiot for trusting my dad.

"They did. And I don't know whether to smack you upside the head or hug you."

I rubbed the back of my neck. "Story of my life, right?"

"You have no idea," she said.

"What did the cops want? Was it about Dad's *crop*?" I made air quotes when I said *crop*.

"Yes, but all they had was an anonymous tip," she said. "And since I didn't know anything, I couldn't answer any of their questions. But that didn't stop them from asking the same ones over and over."

"Who tipped them off?" I asked.

"We don't know," Roland said. "Maybe one of the workers Dad had out there."

"So where are we with all this now?" Leo asked. "Coop, have you talked to Ben's contact at the DEA?"

"He's supposed to call any minute." My phone rang and I pulled it out of my pocket. "Nice timing." I swiped to answer, putting him on speaker. "This is Coop."

"Hi Cooper. Agent Rawlins."

"Hey. I've got my mom and my brothers Roland and Leo here. Is that cool?"

"Yeah, that's fine. Listen, I'm sorry about yesterday. I was in the field. I'm getting caught up now. It sounds like the local sheriff's office stuck their noses in. But am I reading this right? Someone had the state attorney general call and get things straightened out?"

I puffed up a little, knowing my girl rocked it yesterday. "Yep. They took my mom in for questioning, which pisses me the hell off, by the way. They were going to search the property, but thankfully that didn't happen."

"Okay. Sometimes we run into this kind of thing with local law enforcement, so I'm glad it was resolved quickly."

"So what's our next move?" I asked.

"The point of all this is to get to the people your father is working with. Your dad is small potatoes, but if he's trying to offload an entire crop of opium, he must be working with someone big. But if there's any chance your dad, or his contacts, know about the sheriff's office getting involved, they might bolt. At best, they'll take extra precautions. But if Lawrence's deal goes south, we don't have a case."

"No, no, no," I said. "They're not getting away with this."

"I don't want them to walk any more than you do," Rawlins said. "But I need to know if the deal is still on. And I need to find out who your dad's contacts are. Who's on the other end of this deal. We've been waiting it out until the crop is ready to harvest, which should be soon. But if they got wind of what happened yesterday, we might be out of luck."

"Can we find out if Lawrence knows?" Mom asked.

"Coop, are you supposed to meet him again soon?" Leo asked.

"No, I'm just supposed to make sure his guys can get in to harvest when the plants are ready."

"We need this information somehow," Rawlins said.

"It's not like Cooper can call Dad and ask him if his deal

is still on," Roland said. "We don't want to make him suspicious."

I snapped my fingers. "Fungal mycelium."

"What?" Roland asked.

"I need an excuse to meet Dad, so I'll tell him we're fighting fungal mycelium. Powdery mildew. It spreads on the wind—I'll say we're dealing with it in one of the outer vineyards, and it could have spread to his crop."

"Okay," Rawlins said. "You need to at least find out if his deal is still on. Do you think you can get me more information about who he's working with?"

"I'll try."

"All right. Sooner is better. Call me when you have something set up."

"Got it," I said. Rawlins ended the call, so I stuffed my phone in my back pocket.

Roland and Leo were both staring at me.

"What?"

"Are you sure about this?" Roland asked.

"Of course I'm sure. What part should I not be sure about? We need to find out if Dad knows, and if his deal is still on. I can do that. Bam. Done."

"Okay, but that means keeping your head on straight," Roland said. "You can't lose your cool on Dad."

"Trust me, there's nothing I'd like better than to punch that asshole in the face," I said. "Sorry, Mom. But I've got this. I know I was a total freak-show yesterday, but I'm telling you, I can do this. I *need* to do this."

"All right," Roland said. "Let us know when and where. I don't want you doing this alone."

"I'll keep you posted," I said.

"And tell Amelia thanks again," Roland said. "She saved our asses last night."

I grinned. "I will. Mom, you going home?"

"I am. I'm taking today off, so I think a hot bath and a mug of tea is in order."

"I'll walk you."

Mom hugged my brothers—even Leo. She was one of the few people he would let touch him, and even then, he always looked uncomfortable. I said goodbye, then offered my arm to Mom. She tucked her hand in the crook of my elbow, and we went outside.

When we'd walked a little way up the path toward her house, I broke the silence. "Mom, I'm sorry. About everything. I'm sorry I let this happen."

She stopped and turned to face me. "It's okay, honey. I hate that I have to tell you never to trust your father. But never trust your father."

"I won't make that mistake again."

"Neither will I." She squeezed my arm. "How's Amelia? Is she staying?"

"Yeah, she's staying."

She smiled. "I'm glad to hear it. I like her. She's good for you. You know that, right?"

"She really is." I shoved my hands in my pockets and rocked up onto my toes and back again. "I'm in love with her, Mom. It's the coolest thing."

"She's a very lucky girl." She patted my cheek. "Don't mess it up."

I laughed. "Come on, give me some credit."

"You're very charming, Cooper, but I'm not as blind to your *habits* over the last few years as you think I am."

I cringed a little. My *habits*, as she called them, had been going on a lot longer than the last few years. But it didn't matter anymore. I was a one-woman man now.

"Well, I'm glad you like Amelia, because I'm going to

marry her someday and she's going to have all my babies. And I'm going to build a house next to Chase and Brynn so our kids can grow up here like I did."

"Does Amelia know about all this?"

"Slow down, Mom, we just met a couple of months ago. I don't want to scare her off. She's still getting used to my sweet boyfriend t-shirts."

Laughing, she took my arm again and we started walking. "You're something else. But I've always been so glad you're mine."

"Okay, enough. I'm trying to use humor to deflect your poignant remarks about what a great son I am, but if you keep talking like that, you're going to make my eyes leak. And we can't have any more hits to my manhood right now. I've already taken enough damage."

I walked her up onto her porch and she squeezed my arm again. "Fine, I'll stop. Just promise me you'll be careful."

"I promise."

She popped up on her tiptoes to kiss my cheek. "Love you, buddy."

"Love you too."

Mom went inside, and I hesitated on the porch. It felt wrong to leave her alone, and Amelia had already gone back to the cottage. With everything that was happening with my dad, I was worried about her. Worried she was going to face something worse than the cops questioning her. I'd have to talk to Leo about what kind of security he had around the grounds. He was probably all over it, but I wanted to make sure.

I caught sight of Ben walking up the path and my worry eased. Mom's sons weren't the only ones keeping an eye on her. And that was priceless.

After filling Ben in on what was happening, I stepped off the porch to call Dad. I'd set up this meeting, then get back to my Cookie. We had a lot of catching up to do.

ONCE AGAIN, I felt a little bit like I was in a movie, heading out to meet a secret contact. I parked and walked across the empty lot toward two men on the far side. They were little more than shadows from this distance, but I recognized my dad. My heart rate ticked up a notch and my body buzzed with adrenaline. Who was the second guy? Dad hadn't mentioned anyone else being here.

When I'd told my dad we might have a problem with the crop, he'd demanded I meet him tonight. I could tell he was worried. People reacted to stress in different ways, and my dad had always gotten angry. He'd barked at me, as if it were my fault, and told me where to meet him.

It hadn't even pissed me off, which was weird. I hated it when Dad yelled at me. I always had. But a calmness had settled over me ever since I'd woken up next to Amelia this morning. Nothing was going to rattle me. Not my asshole of a father. Not the risks I was taking tonight. I was going to fix this, and I was going to do everything in my power to make sure it was my father—and not my family—who took the fall.

I put my hands in my pockets to keep from fidgeting and approached my dad. The man standing next to him was young, maybe thirty, dressed in an expensive-looking shirt and slacks. Dad looked like shit. He'd aged a lot in the year and a half since Mom had kicked him out. His hair had more gray and he had bags under his eyes.

"Dad."

His eyes flicked to the other man and a vein stuck out in his neck. The other guy, whoever he was, was making Dad nervous. Which probably should have made me nervous, but I felt that sense of clarity I sometimes did in a crisis. Like the rest of the world fell away and my mind focused on the problem at hand.

"Cooper," he said.

"Who's this guy?" I asked.

Dad hesitated before answering. "This is one of my associates."

"Joe," the guy said.

"Joe? Just Joe? We're dealing with some sensitive shit, here, Dad, and I'm supposed to speak freely around *Joe* without knowing who the fuck he is?"

"You'll have to excuse my son," Dad said. "He doesn't know when to shut his mouth."

"Joe Smith," the guy said.

"Okay, I don't really think that's your name, but whatever."

"Jesus, Cooper," Dad said, pinching the bridge of his nose.

"Now that we're all friends, let's cut the bullshit," I said. "I know what you're actually growing out there. It's fucked up that you lied to me about it, and let's be honest, even more fucked up that you're doing it. But whatever. We're here now, and it is what it is. My priority is to get this done so you can get the fuck out of our lives."

Even in the low light, I could see Dad's face redden. His eyes flicked to the other man again. "I just need your assurance that the crop isn't failing."

"It's not failing," I said. "It would be in a lot better shape if you hadn't planted your rows so close together, though. Mildew loves shade and dampness. You have to give those babies room to breathe. As it is, everything is packed so tight, if you get spores in there, you're fucked. But at this point, you're not fucked."

Yet. I was going to make damn sure he *was* fucked. And so far, he hadn't mentioned the sheriff's office. It seemed like he didn't know.

Dad let out a breath and turned to the other guy. "See? He's an expert. You can trust his opinion."

It was a very sad fact that the nicest thing my dad had ever said about me was to a drug dealer about an illegal opium crop.

The guy crossed his arms. "Okay. We'll move forward. How long until harvest?"

"A few weeks," Dad said.

"He better be right," the guy said. "I wouldn't want to be you if this crop goes. Suppliers are expendable."

I hated my dad—a lot—and I didn't hate many people. But I didn't like this guy basically threatening his life, either. My first instinct was to lash out and tell this guy to go fuck his drug-making self in the ass. That he was what's wrong with humanity and he should die a slow death in a box full of scorpions.

But I didn't. I kept my head, because making an enemy of this sort of dude would have been enormously stupid. I kept my hands still and my mouth under control.

"Is that all?" I asked.

"I'll text you when my guys need access," Dad said.

"Fine."

I turned on my heel and walked away. It sucked that I didn't have the guy's real name, but I'd tell Rawlins what he'd said. It wasn't like I could have gotten away with pushing harder for information. For all I knew, the dude had a gun on him and would have shot me right there. But at least it was clear Dad did have a buyer, and the deal was still on. Hopefully the DEA could handle it from here and take those fuckers down. I'd sleep a lot better when I knew my family—and our land—was safe.

Back at the winery, I went straight for Amelia. I wished the DEA could move faster and we could put this shit with my dad behind us. But I'd do what I needed to do to protect my girl, my family, and our land. Those were the things that meant most to me.

And when Amelia opened the door of the cottage, her hazel eyes as bright as her smile, I knew everything was going to be okay. Because with my Cookie at my side, I could do anything. Face anything. She was my calm. My peace. My love. And there was nothing in the world that was better than that.

EPILOGUE

AMELIA

TWO YEARS LATER...

Keeping a secret from Cooper was almost impossible. It didn't matter what it was. He had a sixth sense about surprises. When he'd left for work this morning, he'd given me a mischievous smile. I wondered if he knew.

Then again, when *didn't* Cooper wear a mischievous smile? Maybe he wasn't on to me. It was hard to say. Regardless, I'd decided something. Something big. Enormous, even. I was going to ask him to marry me.

Cooper reminded me at least once a week that he was going to marry me someday. He didn't ask. He hadn't given me a ring, and we weren't actually engaged. In fact, we were the only people in the family left who weren't engaged or married. But sometimes he called me *future wife*, and he'd tease me about making an honest man out of him. And every once in a while, in a quiet moment, he'd touch my face and say, "I'm going to marry you someday, you know that, right?"

I did know. I'd always known, although neither of us had ever been in a hurry to get married. I also knew about the stash of *World's Best Husband* t-shirts he'd been keeping in the back of the closet.

The hardest part was going to be getting him to Mountainside Tavern. I had a plan, but I needed help to pull it off. For that, Brynn and Chase were my best bet.

I texted Brynn to see if they were home or at Chase's shop. She texted back to say they were at home, so I drove over to Salishan.

They'd spent nearly a year building their house from the ground up. It was a beautiful two-story craftsman style with a big front porch, hardwood floors, and an amazing kitchen. Their dog, Scout, came bounding down the front steps when I pulled up.

"Hey buddy." I got out of the car and crouched down to pet him. Scout was a rescue dog they'd adopted about a year ago. They weren't sure about his breed—he was a mix, but we could see some Lab in him for sure. His chocolate brown fur was soft, and he had one ear that liked to flop over. "Such a good boy. Who's a good boy?"

His tail wagged furiously as I pet him.

"Where's your mommy and daddy? Go find Mommy, Scout."

I followed him in as he bounded up the stairs and through the partially open door.

Brynn came downstairs. Her hair was pulled up and she wore paint-splattered clothes. "Hey, you. What's up?"

"What are you guys up to today?"

"Painting one of the bedrooms." She wiped her forehead with the back of her arm. "I swear, this house is never going to be completely finished. Just when I think we're done, I realize there are five more projects left to do."

"It's so beautiful, though."

She smiled and glanced around. "It is, isn't it? Kind of hard to believe."

Cooper had been disappointed that we couldn't build our house right next to Brynn and Chase. But there were zoning laws and permitting considerations, so we'd chosen a lot that was walking distance a little further down. We'd only just broken ground. The foundation was in and Cooper, Chase, and Ben were getting ready to start framing.

"You guys have done an amazing job."

"So what's up?" she asked, reaching down to pet Scout. He sat next to her, his tail brushing the floor as he wagged it.

"Okay, so I have a thing, and it's a big deal, and I've been keeping it from everyone except my friend Daphne, because I didn't want to spoil the surprise. She's still in Europe on tour with Harrison, so she wouldn't be able to tell anyone, but you guys are here, and I just figured it would be better to keep this to myself until it was time. And now it's time."

"Wow. Okay. I think I followed all that."

My tummy tingled with anticipation. "Sorry, I'm just getting nervous all of a sudden."

Chase appeared from the stairway. "Hey Amelia. What's up?"

I took a deep breath so I could slow down a little. "I need your help. I'm going to ask Cooper to marry me."

Brynn's eyes widened and her mouth popped open.

"Holy shit," Chase said.

"I know. It's such a big deal. And he's probably suspicious, but I'm not sure. I need your help getting him to Mountainside tonight. I just know if I ask him to meet me there, he's going to know I have something planned. Why would I ask to meet him there? Why not go together? But see, we met for the first time there and I want to already be there when he walks in, sitting at the bar just like I was the first time."

"That's actually an awesome idea," Chase said.

"Oh my god," Brynn said. "This is amazing. But are you sure you should be the one to do it? Don't you think he wants to? I mean, there's no doubt he wants to marry you—"

"Nope," Chase said. "He's been sure about that for a long time."

"Exactly," Brynn said. "But he's a guy. Don't guys want to be the one to ask?"

"You know, I thought about that a lot," I said. "I mean, a lot. Like I've been thinking about this for months. And I really think he's going to love this. I just have this feeling. I know him."

Chase nodded. "I kind of think she's right."

"Okay," Brynn said, although she didn't sound certain. "I think you two might be the only people on the planet who really understand him. So if you think he'll be cool with it, I'll trust you. What do you want us to do?"

"I need you to pretend that we're having a girls' night tonight. No boys allowed. That way, he won't be expecting me to be home. And Chase, get him to meet you at Mountainside at seven."

"Got it," Chase said. "We've got your back."

"Thank you guys so much. I'm so nervous."

"What are you going to do?" Brynn asked. "Are you going to get down on one knee or something?"

"Not exactly," I said. "But I do have a plan."

"Wow," Brynn said. "This is so huge. I'm so excited for you."

I smiled and put a hand over my fluttering tummy. "Thanks. I'm excited too."

Chase nudged her with his arm and winked. I wasn't

sure what he was getting at, but I didn't worry about it. I knew I could count on them to make this work.

The rest of the day went by at a snail's pace. I had some administrative stuff to do for the ranch. Rob and Gayle had retired to part-time, but their heart was still there, so they hadn't left completely. Which was wonderful, if you asked me. They were so sweet and had spent the last two years gently easing me into running the ranch. I'd used a lot of my trust fund to make improvements and expand. We had space for more horses, now, and we'd brought in several rescues to live out their last years in peace.

I'd already texted Cooper to tell him Brynn had invited me out for a girls' night. A few hours later, he texted back to say it was cool, but he'd miss me. Not long after, he texted again to say he was meeting Chase after work, so it all worked out.

I smiled, giggling to myself. He had no idea.

My heart pounded with excitement when it was finally time. I'd called ahead to Mountainside and the bartender was ready for me. He'd put a reserved sign on the two barstools where Cooper and I had met, just over two years ago. On the day my life had taken a sharp turn and changed forever.

We'd both been feeling a little bit lost and alone that night. And we'd taken solace in each other, neither of us realizing we had just met the love of our lives. It hadn't taken us long to figure it out. Even though there had been some bumps in the road, we always came together, faced our challenges, and grew stronger.

True to his word—and his collection of t-shirts—Cooper had always been the world's best boyfriend. He was sweet and fun and loving—and spontaneous and crazy. He loved to surprise me with spur of the moment adventures. We'd played pranks on his brothers. Taught his nephew how to say, "Hey gorgeous," and wink at girls. We still had fun every chance we got. Because why not? Life could be fun. There were serious moments, and that was fine. But Cooper and I enjoyed each other and enjoyed life, and neither of us saw any reason to stop.

And it was only going to get better.

I went into the bar, wearing the dress I'd bought for tonight. It wasn't a real wedding dress—certainly nothing like the monstrosity I'd been stuffed into the night we met. But it was white and pretty—reminiscent of a wedding gown at least. And it made my boobs look great, so I knew he'd love it.

The bartender smiled and nodded when I took my seat. I asked for a water and let it sit, my heart beating so hard I couldn't sit still. I put the package with his will-you-marry-me present on the bar and waited, fidgeting. Hoping he wouldn't be long.

He pushed open the door and stopped, his mouth turning up in a smile when he saw me. He looked freshly showered—his hair still slightly damp—and he was wearing a clean shirt and jeans.

"Hey, Cookie." He looked a little confused as he walked over to the bar. "What are you doing here? I thought you were with Brynn."

I took a deep breath, my hands trembling. God, I was so nervous. "No, it's not girls' night. It's actually a special night, but not for me and Brynn. For me and you. I have something for you."

"Awesome." He slid onto the stool next to me—the same stool he'd been on when he'd kissed me for the first time. "This is pretty cool, and also kind of weird, because I have something for you, too. I was going to wait until we were at home, though."

"Oh, okay. Let me do mine first."

"Go for it."

I handed him the little gift bag I'd brought. "Open it."

"Are you sure I should open it here?"

"Yeah, it isn't naughty."

"Damn." He winked and pulled the tissue paper out of the bag and set it on the bar. Then he pulled out a t-shirt and opened it so he could read it.

His smile fell, and he looked from me to the t-shirt a few times. "Holy shit."

"Cooper, I love you so much. You make life fun and amazing and I want us to be together forever. And I thought this place, where we met, would be the perfect place to do this. So I guess I'll just say it. I'm wondering if you'll marry me."

His eyes met mine, and he still wasn't smiling. Dread poured through me. Oh no. Maybe Brynn had been right. Most guys would want to be the one to propose. But I'd really thought Cooper would love it if I did.

"Are you proposing?" he asked.

I nodded, nibbling my lip.

A wide smile spread across his face. "Oh my god, Cookie. Are you serious? Is this real? You're asking me to marry you?"

"Yes."

He dropped the shirt on the bar and grabbed me, crushing me against his chest. "Yes. Fuck yes. Holy shit, this is the coolest thing that's ever happened to me. Oh my god, I love you so fucking much."

I almost cried with relief. "Yes?"

"Yes. Fuck yes. Of course I will."

He moved back to kiss me, long and slow and deep. When he pulled away, I touched his face, my eyes stinging with happy tears.

"Are you sure this is okay? I was so sure, but then Brynn said maybe you'd want to do it, because most guys do. I didn't ruin this for you, did I?"

"Are you kidding me?" he asked. "What other guy can brag that his girl asked him to marry her? This is the best. Cookie, you're amazing. I love you so much."

"I love you, too. Do you like your shirt? I know it's not a ring, but this seemed better, even though it's just a shirt and isn't fancy."

"I love it so much." He picked it up to look again. It read *Best Husband Ever* in big block letters. "It's perfect."

"I thought so, too."

He put it down and cracked a mischievous grin. "You know what's funny? I have a surprise for you, too. And you aren't going to believe what it is."

"Okay."

"I've actually had this for a while. But I was waiting for the right moment. It was going to be tonight, after you got back from girl's night. I woke up this morning and somehow I just knew today was going to be it."

He pulled a small box out of his pocket and held it up.

"Oh my god, is that what I think it is?"

His smile was so big, his blue eyes sparkling. "It is. Go ahead. Open it."

I took the box out of his hand and opened it, revealing a beautiful engagement ring. "Oh, Cooper."

"See?" He took the ring out of the box and slipped it on my trembling finger. "Today was the day. Our clocks are perfectly in sync."

He leaned in for another kiss, taking his time. His arms slid around my waist and he held me close.

This man. This crazy, wonderful, sensitive, sexy, funny man. There was no one in the world like Cooper Miles. I loved him with everything I had. I loved all the pieces of him, from his fidgeting, to his sense of adventure, to the way he made me feel strong and brave. And loved. So loved. This man loved with every bit of himself. He didn't do anything small, or halfway. He loved me big, and I was going to love him just as big, every day for the rest of our lives.

WANT MORE MILES FAMILY? How about a surprise **Miles Family bonus epilogue**?

VISIT WWW.BOOKHIP.COM/HTAASG to download your free bonus epilogue.

AFTERWORD

Dear Reader,

At this point in my author career, I don't think I've had a book that was more highly anticipated than this one. (Although I suspect that's going to change with the next Miles Family book... Leo...).

Cooper jumps off the pages in both Broken Miles and Forbidden Miles. He's talkative, charmingly full of himself, and never stops moving. Ever since Broken Miles launched, I've had readers begging for Cooper's story.

To be honest, I was just as excited to write it.

Cooper is one of those characters who was magic for me. They come around once in a while and their voice is so strong, their words fly from my fingers. Not to say Coop didn't make me work for this one. He did. More than once I whined that this book wouldn't end. It was challenging, but also ridiculously fun.

I really wanted readers to see that there's a lot more to Cooper than just the fun guy who talks too much. He's layered, with a depth that hopefully surprised you. And when he loves, he loves big. Huge. Enormous. I love that about him.

There was also a lot of speculation about who would wind up with this wild Miles boy. One thing I knew for sure, she had to be someone who understood him. She had to speak Cooper.

Amelia was that girl. I had the image of her sitting in the bar in her wedding dress from the beginning, way back when I was just starting to plan this series. What an unexpected twist for Cooper - his match being a jilted bride. Did you see that coming? He sure didn't.

Once these two crossed paths, it was clear they were made for each other, like two halves of a whole. They're both a little scattered and random. Both have a sense of fun and adventure. And both love with their whole selves, holding nothing back.

It was a pleasure to watch Cooper fall in love. And you'll see more of these two in Leo's book, Hidden Miles, as well as Gaining Miles, a Miles Family novella. Both are coming in 2019.

I hope Cooper's story was everything you hoped it would be! Thanks for reading!

And if you wouldn't mind, consider leaving a review for Reckless Miles on Amazon or Goodreads. Thanks so much!

CK

ACKNOWLEDGMENTS

A big, huge thank you to everyone who was a part of the magic of Reckless Miles.

Thank you to Elayne Morgan for doing a great job editing, as usual. And to Cassy Roop for yet another perfect cover.

To my beta readers, Christine, Nikki, and Jodi. Thank you again for your honest feedback. You helped take this book to the next level and I appreciate it so much.

To David and my kids for always having my back and only teasing me about writing "kissing books" a little bit.

To my girl, Kathryn Nolan, for being an awesome release day twin again! And all my author friends for being so amazing and pretty and talented.

Finally, to all my readers who have joined me on this journey. I love your faces!!

ALSO BY CLAIRE KINGSLEY

For a full and up-to-date listing of Claire Kingsley books visit www.clairekingsleybooks.com

The Miles Family Series

Sexy, sweet, funny, and heartfelt family series. Messy family. Epic bromance. Super romantic.

Broken Miles

Forbidden Miles

Reckless Miles

Hidden Miles

Gaining Miles: A Miles Family Novella

Bluewater Billionaires

Hot, stand-alone romantic comedies. Lady billionaire BFFs and the badass heroes who love them.

The Mogul and the Muscle

More Bluewater Billionaire shared-world stand-alone romantic comedies:

The Price of Scandal by Lucy Score, Wild Open Hearts by Kathryn Nolan, and Crazy For Loving You by Pippa Grant

Dirty Martini Running Club

Hot stand-alone romantic comedies with huge... hearts.

Everly Dalton's Dating Disasters:

A Faking Ms. Right prequel

Faking Ms. Right

A hot fake relationship romantic comedy

Bootleg Springs
by Claire Kingsley and Lucy Score

Hot and hilarious small-town romcom series with a dash of mystery and suspense. Best read in order.

Whiskey Chaser

Sidecar Crush

Moonshine Kiss

Bourbon Bliss

Gin Fling

Highball Rush

Book Boyfriends

Hot romcoms that will make you laugh and make you swoon.

Book Boyfriend

Cocky Roommate

Hot Single Dad

Remembering Ivy

A unique contemporary romance with a hint of mystery.

His Heart

A poignant and emotionally intense story about grief, loss, and the transcendent power of love.

The Always Series

Smoking hot, dirty talking bad boys with some angsty intensity.

Always Have

Always Will

Always Ever After

The Jetty Beach Romance Series

Sexy small-town romance series with swoony heroes, romantic HEAs, and lots of big feels.

Behind His Eyes

One Crazy Week

Messy Perfect Love

Operation Get Her Back

Weekend Fling

Good Girl Next Door

The Path to You

Sign up for Claire's newsletter at **www.clairekingsleybooks.com** to be the first to hear about new releases, as well as exclusive content, the Ask Cooper Miles advice column, and more!

ABOUT THE AUTHOR

Claire Kingsley is a Top 10 Amazon bestselling author of sexy, heartfelt contemporary romance and romantic comedies. She writes sassy, quirky heroines, swoony heroes who love their women hard, panty-melting sexytimes, romantic happily ever afters, and all the big feels.

She can't imagine life without coffee, her Kindle, and the sexy heroes who inhabit her imagination. She's living out her own happily ever after in the Pacific Northwest with her husband and three kids.

www.clairekingsleybooks.com

Printed in Great Britain
by Amazon